"Chief Cavanaugh of the Bar Harbor Police Department, ma'am."

He looked down at his portfolio and then back up at me, eyes cold. "You trashed your husband's car and then ran, is that right?"

I thought it would be different if I left, if I came to the place I'd been the happiest. Even without Gran, I'd imagined being here would comfort me and help me figure out what the hell to do with myself now that I understood what was apparent to everyone else, that my life was a pathetic sham. I leaned forward, dropping my head to the table. Repeatedly. My brain needed a reboot.

A large, warm hand settled on my shoulder, the heat sinking into my bones. I looked up through wet lashes, and I saw it. I knew who he was.

"Aiden?" I sat up straight to better study him. "Aiden Cavanaugh?"

His hand fell away, and I missed its weight and warmth at once. Unbelievable. How the hell had sweet, oddly geeky Aiden Cavanaugh morphed into tall, dark and forbidding?

Dear Reader,

I'm excited—and more than a little terrified—to share with you my debut novel, *Welcome Home, Katie Gallagher*. At its core, this is a story about second chances, a story about starting over. We all deserve a do-over.

I love writing strong, funny women who fulfill their dreams on their own terms. For instance, when Katie envisioned what her life would be, she never once imagined depression-induced insomnia, being wedged into a battered car with a one-hundred-and-forty-pound dog, grape soda splattered in her lap, a fecund, mushroomy odor she wasn't entirely certain she could pin on the dog, and a cop tapping at the window. Nope, she sure didn't see that coming.

But it's in times like these that we learn who we are. Katie could have stayed with a cheating husband who never looked at her except to find fault. She could have. Or she could have taken his expertly weighted and fitted golf clubs to his beloved BMW. Some of us find clarity through yoga, others through criminal behavior. And, let's face it, a mug shot is a pretty clear indicator that different choices should have been made.

I hope you enjoy Katie's fraught journey. Warning: there is a hot, grumpy cop, an adorably massive dog, snickering marmosets, cupcakes, and a woman trying like hell to make a home for herself.

Seana Kelly

SEANA KELLY

Welcome Home, Katie Gallagher

HARLEQUIN® SUPERROMANCE®

Recycling programs
for this product may
not exist in your area.

ISBN-13: 978-0-373-64036-2

Welcome Home, Katie Gallagher

Copyright © 2017 by Seana Shelby

Printed in U.S.A.

www.Harlequin.com

Seana Kelly lives in the San Francisco Bay Area with her husband, two daughters, two dogs and one fish. When Seana isn't dodging her family, hiding in the garage and trying to write, she's working as a high school teacher-librarian. Seana is an avid (who are we kidding? obsessive) reader who is still mourning the loss of Fred Weasley. What the heck, J.K.? If you had to kill off a Weasley, why couldn't it have been Percy?

For Mom and Dad,
who taught me the importance of
integrity, hard work and storytelling.

CHAPTER ONE

Kate

YOU DON'T ALWAYS know when you're having a nervous breakdown. It's usually later, after being confronted with photographic evidence in the form of a mug shot, that you realize you lost your shit in a truly spectacular way.

The tap of the cop's flashlight on the driver's-side window, combined with a soft woof from the back seat, made me jump and splash grape soda down my sweater. I watched it pool in my lap before fumbling with the can. I searched for a napkin.

"Ma'am, could you roll down your window?" The shield on his coat was hard to miss.

Chaucer lifted his massive head, slowly coming to his paws, needing to hunch in order to fit. He sniffed my ear and then looked down into my lap, no doubt hoping I'd dropped something he could eat.

"Shit, shit, shit. Try to look innocent," I told him as I rolled down the window. I did not need more trouble with the law.

"Ma'am, could you explain why you're parked in the middle of the road? Are you having car trouble?" His voice was a deep rumble, which was oddly comforting, considering the situation. He leaned down, keen eyes taking in everything. God, he smelled good—warm leather and rich wood smoke overpowering the sticky sweetness of artificial grape.

Towering Maine pines, silhouetted against the predawn sky, swayed in the frigid gusts skating off the ocean. I shivered, wishing I'd worn something more substantial than a thin sweater set.

I'd stopped in the middle of the road because I couldn't remember whether to continue straight along the cliff-side road or veer inland up ahead. And that question quickly turned into a paralyzing fear that I had no idea where I was going in my life.

"Um, car trouble? No, Officer. I was just thinking." I hadn't slept in weeks. What the hell was I supposed to say? I was falling apart, and this was merely a bump in the road of the shitlosing lollapalooza that had become my life?

Seemingly unaffected by the freezing temperature, he cleared his throat and leaned down farther, peering into my eyes. "Ma'am? Are you telling me that you purposely stopped your car in the middle of the road, possibly causing an accident, so you could think? Have you been drinking this morning, or late last night? Taking any narcotics?"

Chaucer wedged his head between mine and the window to get a better look, or more precisely a better sniff, of this potential food giver. I'll give it to the cop; he barely registered the shock of seeing a hundred-and-forty-pound Newfoundland squished into the tiny back seat of a small sedan.

I tried to push Chaucer back, explaining around his head, "Unless you can get wasted on grape soda, I'm unfortunately sober." What I wouldn't give for a vat of margaritas and a big bendy straw.

He wore the same look of arrogant disdain that my husband, Justin, wore whenever I'd done something wrong, something worthy of censure. *Ex*, I kept reminding myself. On-the-road-to-being ex-husband. He let me know with one cursory glance that he saw through my carefully cultivated, but ultimately lacking, veneer and what he found wasn't equal to his standards.

The cop rumbled, "Ma'am, can you please explain what happened to your vehicle?" His eyes glinted in the low light.

I was done being patronized, done with the barely veiled condescension. "Look, I'm not drunk, and you need to quit calling me ma'am! I'm twenty-five, for God's sake, not eighty. 'Causing an accident'? Seriously? I've been sitting here for an hour, and you're the first car that's come by!" I threw the door open, trying to tag him in the thigh as I got out.

He moved remarkably fast, sidestepping the initial swing before stopping the door with one hand.

"And—" I turned to look at the dusty, battered car, with its duct-taped rear window and side panels riddled with deep dents. "That? Pfft. They can buff that right out."

"Ma'am, you need to get back in your vehicle. I didn't tell you that you could step out." Steel threaded through his voice now.

Damn, he was a lot bigger than I'd thought. I should have stayed in the car. *No.* I was done agreeing with men who used their size and authority to cow me. I'd had enough.

"I am not drunk and I'm not a hazard, so leave me the hell alone! And stop calling me ma'am! Twenty-eight is not a ma'am. I'm a miss, damn it! A miss!" I'll admit I was kind of shrieking there at the end.

The cop raised his eyebrows in mild surprise. "Looks like we've got ourselves a rip in the space-time continuum."

Fine. I was thirty. Whatever.

He took a step back, resting his hand on the firearm secured at his waist. Okay, in hindsight, screaming at a cop probably wasn't the best way to start putting my life back together, but sometimes it's hard to stop the scream. After years of quietly acquiescing, the pressure had built. Outrage seeped from the fissures. I'd become a little Chernobyl of screaming, in voice and in deed. I needed to give more thought to the fall-out, though.

Chaucer sensed the tension, not that it was hard to miss, leaping over the seat and out the door to stand between the cop and me. I shivered and reached out to weave my fingers through the thick, warm fur of his brown, bearlike head, pulling him toward me. I didn't want the cop to get any funny ideas about my dog being a threat. Plus, he was an excellent windbreak and space heater.

The sun was starting to rise, dark sky bleeding to red. The cop's face was turned away from the light, but he looked vaguely familiar—dark hair, light eyes, a strong, square jaw and a crooked nose. I didn't know him, and yet there was something.

He glared down at me, his jaw clenched. "Ma'am, I'm going to need you and your dog to get back in your vehicle and calm down. You need to give me your license and registration." He slid the flashlight into his belt and waited for me to decide what to do.

The fight in me died almost as quickly as it had flared. I leaned in past the driver's door and snaked my arm around to open the back door, as the handle on the outside was missing. Chaucer hopped back in. I dropped into the soggy driver's seat and reached into the glove box.

I rummaged in drive-through napkins and salsa packets to find the owner's manual with the registration tucked inside. I handed him that, and then started digging through my bag for my wallet. Hands shaking as the adrenaline waned, I surrendered my license. The quirk of his eyebrow told me that he'd noticed. At least he was no longer clutching his gun, so maybe I'd get out of this without being slammed up against the car and handcuffed. That would be nice for a change.

"I'm going to need you to stay right here while I call this in." I started to nod, but then he busted out the *ma'am*.

I stared daggers into the son of a bitch, not that he seemed the least bit concerned. I was almost positive I saw a grin before he turned and walked away.

Part of me was angry, but mostly I was exhausted. I wanted to curl up under one of Gran's quilts and sleep off the last three months. Hell, the last ten years.

When I had opened Justin's Visa bill, it had been an accident. Two envelopes were stuck together. I thought I was opening a phone bill, and instead I discovered that my husband was having an affair. It was either that or he really liked to take naps in the middle of the day at the Embassy Suites while wearing expensive lingerie.

I'd thought for a moment there had been an error. The credit card was under his company's name, but those were charges for hotel rooms, restaurants, jewelry stores… Where the hell were the OfficeMax and FedEx charges?

White noise had filled my ears and my head began to throb. I was pretty sure I'd forgotten to breathe. Right before I'd passed out, I wondered if he'd get in trouble with the IRS, if he'd actually written off his skank-related expenses and whether or not I was in trouble, too, since we'd filed joint returns. Weird, the things you think about as you go under.

When the cop strode back, I took a moment to appreciate the thick, muscular thighs his uniform couldn't hide. "Chaucer, I've recently discovered it's the little things that make life worth living." Objectification may be wrong, but it sure was fun. Asshole or not, the man was beautiful.

I turned to the cop and said, "Everything all right, Officer?" *I hope, I hope.* Last I heard, charges hadn't been pressed. Or they'd been dropped. One or the other.

He stared, and I felt sweat beading on my upper lip. "Ma'am, there's a notation on your license about a destruction of property allegation." He looked significantly at the abused sedan I was driving. "And resisting arrest. Do you know any-thing about that?"

I rolled my eyes. "Resisting arrest? What kind of whiny cops complain about having their hands slapped? I'd be embarrassed if I were…" I trailed off as I watched his fingers drumming the handle of his gun. "I mean, resisting what?"

"And destruction of property," he reminded me.

I looked up into his light blue eyes and felt a familiar jolt. "Well, see, I contend that since this BMW is in my name, too, it's not destruction of property so much as adding air holes to better ventilate my portion of the car. Allegedly."

He appeared as stern as ever, but I could have sworn the corners of his eyes crinkled. "I see. Do you have a lawyer you'd like to call before you follow me to the station?"

I'd met with a divorce attorney before I'd left California and headed east. She was not going to be pleased with me if I ended up in cuffs again.

"I do, but as she's on the West Coast, and it's two in the morning her time, I should probably go it alone, although you can expect to hear 'I've been advised by my attorney to remain silent.' A lot. I'm sure if she were here, she'd tell me to keep mum."

The cop's mood seemed to have shifted. He leaned one arm against the roof of my car, gazing out toward the ocean. While he contemplated life and whether or not he was going to allow me to continue partaking of it, I flexed my superficial, objectifying muscles. His jacket was hanging open, so I could see that those broad shoulders narrowed to a flat stomach. I tried not to look below the waist, but it was right there, framed by his big utility belt. I may have been new to this, but I was a fast study.

He cleared his throat. When I peeked up, he was staring back at me, eyebrows raised. Busted.

CHAPTER TWO

Aiden

SITTING BACK IN the cruiser, I watched Katie shove her dog's head out of her lap. Her mouth was moving like she was talking to the damn thing. She glanced up, noticed me watching her and gave me a big, fake smile before finally starting that heap she was driving. She spun it around, kicking up rocks, and then waited for me to lead her to the station.

Unbelievable. Katie Gallagher was back in Bar Harbor. And apparently, she'd become an actual criminal. It had been fifteen years, but looking at her was like a punch in the gut. Katie Gallagher had dominated my puberty, with her curly red hair, big green eyes and that little dimple near the corner of her lower lip. My best and worst memories of adolescence had been connected to her in some way.

Yet she stood there a few minutes ago, glaring at me, and had no idea who I was. I didn't know if I should be flattered that I bore no resemblance to the creepy little stalker who'd followed her around, or offended that she had no recollection Aiden Cavanaugh ever existed.

I checked the rearview mirror, wondering what the hell she was doing back in Bar Harbor. She and that moose of hers followed closely down Main Street to the station. I picked up my radio. "Heather, can you move all those Halloween decorations out of the interview room? I'm bringing in a suspect for questioning."

She came back quickly. "Well, sure, Chief, but what should I do with them? Nancy's coming by tomorrow to pick them up. Do you want we should put them in an empty cell until they're taken over to Agamont Park?"

Did I? No, damn it. I realized I was doing the professional equivalent of stuffing dirty laundry under the bed when a date came over. Had Alice taught me nothing? Women weren't to be trusted. This one in particular. Katie'd only been back in my life a few minutes, and I was already falling into that same old morass of lust, stupidity and disappointment. I was an adult and long past chasing after Katie Gallagher.

"Never mind, Heather. Leave it. Shove everything down to the end of the conference table so there's room to conduct an interview."

"Sure, Chief, no problem. I'll get Mikey right on it."

CHAPTER THREE

Kate

I TURNED THE CORNER, following the cop toward the small police station on Firefly Lane. Was there ever a street that struck less fear in the hearts of its citizenry? *Watch out, buddy, or they'll drag you to Firefly Lane. Did you hear they busted a crack house on Firefly Lane?* I thought a name change was in order, perhaps Gulag Terrace.

Possible incarceration aside, it was good to be back. The town hadn't changed all that much. The downtown was quaintly charming, vibrant shop fronts lining Main Street down to the water. An older man was hosing down the sidewalk in front of a neighborhood market, carts of fresh fruit and vegetables already flanking the door.

I tapped my fingers on the cold steering wheel. "Think he sells forty-pound bags of dog food in there?" Hopefully that big feed store was still on the other side of town. "We'll need to find out soon. You've almost finished the bag we brought with us."

Chaucer sniffed around at the mention of food, but when none was forthcoming, he sat back, no longer blocking the rearview mirror.

Stopping at a red light, I caught myself checking out shoes in a store window. What the hell was wrong with me? I was following a cop to a police station to be questioned in a criminal case, but instead of concerning myself with my own defense, I was considering whether or not I should buy a pair of cute new boots with a wedge heel. I was clearly unhinged.

"Look, Chaucer. I had my first kiss in the park down that street." Michael Emerson. He'd been sweet and shy, smelling of fabric softener and freshly mown grass. Looking around, I began to relax. This was a good decision. I'd done the right thing for once.

I followed the police cruiser into the station parking lot and stepped out of my car. I'd been happy here once. I would be again. I took a deep breath. I'd missed the cold, salty ocean air. I closed my eyes and let the feeling settle. I hadn't realized how beaten down I'd become, how hollow. Being back in Gran's hometown made me feel steady and hopeful.

The glowering cop standing by his car took care of that feeling quickly, though. I couldn't see his eyes through the reflective sunglasses he wore, but I could see the disapproving scowl. Years of a scowl like that had been part of what had beaten me down. I wasn't bowing to that disapproval anymore. I turned on my heel, jogging around the back of the car. Pressing my key ring, the lock on the passenger side back door popped up. I opened the door for Chaucer.

The cop stepped forward. "Why don't we leave him in the car while we talk?"

Chaucer stepped down and leaned into me. "Are you kidding? You don't leave dogs alone in cars. Do you want him dying of heat exposure?" Not to mention the poor pup needed to use the facilities. Hopefully we could make a quick detour to the lawn.

"Well, as it's in the high thirties with a forecast of getting into the low fifties today, I'm pretty sure he can avoid heat exposure." He held his hand in front of Chaucer, who sniffed him thoroughly before stepping forward to let the cop pet him. "Fine, you can bring him." He turned to lead us.

"Right behind you," I said, as Chaucer and I headed in the opposite direction toward the lawn. The russet colors of autumn dripped from the trees. We walked on stiff, crackling leaves until Chaucer found a perfect spot. During a ridiculously long potty break, I sensed the cop's eyes on me. It was strangely comforting, like he was watching over me rather than keeping me under surveillance. When Chaucer finally finished, we met the cop at the door to the station.

He'd taken off his sunglasses. "Impressive," he said, while scratching the top of Chaucer's head.

"Good morning, Chief!"

He turned to a pretty woman with light brown hair. She was bundled up in a long, ivory sweater coat and was wearing an adorable pair of high-heeled boots that put her close to the cop's height. He grinned at her, and my stomach fluttered. No, no. Men were strictly verboten, especially the ones who liked to mock and criticize. New me, new choices.

He nodded. "Nancy."

She was breathless, as though she'd run to catch up with him. She placed a hand on his sleeve. "Chief, I'm so glad I caught you." She glanced at me. "I'm not interrupting anything, am I?" She shifted her stance, partially blocking me. "I had a quick question about the festival. I need your opinion…"

Honestly, I stopped listening at that point. I leaned over and whispered in Chaucer's ear. "He's distracted. Now's our chance. You run that way and I'll run this way. I think we can totally get away if we act quickly." I glanced around to make sure he was still engaged in chatting up the brunette.

He'd moved away from the woman who was still talking, a hand *still* on his arm. All his attention was on me; eyes squinted, he was practically daring us to make a break for it. Focus never wavering, he said, "Nancy, I'm in the middle of something. You can discuss all this with Heather. She'll know the answers better than me, anyway."

I leaned back down. "Abort. Abort." Stupid, observant cop.

He moved to the steps of the station house, extending his arm to us. "After you." As Chaucer and I passed, he gave a low grumble. "Not exactly a criminal mastermind, are you?"

I paused, eyebrows raised in question.

He smirked. "Your plan was 'run.' Really?"

I gave him my most dismissive hair flip and walked through the door. I had Chaucer on a leash, but he would have stayed with me, anyway. And honestly, as the dog outweighed me by at least thirty pounds, if he ever wanted to get away, there's not much I could do. Luckily he was devoted to me, almost as much as he was devoted to never exerting himself.

Inside, a soft, middle-aged woman wearing a headset looked up from her cluttered desk. Her eyes comically rounded at seeing Chaucer walk in.

"Heather, this is Katie Gallagher. We'll be using the conference room."

I started at hearing the name Katie Gallagher. The name on my license was Katherine Cady. No one had called me Katie in a long time. Justin called me Katherine, and I insisted that my friends call me Katherine or Kate. I'd refused to be known as Katie Cady. That was too ridiculous, not to mention redundant.

As I walked through the police station, I knew I should be feeling fear, concern, abject terror, something. But I wasn't. It was like a dream. Weird, bad things kept happening, but they didn't touch me. I floated through. Maybe I was in shock, or that grape soda was laced with quaaludes. One or the other.

"It looks different," I observed.

"Make a habit of studying the insides of police stations?" He led me past desks toward a rear hall. A few cops watched my perp walk, or maybe it was the Newfoundland trying to sniff out forgotten food that caught their attention.

"Not a habit so much as a hobby," I said, studiously regarding the tips of my shoes. My eyes were definitely *not* drifting up to watch the world-class butt directly in front of me. Nope. "My Gran brought me here when I was thirteen as part of her scared-straight campaign. A couple of kids were busted for pot, and she was certain I was a member of their drug-guzzling gang. Never mind that I had never met any of them, nor had I ever been high."

"Nor did you realize that drugs weren't guzzled." He opened the door to the interview room, which, I must say, was far less frightening than I had been trained to expect watching cop shows on TV. It was a very cozy, pleasant room with an unusually large number of cardboard ghosts and pumpkins strewn across the far end of the table.

"Yeah, yeah. Anyway, Gran decided it was better to punish me before I did anything, in case she missed it afterward. I spent a Saturday afternoon locked up in a cell back there while Gran sent in random folks she'd found in the shops to come scare me straight with their stories of prison." Chaucer flopped down on the floor, rested his head on my foot and fell asleep. It had been a big day for him.

"You're making this up," the cop said as he sat down.

"No, not at all. It was kind of fun for me. As they told me their stories of depraved incarceration, I tried to identify which shows they were stealing from." I smiled, remembering. "Mr. Wilson told me he had tunneled out of Shawshank Prison with nothing but a rock hammer. Oh, wait, do I get the same number or a new one?"

His brow furrowed. "Number?"

"For my mug shot. The bottom of the picture. Will I have the same number I did when I was thirteen? Is it like a Social Security number that follows you around, or is it the case number or something?" This was knowledge I hadn't realized I'd ever need to possess.

"It follows you, but according to your record,

you've never actually been booked. Unless you have an alias."

"Oh." *Bummer.* I kind of liked the idea of being a hardened criminal, a total badass with a record. I needed a leather jacket and maybe a tattoo—not one of those prissy deals. No dragonflies or mermaids for me. I wanted a skull or tribal pattern around my biceps. I also needed a biceps, preferably two. I was going to go all Sarah Connor, build up my guns and wear tank tops to show 'em off…

"Katie?"

Hmm? "Sorry, what?"

He sighed and tapped the screen on his phone right before a flash blinded me.

"Seriously, with your phone? Is this some kind of pity mug shot?" He was making fun of me. Man, he was going to be sorry when I became a badass. We didn't forget shit like that.

He smirked and returned the phone to his pocket.

"I wasn't ready!" Damn, I didn't scowl or sneer or anything. "Do over!"

"No." He pulled out a portfolio and opened it. "You haven't changed," he said as he stood, removing his jacket before resuming his seat.

"You know me?" I wondered over the planes of his face again. Had I met him when I'd visited Gran all those years ago? I considered the dark hair that curled near his collar, the Paul Newman blue eyes, the tall, muscular body, the cleft in his chin… Wait. The eyes, the cleft…those were familiar.

He tapped his pen rapidly, ignoring my question. "Now, could you tell me why you tortured that poor car?"

I wilted. Why was I the one in the police station? All I did was take Justin's expertly fitted and weighted golf clubs to his beloved car. I didn't lie to him day in and day out. I didn't betray him. Nope. I broke a thing, not a person. Why the hell wasn't *he* the one staring down a cop and answering questions?

"I'd really prefer not to, and I don't understand why I should have to. Taking a golf club to your own property is not against the law. It's not like I went on a spree and destroyed all the cars in the country club parking lot. It was a surgical strike. I was a Tomahawk missile of tactical fury. And anyway, shouldn't you have to identify yourself before you start asking me questions?" I clenched my trembling hands in my lap, trying to maintain my new, hard-ass persona.

"Chief Cavanaugh of the Bar Harbor Police Department, ma'am." He looked down at his portfolio and then back up at me, eyes cold. "You trashed your husband's car and then fled, is that right?"

I thought it would be different if I left, if I came to the place where I was the happiest. Even without Gran, I'd imagined being here would comfort me and help me figure out what the hell to do with myself now that I understood, what was apparent to everyone else, that my life was a pathetic sham. I leaned forward, dropping my head to the table. Repeatedly. My brain needed a reboot.

A large, warm hand settled on my shoulder, the heat seeping into my bones. A shiver ran through me. I looked up through wet lashes, and I saw it. I knew who he was.

"Aiden?" I sat up straight to better study him. "Aiden Cavanaugh?"

His hand fell away, and I missed its weight and warmth at once. Unbelievable. How the hell did sweet, oddly geeky Aiden Cavanaugh morph into tall, dark and forbidding?

"Wow," I said. "Look at you with your big-boy muscles and your lumberjack build. You must have had one hell of a growth spurt. I knew there was something familiar about you. It was the eyes. You were always cute but holy shnikies. I'm feeling kind of dirty now for some of the things I was thinking about you up on the cliff."

CHAPTER FOUR

Aiden

Disturbing sisterly attitude aside, it was nice to know that the girl I'd obsessed over as a kid appreciated what she saw enough now to mentally grope me.

I gave myself a mental slap. Women, for more than a couple of hours, were off the table. They couldn't be trusted, and trust was vital. "Thanks. If we can get back to the destruction of property issue..." I said, and her smile dropped.

She sighed. "He cheated on me. A lot. I moved out, met with a lawyer, but then..." She looked up at me. "Do I have to tell you all this? Can he really have me arrested for beating up his car?" Her bottom lip quivered before she stiffened it.

"If you're in the process of a divorce and you took a golf club to his things? Yes."

She looked down into her lap.

"Would he willingly air the dirty laundry to punish you?"

She sat up straight, her head cocked, considering. "No. Image is everything to him. The

Asshat used to go shopping with me to make sure I dressed like a successful man's wife." She paused, her fingers tapping on the tabletop. "I doubt he'd want his clients to know why I did what I did." She nodded slowly. "I hadn't thought of that."

My hand twitched, wanting to touch her once more. Damn it. I wasn't going down that road again. Not after Alice. "Are you visiting or planning to stay awhile?"

"I want to stay. I don't have anywhere else to go. I know Gran's gone, but I was hoping—I don't know. I was happy here once."

I laughed. "You were a menace here once, Katie."

Outraged, she said, "Menace? I was a sweet and charming addition to this community for two months every summer!"

Choking, I stood. "Sweet and charming? How many Fourth of July parades did you ruin?"

"Enhanced. The word you're looking for is *enhanced*."

Dropping back down in the chair, I fixed her with a stare. "Enhanced? When you stole Old Man Benson's crickets and released them into the crowd, you believed that it improved their parade-viewing experience?" I paused, considering. "And how the hell did you end up on different floats every year? You were a member of the Kiwanas? The Elks? A volunteer firefighter?"

She laughed, relaxing. "Good times. The kind and trusting people of this community welcomed me with open arms. It helps that they have short memories. Every summer, I'd promise that I'd learned the error of my ways and they'd let me climb on their floats." She grinned at the table, remembering.

"Crickets?"

"Do you know what he planned to do with those poor little crickets? He was going to skewer them with a fishing hook. I heard him talking to Gramps outside the bait shop. He had a big container of live crickets that he and his buddy were going to use the next day on their fishing trip!" She shook her head. "While they chatted, I grabbed the bin out of the back of his truck and ran to the parade. It was a crime of opportunity. Anyway, I was like seven or eight at the time. Hasn't the statute of limitations run out on that one?"

"Perhaps. What about the rubber balls?"

She tried to hide her guilty expression. "Who doesn't like bouncy balls?"

"Off the top of my head, I'd say the guy driving the tractor directly behind your float. When you sent hundreds of bouncy balls in every direction, quite a few bounced into his engine. You broke his damn tractor."

Cringing, she said, "Not broke. They were able to fix it. I screwed up the parade, though.

It took a while to get the tractor moved so the rest of the floats could go by. On the bright side, people had bouncy balls to play with while they waited!"

"Where did you even get hundreds of balls?"

"Brought them with me. It was some kind of ordering mistake at my parents' university. I think they were supposed to be ordering condoms, but checked the wrong box. I don't know. I was nine. There were boxes of bouncy balls sitting in the back of the administration building." She looked at me, wide-eyed. "What was I supposed to do? Just leave them there?"

"Yes."

"Pfft. I filled my backpack and a plan began to form."

I shook my head. "Like I said, menace."

She waved away my concerns. "I worked all summer at Mr. Sheets's ranch to pay for the tractor repair."

"You did?"

"Oh, sure." She grinned. "He was only annoyed with me that first day, though. I went from mucking out the stables and polishing the tools to apple picking and horse brushing. Fun summer."

Her expression shifted, memories scattering. "I thought—with everything going on—I could start over here." She shook her head, shrugging. "I didn't know what else to do."

I ignored a twinge of sympathy for Katie, closing my portfolio. "You're going to your grandmother's?"

"Yeah. She left me her house. Not *him*, not us, just me." She clenched her hands in her lap. "I don't know if that'll work, though. California is a no-fault, community-property state. My lawyer is—well, she's doing what she can." She moved her foot, and her dog groaned at having his pillow taken away. "So, is it okay? Can I go?" She bit her lip, and I looked away.

I stood and moved toward the door. "Yes, but only because charges were never actually filed. I guess your husband forgave you."

Pushing up from the table, she rolled her eyes. "Sure. We can go with that."

What did that mean? I put my coat back on and waited for her to collect her dog and bag. "What happened to your hair?"

She laughed, a quick outburst of breath, and shook her head. "I see your skill with compliments hasn't improved. I believe you once told me I had very straight shoulders." She walked past me without answering the question.

She had beautiful shoulders—ones I'd wanted to kiss, but hadn't known how to talk about as a kid. And her hair had been a mass of curls when she was younger. It hung straight now. I followed her back through the station house, scowling when I noticed Mikey, my newest officer, checking out her ass. Her ass was none of my business, but that didn't keep my jaw from clenching. "Still waiting for that report, Officer." That did it. Eyes back on his desk where they belonged.

I trailed her through the front door, stopping on the steps. "Okay, fine. Your hair was really curly when you were younger. How can it be straight now?"

"Oh, well…" She spun away from me but not before I noticed a tinge of red touch her cheeks. "I've been straightening it for years."

Hands on my hips, I studied her. Her embarrassment was clear. "Why the hell would you do that?"

She turned back quickly, surprised. "You *liked* my hair?"

"What's not to like? It was beautiful. I mean, it's nice now, but—hell, it's your hair. Do whatever you want with it." Damn it, what was it with this woman? I might as well have been eleven again.

She opened the rear door of her car, letting Chaucer trundle back in. She had her back to me when I heard "He didn't care for it, thought it was too much." She turned back around, a hand unconsciously smoothing her hair before she dropped it heavily to her side.

"Too much," she echoed, shaking her head.

"You could shave your head, and you'd still be one of the most beautiful women I've ever seen."

Note to self—shut up.

CHAPTER FIVE

Kate

"DID YOU HEAR THAT? He said I was beautiful."
I grinned stupidly, but then remembered. "Unfortunately, I'm pretty sure he also thinks I'm a
nutjob."

Chaucer stood up and rested his head on my
shoulder. He rendered the rearview mirror moot,
but the weight of his head was comforting. I
scratched his ruff. He'd witnessed my humiliation and still loved me.

"Scowling, leering, crying. What do you
think, buddy? Could I have added to that fairly
impressive list of asinine behaviors? I suppose I
could have wet myself. I'll try to take comfort in
the fact that my pants are dry." Sniffing grape, I
added, "You know, mostly."

I rolled down the windows and breathed
deeply, the air crisp and biting. Driving back
through the leaf-strewn town, my eyes were
drawn to a woman with a stroller. I hugged
Chaucer once more, pushing away unwelcome
memories, and headed up through the hills.

Gran's house, a charming stone cottage, was nestled back against the forest. I found it surprisingly easily, my mind no longer consumed with self-doubt, listening instead to the gruff-sounding *beautiful* echoing through my thoughts.

To one side of Gran's house, the cliff dropped to a rocky shore below. From the wraparound porch, rolling emerald hills ran down to the town and the harbor beyond. The far side, opposite the ocean, was Gran's baby, her garden. Hydrangea blossoms floated down like pink snow, settling on the peonies below. At the back of the house, Gran kept a large vegetable patch, preferring the old practice of stepping out the kitchen door to pick the food for that day's meals.

As I crested the driveway, taking it all in, I worried that in the month since her death, her house had been damaged or broken into. I still couldn't believe Justin, the selfish bastard, hadn't told me she'd died until after her funeral.

They'd called the house about Gran, but it was after I'd already moved into my friend Christine's apartment. Justin had apparently taken the message that Gran was really sick, and that I needed to come now. However, he'd never bothered to pass it along to me.

When the lawyer finally tracked me down through my mom, I'd learned of Gran's passing and of her bequest. Rage and guilt warred. I should have been there, should have told her how much I loved her before she died. That *fuckknob* had kept her from me. I'd been ready to tear his balls off when I'd tracked him down at his country club. He was in his car on the phone, turning away from my knock. He thought smugly ignoring me would work when my grandmother was buried without me? I put an end to that shit.

His golf bag and clubs were standing by his open trunk. I grabbed one of his clubs, put all my weight and fury behind it and swung for the bleachers. I'd intended to break his clubs, but instead broke his back window. I stopped and stared at what I had done. Never in my life had I engaged in vandalism. I was a vandal. It felt good. I was terrified of myself, but swung again to check my response. Yep, still felt good.

Years of pent-up frustration and betrayal fueled my frenzy. At some point he jumped out of the car. I heard him yelling, but he was like a yapping dog in a neighbor's yard. Annoying but easily ignored.

The cops showed up. I never knew if it was the country club who called or Justin. It didn't matter. One of the officers drew a gun on me. That sobered me up real fast. His partner stepped in front of the gun, telling the other guy to put it away. Good cop asked me questions, looking in my eyes, trying to determine if I was hopped up on PCP. That's what I assumed, anyway. His expression was a combination of concern and wariness. I would have answered his questions, but I couldn't hear anything over the buzzing in my head.

Bad cop grabbed at my arms. I slapped his hands away, so resisting arrest was added, and I was handcuffed. I don't remember anything about the drive to the police station. One of them apparently snagged my handbag from my car, so at least I had my ID and phone.

Once we got to the station, bad cop took off to do bad-cop stuff. Good cop told me his name was Officer Kinney. He had dark skin, kind eyes and a soft, deep voice. He let me call my mom for help, but warned me that Justin could still press charges, and that the country club was deciding if they were going to, as well. He said he'd talk to his partner and try to get the resisting charge dropped.

I broke down and told the poor guy everything. I sobbed on his desk. He patted my back reluctantly, but I appreciated it all the same. Mom showed up and drove me back to the country club to pick up my car. It was gone, although Justin's was still there. I stared at it, shocked. I had broken and dented a gem of Bavarian automotive engineering. Holy crap! I was kind of scary.

I brushed the glass off the seats and drove to the house, wanting to confront the asswipe. I sat steaming in the driveway for an hour, and then rethought my plan. Talking to Justin never helped. I reluctantly went into the house that had never truly felt like mine to pack and leave for good. Justin didn't come home that night, which made the process easier. I traveled from room to room, picking up a photo here, a book there. Everywhere I looked, I saw Justin's stamp.

I was done there. I didn't want to ever see him, or this house, again. I found boxes in the garage and started packing what was mine. The fact that it all fit in the trunk demonstrated how little of my life was actually my own.

Good or bad, my life was my own now. I stopped the car when the drive leveled out. I took in Gran's house. "Look at it, Chaucer. Isn't it beautiful?" I closed my eyes and let out the breath I'd been holding. Home.

I parked to the side of the front steps, near a pear tree, and let Chaucer out. I stretched, slamming the car door before sitting on the white-washed front steps. I inhaled the sharp scents of hemlock and salt water.

Home. "Thank you, Gran. You knew even when I didn't how much I needed to be here." Chaucer walked up the steps and lay down on the porch, his front paws and head hanging over the edge.

A moment later, his head popped back up. He found his feet, standing alert and still. I heard it, too. It sounded like it was coming from the backyard. I walked up the last step and followed the porch around the side of the house. White wicker furniture still sat out, facing Gran's magnificent garden.

Whack. I scanned the tree line, trying to locate the sound. Chaucer stood beside me and gave a quiet woof while looking toward the rear of the house. I saw him, too—a man with his back to us, holding an ax and splitting wood.

Normally, a strange man swinging an ax would be enough to send me scrambling in the opposite direction, but there was something familiar about him. He had a shock of white hair and was wearing a red plaid work shirt. He had strong, broad shoulders, although time had worn away at his posture.

I walked down the side steps, Chaucer at my side. "Mr. Cavanaugh, is that you?"

He spun around, startled and staring, his eyes getting wider. "Nellie?" he asked breathlessly. His hand rose to his chest and rubbed.

"No, Mr. Cavanaugh. Nellie was my grandmother. I'm Kate." I'd heard before that I favored my grandmother, but the only pictures I had of her were as an old woman.

The poor man dropped down heavily onto the stump he was using to split wood.

I rushed forward, kneeling in the soft, dark soil before him. "I'm so sorry. I didn't mean to give you a start," I faltered. He appeared pale and drawn, shaky. I feared I'd given him a heart attack. "Can

I get you a drink of water, call someone? Anything?"

He reached out and touched the side of my face. "Remarkable…you look like my Nellie… except the hair. She had curly hair, same color, though. Same green eyes." He shook his head and dropped his hand. "I'm sorry, Katie. Of course, I know who you are. For a minute there, I thought that Nellie had come back for me. Thought maybe I'd died chopping wood and Nellie had come to take me with her."

"Sir, why don't we go sit on the porch for a few minutes? I can grab you a glass of water, and we can get reacquainted." I helped him to his feet and took his arm, surreptitiously lending support. My throat tightened when I felt his trembling hand.

After helping him up the stairs and into one of the chairs that overlooked the flower garden, I excused myself. The front door was locked. I searched my pockets. The lawyer had given me the key. I'd been holding it like a talisman for days.

Once open, I ran through the door, registering dust and leaves. Something took flight, flapping loudly, but I was moving too fast to see what it was. *Please, don't be a bat. Please, don't be a bat.* The kitchen counters and floor were grimy, but the dishes inside the cabinets appeared clean and untouched. I pulled a cup down, filled it quickly, but then my eyes fell on the phone at the end of the counter. I picked it up, got a staticy dial tone and speed-dialed the police station.

"Bar Harbor Police, can I help you?"

"Yes, please. Is Aiden Cavanaugh in? I need to speak with him right away." My heart raced. *Please, don't let his grandfather die on my side porch.*

I heard a click. "This is Chief Cavanaugh."

"Aiden, it's Kate. Your grandfather is here. I think I scared him pretty badly. He's pale and shaky. I'm worried it might be serious. Does he have a weak heart?" Shit, I was rambling. Did I mention the heart thing?

"Kate? Are you at your grandmother's house?"

"Yeah, I just got here."

"I'm on my way." He hung up.

I placed the receiver in its cradle and tried to pull myself together. I picked up the glass, walked back through the house, detouring through the dining room. I yanked repeatedly at the French doors leading to the side porch before they screeched in protest, giving way. Mr. Cavanaugh was right where I'd left him. I handed him the water, and he appeared surprised all over again at my appearance.

"Sorry. You look so much like Nellie, it's a bit of a shock. Everything, except the hair. I thought you had curly hair, too. I must be misremembering." He studied me, unsmiling. "I'm seventy-four now. Sometimes my memory fails me."

"No, it's not your memory. You're right. My hair was curly. I straighten it now." What was it with Cavanaugh men and my hair?

He grimaced and looked away. "Denying the gifts you were given. Make a habit of that, don't you?"

Right. I had abandoned Gran. "My husband hated it."

"What kind of an idiot did you go and marry?" He watched me, waiting.

"The controlling kind."

He shook his head, as though it was no more than he expected. "Did you leave him, too?"

My stomach dropped, thinking of Justin's betrayal, the women he'd leer at and how he'd wonder aloud why I couldn't look more like that one, behave more like this one.

I nodded. Yes, I'd left him. Years too late, I'd realized.

He grunted a response.

His color was back, and the tremors seemed to have subsided, thank God.

"Visiting one week a year." He shook his head, disgusted. "Phone calls and emails aren't the same thing. You didn't even come to her funeral. You think I don't know why she was so sad when she talked about you? She kept asking for you at the end, and you couldn't be bothered to fly back and let her see you. Hold your hand."

"You're right. I let Gran down. She was nothing but loving and supportive to me, and I…" I held my tears in check. Barely. "Doesn't matter now."

"It matters to me." Anger threaded through his voice, but his eyes held nothing but pain.

I pulled at the wrist of my sweater. "It was hard." I didn't want her to see who I'd become. "My husband needed me." *To cook and clean and throw dinner parties while he cheated on me.*

"But you left him?" He shook his head and took a sip of water.

I let out a gust of breath, an almost laugh. "Don't worry. He has lots of women to console him."

He pinned me with his gaze. "She didn't think he was the right man for you, but she never blamed you for choosing to marry him." He took another sip of water, watching me over the glass. "Your mother wasn't the attentive, responsible type. Nellie knew that. After your father died, well, it worried her the way your mother neglected you."

"No, not neglect. I was provided for. Dad's loss hit her hard. She couldn't deal with people and emotions after that. Impersonal academics, she could handle." I caught his eye, not wanting him to think poorly of her. "She's a brilliant professor. In her personal life…" I shrugged. "She was emotionally absent, I suppose." Truth was she didn't know what to do with me. She became flighty and forgetful, so I started doing the shopping and cooking, the bill paying and the cleaning.

He looked away again. "Call it what you want."

"About the other thing…I didn't know Gran had passed until after the funeral."

A car raced up the drive. Oh, right. "Sorry, Mr. Cavanaugh. I was worried about you and called your grandson." I stood to meet Aiden.

"You gave me a start is all, Katie. I'm fine," he grumbled as I made my way down the porch.

Heavy footfalls sounded on the front stairs. "We're over here," I called. "He's all right now."

Aiden came around the corner, concern etched on his face. "Where?"

I stepped out of the way so he could see his grandfather.

"Pops, are you okay?" He strode forward and sat in the seat I'd vacated. "Katie said you were having some trouble." He leaned forward, studying his grandfather.

"I'm fine. She startled me, looking every inch like her grandmother." He gave me a disgusted look. "Except for the hair. I thought I was dead. Took me a minute to settle. I'm fine."

Aiden stood. "How about I take you home now?"

"I don't need any help getting home." He spoke grudgingly to me. "I live right through those woods there, over the ridge. I come by most days to tend Nellie's garden. I don't go inside, but I take care of her garden. She thought you might be coming soon and wanted it to look nice. That was important to her." To Aiden he added, "I've still got wood to split in the back."

"Katie can cut her own wood." At his grandfather's glare, he added, "Fine. I'll come back and split the wood myself if you let me take you home now." Aiden stood in front of his grandfather, blocking my view.

Something must have been communicated silently between the two men, because a moment later Mr. Cavanaugh relented. "All right, I'll let you see me home." He stared at me, as though weighing his words. "Nellie would be glad to have you back." He nodded, apparently feeling as though he'd said what he needed to. "I'm glad you have that dog with you. He doesn't seem like much of a guard dog, but his size should scare off most thieves."

Mr. Cavanaugh stood, and Aiden stepped over to take an arm. "What are you doing, boy? I can walk fine on my own." He stopped, looking at me closely while speaking over his shoulder. "Aiden, what do you think of Katie's hair?"

If Aiden was surprised by the question, he didn't show it. I felt his gaze move over me. "It's beautiful, although I liked it better curly."

Mr. Cavanaugh nodded. "Just so."

CHAPTER SIX

Aiden

GETTING POPS IN the car proved more difficult than I'd expected. And not because he was ill. He kept trying to get me to go back, finish splitting the wood. Instead, I drove us down the narrow, graveled road. "Leave it. I'm taking you home."

There was a disgruntled tsk, and then Pops smacked his fist against his thigh. "I'm done pussyfooting around this. Every time I try to bring it up, you change the subject or leave the room. No more, Aiden." He paused to gather his thoughts, and I wished I hadn't offered to drive him home. "You've changed. You're harder, meaner. You told a tiny woman, Nellie's granddaughter, to chop her own wood. It's not you, and I don't like it. Son, I know Alice's leaving was difficult, but isn't it better that she did it *before* you were married?"

"Yeah, Pops. She was nothing if not kind and considerate. I'll be paying off that not-a-wedding for many years to come. I'm reminded every month as I transfer funds for the altered designer dress, the out-of-season flowers that needed to be flown in, the gourmet food, the banquet room at the Bar Harbor Inn… At least I got to keep the cases of wine. Too bad I don't particularly like wine. I think she vetoed beer at the reception, so I wouldn't be left with anything I actually liked."

Pops tsk-tsked again.

"And, yes, I will return the ring soon." I squirmed at the thought of everyone in the jewelry store carefully not looking at me as I return a $10,000 ring for the woman who took off a year ago, the day before our wedding. She left me an empty apartment and a note.

"Sorry, Aiden. I just can't" was all the explanation I'd been given. Sorry, I just can't marry you? Sorry, I just can't love you? Sorry, I just can't stand the sound of your breathing? What the fuck was it that she just couldn't?

"You've been saying that for almost a year, but I can still see that damn box in your pocket." His fingers tapped on his thigh. "I told you I'd help you pay off that debt—"

"Stop. You're not paying my damn bills. I was the idiot who thought Alice loved me. The bills are a monthly reminder of why I shouldn't trust women." My hands tightened on the wheel.

"You don't really think that, do you?" Pops actually sounded concerned about my sanity.

"I don't know. I guess some of them are okay.

Mrs. MacPherson, the old librarian, seems pleasant enough."

Pops tsk-tsked in annoyance again, prodding a grin out of me.

"Well, you know that Katie—"

"Ran out on her husband? Yeah, I'd heard that. Apparently, she wasn't considerate enough to realize that she just couldn't *before* they got married."

Pops gave me a disgusted look. "That was not what I was going to say. Nellie doted on her—"

"Yeah, and how often did she visit Nellie? I haven't seen her since she was fifteen. You said she visited, but she was clearly never in town long enough for anyone else to notice. Hell, she didn't even come to Nellie's funeral."

When I pulled up to his front steps, I turned off the engine, rolling my shoulders, to relieve the tightness. "Listen, Pops, I know you mean well, but, no. Stop, okay? I'm not interested in that one."

"I'm not saying you should be. I'm angry with her for not being with Nellie more, especially at the end, but if what she said was true... Nellie loved that girl to the moon, and I think she'd be mad as hell at me if I didn't try to help her." He touched the door handle, but then turned back to me. "You used to be so sweet on her, you couldn't take your eyes off her."

"That was a long time ago. People change."

CHAPTER SEVEN

Kate

I WANDERED THROUGH Gran's house. It was exactly as I remembered, but with a new horror-movie feel. Heart pine floors, tall windows overlooking the ocean and town, walls the color of butterscotch, furniture in blues and whites, but all of it was covered in a combination of dust, dirt, feathers and droppings. What the hell?

I walked through the tiny house, terrified of what was living in it. Chaucer sniffed everything. Although he wasn't barking, he raced from room to room, ears twitching at every skitter and squeak. I prayed I wasn't in immediate mortal danger. I found three windows that had been left wide-open, their screens chewed and ripped. I guess that accounted for the apparent influx of woodland creatures taking up residence. I closed the windows, but then worried that I'd probably just trapped them in with me.

When I made it back to the living room, I surveyed the mess there. "This is going to take forever." I just wanted to lie down and sleep for a week. Judging by the beds upstairs, some of my forest neighbors had felt the same way. Looking warily at the couch, I approached it slowly, reaching out and carefully lifting a cushion. Something small and furry with a long tail raced across my foot and down the hall. Chaucer barked and bounded after it. I may or may not have shrieked. I found myself with my back against the front door, watching the room, terrified.

"We're sleeping in the car!"

I eventually pried myself from the door and went in search of cleaning supplies. I swept and mopped, washed down walls, dragged chewed and soiled mattresses down the stairs and out the front door. The only bright part of my day was finding love letters Gran had exchanged with Mr. Cavanaugh. I had a flash of worry that they'd contain passages more graphic than I could deal with in relation to Gran. Luckily, they were charming and considerate, loving and funny. I sat in the middle of her bedroom, tears streaming down my face, so happy that Gran had had this man in her life, but hollowed out by my own inability to inspire that kind of devotion in another person.

By nightfall, I was sweaty, depressed and covered in substances best not to consider. My last task of the day was to clean the bathroom, and then take a long, scalding shower. I stood under the water, tension leaving my muscles, and I finally let go of what I'd been holding tightly in check. My Gran was dead. She'd called for me on her deathbed, and I wasn't there. I wasn't there to pray over her grave and say goodbye. I wasn't there. Instead, I was feeling sorry for myself a country away because I'd chosen to marry a faithless bastard. I was a fuckup, plain and simple. I sobbed against the now-white tiles, drowning in self-loathing.

Cleaned, dried and wearing sweats, I walked back downstairs, Chaucer at my heels. I'd put out his food and water bowls as soon as I'd started cleaning, so at least *he'd* been fed. My stomach growled. I hadn't eaten anything all day. I found a plastic container of granola. It had been gnawed upon, but the rodent hadn't made it through. I'd already thrown out all the boxes of foodstuffs. They hadn't survived the critter-pocalypse.

I stuffed a few handfuls of cereal in my mouth and choked. I washed it down with tepid tap water, while dreaming of mashed potatoes. Maybe some baked mac and cheese. I needed comfort food, stat! Instead I ate another handful of granola and called it good. My stomach hurt. Apparently, it was disgusted with me, too.

I'd found some blankets in the upstairs linen closet. Gran's water and electricity were still working, so I'd been able to wash them. I knew I'd freeze, sleeping in the car, without something to keep me warm. I considered sleeping on the living room floor, with Chaucer curled up next to me, but then I thought about all the creatures still hiding somewhere in the house, and me sleeping down where they'd have easy access to my face. Just nope.

Chaucer followed me outside. I moved the front seats as far forward as they would go. Chaucer took the back seat, as he had every time he got in. I felt bad making him sleep on the floor of the car, but I did put a blanket down first to cushion it. I lay across the back seat, one blanket cocooning me, while another served as my pillow. I fell asleep with a hand on Chaucer's head.

Sometime later, I was jolted out of sleep by a bark and a bang. Again, I might have shrieked. A flashlight beam cut through the pitch-black. I sat up, plastered against the far door, the blanket pulled up to my nose. Chaucer's deep bark boomed in the too-small car. The light spun and illuminated a hideous face. That time I knew I'd shrieked—I was aware of it at the time in a huh-I-didn't-realize-that-I-actually-made-that-sound kind of way.

He put his fingers over the top of the flashlight and then pointed it at himself again. Without the under glare, he wasn't hideous, just really freaking annoying.

"What the hell, dude? Is this your thing? Do you sneak up on people in the middle of the night, peeking in windows, trying to scare the crap out of them?"

"Why are you sleeping in your car? It's thirty degrees, and this back window has holes in it." His voice was a rumble in the dark, clearly audible through the cracked and broken windows.

"It's brisk. Chaucer and I sleep better with an open window."

He grumbled something I didn't hear. "Katie, why aren't you sleeping in the house?"

"It's infested. Rodents, bats, who knows what else. I cleaned all day, and I'm not even close to done." Wait a minute. "Why do you care? I'm on my own property." I checked my watch. "And it's four in the morning. Why are you even here, freaky stalker cop?"

More grumbling. I'm pretty sure I heard some cussing, too. "I'm not stalking you. I got into the habit of driving by Nellie's house to keep an eye on it over the last few months. I forgot about you until I saw the car. Then I saw the mattresses and junk on the porch. I got out to investigate and saw you, sleeping in your beat-to-shit car."

Humph. "A likely story."

I think he was grinding his teeth now. Weird sound. "One more time. Why are you sleeping in your car? If the house isn't habitable, why didn't you go to a hotel?"

"Hotels are expensive, genius. I'm just going to go back to cleaning when I wake up, which is apparently now, fricking Nosy Parker." I pulled the blanket tighter around myself.

He turned, and his flashlight beam lit up the porch and house. "How did animals get in?"

I blew out a breath. "Three windows were left open, the screens chewed through. From the looks of it, they had quite the kegger."

"I didn't think to check all the windows. When Nellie got sick, Pops moved her into his house so she wouldn't have to climb stairs, and so he'd be there when she needed him. Her house has been empty for months."

The night was becoming more gray than black, allowing me to see the annoyance written all over his face. "Do you want me to go in? Try to get rid of whatever's taken roost?"

"No, thanks. Bye now!" My stomach chose that moment to rumble. Chaucer shifted, putting his head in my lap to investigate the sound.

More swearing. "Have you eaten?"

"You bet. See ya!" The damn cop would not take a hint.

He started to back away, thank goodness, but then stopped. "I can come back with my pickup. Take all that stuff to the dump for you."

I leaned forward again, trying to get a better look at his expression. "Why would you do that? You don't like me, remember?"

"I don't care enough to not like you. Anyway it's Nellie I'm thinking about." He exhaled sharply. "I should have checked the windows. I've been driving by every day to check on her house and never once thought about the inside."

He turned back to me. "Listen, don't let Pops know, okay? He's been killing himself tending the garden for her. Just...don't tell him. Okay?"

"I won't."

"I'll go get my pickup now. Can you pull out anything else that's been destroyed? And I'll haul it all away. He may stop by to check on the plants. I don't want him seeing any of this."

"Okay."

He jogged back to his cruiser and left without another word.

"I guess we're getting started early this morning," I said to Chaucer.

I fed him with what was left in the bag of dog food. "We need to go shopping today, buddy."

I cleaned out the rest of the pantry and then the closet under the stairs. Most of the jackets and things that were hanging had been shredded, as though something was searching for food. One looked in decent shape, so I put it aside to wash.

There was a box on the floor that squeaked. I dragged it out of the closet and quickly stuffed a stray scarf into the hole that had been chewed in the side. If there was a nest of rats in the box, I didn't want to know anything about it. Ever. I hauled it out to the porch, and then pushed it to the extreme end, wanting it as far away as possible. I pretended not to hear the scratching coming from inside. Nope. I didn't hear a thing.

I stuffed all the sheets and towels that had been used as varmint beds into a large garbage bag, and threw it down the stairs. After I'd gone through the closets and tossed everything that had been gnawed or defecated on, I went back downstairs and stared at my nemesis, the couch. That rat had probably come back during the night, burrowing into the soft, warm couch, laughing its little rat ass off at my sleeping in the car. I wasn't letting that asshole win. That couch was out of here. I didn't care if I lived on lawn furniture for the next year, I wasn't settling for a rat's sloppy seconds.

I glared at the piece of furniture another minute, and then started pushing it toward the door. Chaucer hopped up on the couch, because rides are fun, and let me struggle to get the damn thing across the room.

"Not helping, buddy," I gasped. He grinned at me and rolled over.

"Need some help?"

My heart seized. For one terrifying moment, I thought the rat was taunting me. Aiden stood in the doorway, watching me. I looked down at Chaucer who was still pretending to sleep. "Some guard dog you are." His rear paws kicked into the air.

Aiden didn't wait for an answer. He walked

in, nudged me out of the way and pushed the couch across the floor, Chaucer and all. At the doorway, he tipped my dog out and looked at me. "Can you get the other end, help me get it out?"

As long as he was going to do all the heavy lifting, fine by me. I climbed over the end, leaned down to grab the couch arm and yelled, "Pivot!"

Staring at me a beat, he shook his head. "I can't decide if you're insane or…"

I raised my hand in the air. "Oh. Oh. I know!"

Rolling his eyes, he shoved the couch out the door. He pushed it all the way down the porch steps, dragging it up into the bed of his truck. When he was done, he jogged back up the steps and picked up a mattress, shouldered it back to the truck and tossed it in.

I watched as he did the same with the other mattress and the bags of chewed-up linens. When he went for the rat box, I felt the need to advise caution. "You'll want to be very careful with that box. You may hear squeaking and scratching. Ignore it. And for goodness' sake, do not open the lid!"

When he studied the box warily, I knew we were on the same page. He glanced at me and then at his truck bed. "Is this all of it?"

"Nope."

"Then why are you just standing there watching me?" He placed the rat box securely in a corner, where it wouldn't be jostled. Smart man.

"It's fun to watch other people work. Duh."
I walked back in the house to see what I had
missed.

"Insane!" he shouted from the front yard.

"Pfft. As if." I walked through the living room,
dining room, kitchen and bath on the first floor.
I would need to mop the floors again, but just
about everything seemed to be cleared out.

"Are we done?" Aiden was back in the doorway, looking at the empty rooms.

Pointing at the squashy chair, I said, "I haven't
had the nerve to check that yet."

He strode over to the chair and cautiously
lifted the cushion, looking underneath. When
he jumped and threw the cushion, I screamed
and ran for the porch. I was hiding around the
corner when I heard his booming laugh. Bastard.

Strolling back in, my arms crossed, I said,
"Hilarious."

Chuckling, he put the cushion back. "Good
news. You have somewhere to sit."

"Yay, me." I looked around the empty rooms,
wondering if I'd be able to sleep in that chair. "I
couldn't lift the box springs upstairs. Getting the
mattresses down just about killed me."

He looked me up and down. "How *did* you get
the mattresses down the stairs and out the door?"

"Terror is a great motivator."

He jogged up the stairs. "Okay. Two box
springs coming down." When he returned a few

minutes later, he said, "You're going to want to pick up some traps. Oh, and don't go in the bedrooms for a few minutes."

"What? Why?" It'd probably be easier to just sell the house and start again.

"No reason." He tossed a box spring onto the tower of crap in his truck. When he came back in, he detoured by the dining table, picked up two empty garbage bags and checked the gun in his holster.

"What the hell is up there?" That settled it. I was living in my car.

He trotted down a few minutes later, two big bags held tightly in his hands. I swear I saw one of them move.

"What is it?" I backed away as he went out the door, placing them gently in the back of his truck, before holding them down with a box of shredded books. "Seriously, Aiden. You have to tell me. I'll never sleep again. And how do you know there aren't babies or eggs or some other smaller version of those things that are going to grow up and bite my head off?"

He watched me panic, backing farther away from the house. His lips twitched, and I stopped. What. The. Hell. He turned his back on me, shoulders shaking.

"You're screwing with me?" I screeched. I stalked across the yard and proceeded to smack every inch of him that I could reach. "You ass! I was planning to spend the next few years living in my car because of you!"

The bastard was laughing so hard, he had a difficult time fighting off my slaps. Finally, he grabbed both wrists and held them together in front of me. "This position probably feels pretty familiar, huh?"

I glared. I couldn't move my arms, so I kicked him.

"No kicking. Or slapping. You already have a record of accosting police officers. I'd hate to have to lock you up again."

As a child, he'd been a hero, facing down bullies. As an adult, it looked like he'd become one. "That hurts," I said, voice low and expressionless.

He loosened his grip immediately and began rubbing my wrists with his thumbs. I could feel tears gathering. I wouldn't look at him. I pulled my arms away and strode back into the house, slamming the door after me. I realized too late that Chaucer was still sitting on the porch. My dramatic exit lost a few points when I had to open the door and call him in.

Aiden

I KEPT CHECKING my rearview mirrors to make sure nothing was slipping off the truck. I couldn't believe it had never occurred to me to check inside

Nellie's house. Pops hadn't stepped foot inside since she got sick. I doubt he'd change that status today, but I didn't want him to know what we let happen.

Walking through the place, it didn't feel like Nellie's anymore. Her furniture was missing. Her walls were dirty. The paintings and photos had been taken down. It was a shell. Nellie was absent, and the loss of her hit hard.

Honk. I turned to see Nancy driving in the other direction, waving at me. I lifted one hand in acknowledgment. Nancy was a mistake. I'd been paying for that lapse in judgment ever since I'd slept with her. Once. Almost year ago now. She wouldn't leave me alone. Every time I turned around, there she was, talking too close and touching my arm. I needed to figure out what to do.

And why was Katie back in Bar Harbor and sleeping in her car? When I saw furniture piled up on the porch, I'd thought Nellie's place was being robbed. It wasn't until I'd driven close enough to see her trashed BMW that I'd remembered.

I was sorry to have scared her, but why wasn't she at a hotel? That house wasn't going to be livable for a while. The floors would need to be stripped, sanded and resealed. The walls and ceilings would need to be painted, furniture replaced. But before any of that could happen,

she'd need an exterminator. I saw enough movement walking through that house to know she
had a major infestation problem. I heard scratching in the ceiling, too. She probably had raccoon
or opossums living up there. What's she going to
do? Sleep on the floor through all that? Nah. She
found herself a rich husband, trashed his $60,000
car and then made jokes about being arrested. It
was all a big joke to her. She'd figure things out.

A twinge of regret poked at me. I didn't mean
to hurt her wrists, though. I was just playing
around.

Huh. I couldn't remember the last time I'd
played.

She was fighting back tears at the end. Was I
being a dick, or was she just not used to being
teased? Oh, hell. It was done, and I wasn't seeing her again, hopefully. What difference did it
make?

Still. Even after all these years, looking at her
took my breath away. Four in the morning, hair
sticking out in every direction, scared out of her
wits, blanket pulled up to her nose, and I wanted
to drag her into my arms and kiss her senseless.
Oh, fuck me.

CHAPTER EIGHT

Kate

Sitting at the freshly washed worktable with a notepad and pen, I wrote a list of what I needed for my new life.

1) NO MEN! My life will be greatly improved by their absence.
2) A clean, animal-free (except for Chaucer) house.
3) Food.
4) Money to buy aforementioned food.

Sighing, I considered my needs. I *needed* Gran to forgive me for not being here when I should have been. One week a year hadn't been enough. I hadn't fought Justin the way I should have, the way Gran would have for me. I needed…

5) Forgiveness. Someday.
6) Better decision-making skills!

Seriously, was I absent from school when they taught that unit?

6b) Stop making fear-based decisions!

After Dad died and Mom fell apart, fear had consumed me. I no longer ran toward what I wanted. I ran away from what I feared. Dad was gone. There one minute and gone the next. Stroke. Anyone at any time could disappear, and I'd be left alone. I'd trailed after Mom, doing everything I could think of to keep her afloat. I couldn't lose her, too. I think that was how Justin wormed his way into my life. He seemed solid and dependable, protective. It took me too long to realize that *controlling* and *protective* were two very different things. And solid? Dependable? Not so much.

7) A job. To get money. To buy food.

Doing what, though? I'd only ever done research work for Mom. Cleaning out her office, grading undergrad tests, returning books to the library. Hmm, I did pretty much the same for Justin, minus the research, tests and library. I ran errands, cooked, cleaned, paid bills. Did anyone in town need a personal assistant?

8) Cleaning gloves.

The mold in Gran's fridge had been epic.

9) Traps, big and small.

Crap, I was going to have to throw out crit-ters stuck in traps, wasn't I? I thought longingly of the car. Maybe I really should live in the car.

10) Dog food.
11) Every cleaning and disinfecting prod-uct they sell.
12) A sleeping bag.
13) A dog bed.
14) A pillow.
15) Chocolate, lots of chocolate.
16) Toilet paper.
17) Shampoo and conditioner.
18) Razor blades.
19) Chips, every kind of chip.

As the list got longer, one thing became very clear. Starting completely from scratch was im-possible. Oh, and ten years of having my every move and meal monitored had turned me into an irresponsible teenager given a hundred bucks for food on a weekend her parents were away. Ice cream was a perfectly acceptable dinner, right?

Once I'd completed my list, I collected my

dog and headed for town. "Listen, buddy, you have to stay in the car while I shop. Don't try to hot-wire it and leave me stranded, okay? That is not good puppy behavior." I left Chaucer with a large rawhide stick and went in.

The pile in my cart grew quickly, becoming precarious. The contents of said cart also put me on the receiving end of some strange looks, but if they thought I was an exterminator with an eating disorder, then who was really hurt? Ten years of low-fat, high-protein, low-carb organic with a side of steamed vegetables may have made me healthy, but it definitely hadn't made me happy. I figured it was time to give high-fat a try. One hundred million obese Americans couldn't be wrong.

Third in line at the checkout stand meant I could do a little people watching, all in the name of acclimatizing to my new environs, of course.

20) Wear more plaid.
21) Get good, warm boots.

Shit, I needed clothing for snow. I'd never lived where it snowed. My cold-weather gear was already at its warmth limits, and it was only October.

The cashier was working a sister-wife vibe, but if she liked long-sleeve, high-neck chambray dresses with World War II hair, who was I to comment?

Three-hundred sixty-two dollars and fifty-nine cents of traps, poisons, bleach and junk food sat on the counter, waiting to be bagged. I felt a strange mixture of horror, embarrassment and pure pleasure. Until sister-wife swiped my card and it was declined.

"I'm sorry, ma'am, the card isn't going through. It says I should confiscate it." She was gleefully apologetic.

He'd canceled my credit card, the Nutsack. Sure, why not? It wasn't like I was the one who had cheated. Fidelity should be punished.

I handed her my debit card. There was roughly eight hundred dollars in my checking account. She swiped it, and I waited to see if he was angry or if he truly hated me. Her computer buzzed. I recognized the schadenfreude making sister-wife's eyes bright while the enormity of what was happening rolled over me. My husband of ten years wanted me broke, unable to care for myself or for the dog he hated. He wanted me… What, on the streets? No, he wanted me to come crawling back to him, to apologize, to suffer for having embarrassed him. Forget about love. Would he treat me this way if he even *liked* me? I was having a humiliating revelation while sister-wife looked on, taking notes for the retelling.

"I see," I said, and I guess I did. I saw exactly what I meant to him. I checked my wallet. I had eighty-seven dollars in cash, but I still needed to pick up Chaucer's food. That meant I had about forty-five dollars I could spend here. Apparently I was also going to need to start selling blood.

I looked up at the annoyed cashier, and then back at the four people waiting in line. Sweat broke out on my forehead.

22) Find a hole. Jump in.

The woman second in line checked her watch. I wanted to run to my car and hide, but I needed traps and food. I stood up straighter and powered through.

"Sorry, everyone. I'll just be a few more minutes." My heart raced, pounding in my ears as everyone watched me figure out how to pay for three hundred dollars' worth of groceries with forty dollars.

Sister-wife watched, but didn't offer any help. I kind of hated her. "I'm sorry. I'll need to put a lot of this back." I pulled out the traps, the big bottle of discount spray cleaner—I could probably cut it with water to make it last longer—the jar of peanut butter and a loaf of bread. I pushed the bags of chips and cartons of ice cream, the pasta and vegetables, all down to the end of her counter.

"I'm sorry. I can't get those things today." I gestured to my much smaller pile. "Could you ring me up for just these items?"

She sighed heavily and turned back to the computer. "I need to void out your original order first." She hit a few buttons and a long tape spit out. She paused and looked at me before she started scanning. "Can you keep an eye on the total as I go? Let me know if I need to stop?"

My eye twitched. A bead of sweat ran down my spine. I nodded.

After another sigh, she began scanning. She did it slowly, checking after each item to see if she should keep going. The people in line shifted, looking around as though trying to will another checker to appear.

My revised total was forty-one dollars. I paid and left as quickly as possible without actually running.

I put the grocery bag in the trunk and then sat in the car for a while, breathing deeply and wishing I could take back the last twenty minutes of my life. If I'd checked my accounts this morning, I would have known what he'd done. I leaned back and let the tears go. Thirty years old and I couldn't pay for my own damn groceries.

Chaucer leaned over the seat, resting his head on my shoulder again. After a minute, he licked my face. "You're right. Humiliating, but in the grand scheme of things, not important. I'll call my lawyer. Let her deal with it." I glanced at the front windows of the stores around me, looking for a help-wanted sign. "In the meantime, I need to find a job. Kibble doesn't grow on trees, you know." I wiped my face and sat up straight. "Enough of that." I had responsibilities, and feeling sorry for myself wasn't one of them. "Let's go see if that feed store is still across town."

Once we were back on the road again, I looked in the rearview mirror at my poor boy, falling off the seat, trying to figure out how to turn around in a space that would have been difficult for a dog half his size. From California to Maine, he'd been uncomfortably squished in the back seat with nary a whimper or whine. I needed to do a better job of taking care of my family. "Someday, I'll get us a big rig, one with snow tires, four-wheel drive and a roomy back seat. Okay?" He sniffed my ear in agreement.

The feed store was right where they'd left it, so once I'd wedged a forty-pound bag of kibble into the passenger seat, I pulled out my phone to call my lawyer. No service. It went right to an emergency screen, allowing for a 911 call. That Shithead had turned off my phone, as well.

I dropped it back in my purse and started the car. "Let's go for a walk, okay? I think we can both use one."

This was good. It was. He was forcing me to start over fresh.

I parked on Main. I figured we could window-shop on our way down to the harbor. We'd just started walking when Chaucer pulled on his leash, which was very unlike him. I looked across the street and saw Aiden. He was talking to the tall, cool brunette who liked to rub his arm. See? She was doing it again. Chaucer wanted to go to him, but I held him firm.

Turning away from Aiden, I pretended to look in the store window; Chaucer sighed and flopped down at my feet to wait. The butthead probably thought I was an idiot, crying over ouchy wrists. I looked past his reflection into the store and saw it was empty, and not a store at all but a little restaurant.

I may not be able to do much, but I could cook. I may never have finished college, and I may have few marketable skills. I may not have held a job since before I was married, but—wait, what was my point? Oh, right, I'm an unemployable loser. Good pep talk. Maybe I'll go into motivational speaking.

I stared in the window, dreaming of opening my own breakfast diner—the colors I would paint, the items on the menu, the name. It was all so much stuff and nonsense, but it felt wonderful and I was reluctant to walk away. The placard in the corner of the window said the location was to lease, and it gave an agent's name and number. Although I recognized it as foolishness, I copied the number on an envelope in my bag before tugging on the leash, letting Chaucer know our walk was continuing.

"Look at the big, lit-up elk. Moose? Deer… What the hell is that on the roof? Moose, definitely a moose. Think they let doggies in their shop? Probably not. Too bad. I could really use a shot glass with a cartoon lobster on it. Come on, baby, we're almost to the water."

The ocean was only a block away. The air was ripe with the tang of the sea. Chaucer shook himself and began to pull again. Newfoundlands were water dogs. If I let him, he'd run to the water's edge and jump without a second thought. It was one of the reasons I'd decided to come to Gran's house. I knew Chaucer would love living by the sea.

Main Street gave way to an expansive view of the Atlantic, blue gray as far as the eye could see. Fishing boats dotted the water along the horizon, their labor and strain taking on a romance with the distance. A masted schooner sat close to shore. Chaucer yearned for the water and gave a little whine.

"Oh, all right. But don't you dare shake all over me," I said, as I leaned over to detach the leash. When he looked up at me, I gave him the go-ahead sign. He barreled over the brick walkway and went flying into the ocean. I followed at a much slower pace, bursting out laughing when he belly flopped. I made my way to the dock and sat to watch my baby frolic in the waves.

The wind was icy off the water, but I was hard-pressed to call Chaucer back to me. The punishing winds cleansed as they tore through my clothes and hair. I closed my eyes, felt the cold of the frigid rocks below me seep into my bones and let the ocean winds blow away the uncertainty and humiliation that filled me.

A furry lick on my cheek made me open my eyes. I grinned up at him and then shot to my feet, backing up quickly. "No. Wait. You promised!" He started to shake, sending water flying. Within seconds I was drenched and sputtering, water dripping off my face. Chaucer laughed at me, as only dogs can when they know they've gotten you good.

"All right, funny boy." I attached his leash. "There's a sunny park across the street. After we dry, we'll go eat. Okay?"

Agamont Park was alive, tall trees showing their fall colors, a bright white gazebo overlooking the harbor, an ornate fountain surrounded by benches. I looked with longing at the mothers and small children playing near the fountain. I wanted children. I wanted them so badly it was an ache that seemed to crush me some days. Justin had refused, had been refusing for years.

After one particularly ugly confrontation on the topic, I'd been informed that he had no desire to watch me get fat and that I hadn't convinced him that I could be entrusted with the care of a child. Perhaps with a nanny...

I'd adopted Chaucer the following week. Justin was angry and indignant that I would do something so ill conceived and irresponsible. Poor Chaucer had had to deal with my babying while Justin had wavered between pretending Chaucer didn't exist and railing against the dog hair on his slacks.

I lay down in the soft grass, Chaucer reclining next to me. I secured his leash under my butt and then around my arm so if he got any ideas about chasing squirrels, he'd have to drag me with him. I watched a red dragon kite trace a figure eight in the sky before multiple sleepless nights finally caught up with me, and I dozed off.

A throat clearing woke me a little while later. When I opened my eyes, a large black shape loomed, silhouetted against the sun. I flinched and shaded my eyes, squinting against the glare. I felt a tug on my arm. I looked up and found Chaucer standing behind me.

"Ma'am, we received a report of a vagrant with a large bear frightening small children."

I knew that deep rumble. "Seriously? You're rousting me again?"

He squatted down so I could see the glint in his eye. "Did you shower in your clothes?"

Chaucer responded by sniffing Aiden's ear, and I'll admit it—if you're not prepared for it—it can be an odd experience. Let's just say that Aiden wasn't prepared. He flinched, losing his balance and ended up dumped on his ass. It made me smile. "Good boy," I said, ruffling the fur behind my baby's ear.

Aiden pulled his sunglasses down his nose, his narrowed gaze studying me over the rims. "You make a habit of napping in public parks, ma'am?"

Today was just getting better and better. "Have we not discussed my feelings about being addressed as ma'am? I'm pretty sure we have. And does your doctor know you've gone off your lithium? Regular use of the proper medication can make these mood swings a thing of the past." I stood and adjusted Chaucer's leash. "Officer, you have a good day now."

Something inside me rebelled against the idea of turning tail and running. No more fear-based decisions. I was divorcing constant disapproval. I didn't need to invite more in.

He stood, still staring at me over his dark lenses, a strange expression on his face.

"Let me ask you something," I said. "Was this necessary? I'm pretty sure I wasn't breaking any laws here. Couldn't you have just said, 'Hi, Katie, how's it going today?' Are you under the impression that I miss the disdain, the mocking?"

Hurt flashed through his eyes before he pushed the glasses back up his nose into place.

"You're wrong." I turned around and made my way across the park and up Main Street. I chanced a look back as I crossed the road. He still stood in the park, his hands at his hips and head bowed.

It's number one on the list for a reason—no men. They're nothing but trouble.

As I continued back through town, I knew it was still a jewel—sidewalks bustling, people browsing and sightseeing—but it had lost some of its luster. We walked toward the car and the vacant restaurant. What was I thinking? I didn't know the first thing about opening a diner or running a business. Stupid.

We'd almost passed it when I noticed the front door was ajar. I pushed it, and it swung open freely. I'd planned to close the door, make sure it locked, but I was drawn in. Instead of doing a good deed, I decided to trespass. Just more of my good decision-making skills at work.

"Hello?" I waited a moment. "Is anyone in here?" I stepped forward, Chaucer at my heels. "You left the door open. Hello?" Chaucer didn't see the need to stand by the door, so when he tugged at the end of his leash, I dropped it, letting it slide along the floor behind him.

I followed my pup's lead and wandered in. The space was empty but completely realized in my mind. I stood in the middle of the room, looking out the big, front windows, imagining that this would be my view every day. I'd cook back there, bring plates of food to people seated around this room and occasionally I'd pause, right here, to gaze out the window and watch the world of Bar Harbor stroll by.

Looking up, I imagined adding tin ceiling tiles, painting them a soft white, with a large, crystal-laden chandelier hanging in the center of the room. Black wrought iron tables and chairs, reminiscent of a Parisian café, and dark, red leather high-backed benches lining the walls completed the picture.

I was just settling into the daydream when I heard a shout from the back. Chaucer trotted toward me from the kitchen area, looking innocent and just as confused as I was by the shout. "Yeah, not buying it for a minute, buddy."

I took a tentative step forward, unsure if I should apologize for trespassing with my big, scary dog or run like hell before anyone saw me. I heard heavy footsteps and a deep voice grumbling. Chaucer didn't seem at all concerned, so I stayed where I was.

A huge mountain of a man walked out of the kitchen, stopping short when he saw us. He appeared to be close to my age, with short brown hair and golden brown eyes. "Oh." He scratched his head. "I thought I saw a bear cub." He leaned down, extending a hand for Chaucer to sniff. "This makes more sense." He looked over at me and stared. "Well, hello." He grinned and his face lit up. Dimples. My kryptonite.

23) If at all possible, find a hunky guy with dimples for making out.

"Sorry. I saw the door open, and I intended to close it, but then, well, it just looked so cute in here. I wanted a closer look. I'm really sorry we barged in and that Chaucer startled you."

He crouched down, giving Chaucer a good strong rub. "Is that your name, buddy? Chaucer? Now, this is a good-sized dog—my size." He whispered, "Those little, yappy ones make me nervous." Standing, he extended his hand to me. "Bear."

I shook it. "Bear?"

He shrugged broad shoulders, and a faint red tinge colored his cheeks. "Levi Berenson. My friends just call me Bear, for obvious reasons."

"Kate Gallagher." I was getting a crick in my neck from looking up at him. He had to be at least six and a half feet tall and was built like a linebacker.

"It's nice to meet you and Chaucer." He studied me. "So, what brings you in? Were you looking for someone?" He stepped away from me so I didn't have to strain to look up.

"Nope. Just being nosy and daydreaming."

He tipped back on his heels, nodding. "I have a healthy respect for daydreaming. I'm a contractor, and without daydreams, I'd be bored stiff most of the day." He turned toward the kitchen. "Come on, then. You should see it all."

I followed him back. Oddly enough, it never occurred to me to be nervous around a man who could break me in two without even trying.

Walking through the open doorway, he said, "This is the kitchen. It was remodeled a few years ago." He tilted his head. "By me. It's a good setup, and all the appliances still work great. I wanted to open up that wall there. Make it a half wall between the kitchen and the wait station and lunch counter. The previous tenants didn't like the idea, and the owner was fine with whatever they wanted."

He gestured to his left. "This is the walk-in cold box and the reason I'm here today. The previous tenants complained about spots getting warm in here. I'd just started checking it out when this guy wandered in and sniffed my leg." His hand dropped to Chaucer's head and began petting.

Leaning forward, I peeked around the corner into the cold room.

He laughed. "I promise not to lock the door on you. Go on in, if you want."

I stepped back, looking at him warily. "Yeah, I'm good right here."

He chuckled again and shook his head. "Okay, let's continue our tour. Pantry's over there." He pointed to the right. "Storage closet over here." He motioned again. "Dumpster and additional parking through the back door." He opened the back door and stepped out. "I always thought this would make a great patio dining area."

"Yeah, I can see why. The Dumpster is lovely. If they painted some flower vines around the graffitied profanity, it would really romance up the place. Good call." I kept a straight face as I nodded, studying the area.

"A smart-ass, eh? Good to know." Grinning, he stepped back inside. "Come on, funny girl. Tour's over. I need to get back to work."

As we walked through the kitchen, I detoured by the stove. It was a gorgeous Viking industrial-grade range. "Ooh, so pretty," I whispered. I ran my fingers lightly over the knobs, wishing I could cook on a range like this.

"Should I leave you two alone?"

I turned, finding Bear watching me, his eyes bright with humor. "Um, yeah, if you could, that would be great. I have knobs to turn, buttons to push, maybe even some cavities to explore."

Bear choked out a laugh. "I like you, Kate,

and your little dog, too." He paused, looking at me thoughtfully. "Gallagher? As in Nellie Gallagher?"

"Yes. Did you know Gran?"

He shook his head, his hands on his hips. "Figures. The first woman I've met in far too long, that I'd like to get to know better—" he stepped closer, only an arm's length away "—a woman I'd love to take to dinner tonight, is related to the only woman I've ever wanted to marry."

I laughed. "Don't you think my grandmother was a little old for you?"

"Nope. My devotion couldn't be swayed by a little thing like forty years."

Gah! Dimples again. He was killing me. "I hope you didn't let Mr. Cavanaugh hear you say things like that. He could still whoop your butt, boy." I leaned back against the stove.

"Don't I know it. Luckily, he was secure in her love and wasn't threatened by my pining for his girl. For some reason, she preferred that old coot." He turned and walked back toward the dining area. "No accounting for taste."

Chaucer and I were right behind Bear when I saw the front door open. "Bear! You working today?" Aiden walked in, taking off his sunglasses. "Oh, there you are. Listen, can you stop by Pops's place later today? He wants a glider on his back porch, thought maybe you could build him—"

Chaucer walked around Bear, his leash still sliding along the floor behind him. Aiden stopped midsentence, pointed, questions written all over his face. Bear crouched down, getting Chaucer in a headlock and thereby revealing me, not that I was hiding or anything. "Hey, Aiden, have you met Chaucer?" He looked over his shoulder at me. "And this is his mom, Kate. Kate was just considering going out to dinner with me. Maybe if the chief of police could let her know I'm not going to tie her up and feed her to hungry cats, she might be more likely to agree."

Aiden stared, his face entirely blank.

I walked over to grab Chaucer's leash and to get the hell away from Officer Buttmunch. "Thanks for the tour, Bear. I'll let you get back to work."

Bear looked up at Aiden, waiting for him to speak. Aiden was still silent as I walked out the door. When we got back to the car, I let Chaucer in first before settling in behind the wheel.

Bear hurried out and leaned against the passenger door. He raised his eyebrows, waiting. I turned the key and lowered the window.

"Sorry. I have no idea what that was about with Aiden, but I really am a nice guy. Promise." He bent down, resting his forearms on the edge of the door. Chaucer leaned forward and licked

Bear's face. Bear chuckled. "Thanks, buddy." Turning back to me, his warm brown eyes were hopeful. "Can I talk you into dinner tonight?"

Strangely enough, even though men were strictly verboten, I wanted to say yes. Then again, dimples were on my to-do list. "That sounds lovely, but I'm going through a divorce right now. I think the timing is—"

"Perfect." He grinned and I felt a flutter. Damn dimples. "It's just dinner. We'll talk. We'll eat. I promise not to propose. It'll be good. What do you say I pick you up at seven?" He stretched his arm through the window, hitting the button to lower the rear-door window. He moved back to Chaucer to give him a full-body rub through the window. "Later, little bear cub. Feel free to come visit me anytime." He stepped back to the front window and leaned down. "So, make any decisions yet?"

WHEN CHAUCER AND I returned home, I curled up on the one chair left in the living room and tried to erase the day's events by slipping into a coma. It worked for about two hours, until the house phone woke me up. I went to the kitchen and warily picked up the receiver. *Don't be Justin.*

"Kate? Are you there?"

Damn! I'd forgotten. "Hi, Mom. Yes, I'm here." I hopped up on the counter, feet dangling and banging against the cupboards.

"My goodness, I've been worried sick. You said you'd call when you arrived. I haven't been able to get a hold of you for days. Your cell is disconnected. What's been going on?"

"Sorry. The drive was really long and exhausting. I finally arrived before dawn two days ago."

"Oh, well, good." The worry faded from her voice. Mom couldn't hold on to strong emotions anymore. They ran like water through her fingers.

"I didn't realize Justin had disconnected my phone until this morning." Shoot. "I'd better call Christine, too. She was checking in daily. I assumed I hadn't heard from her because she was busy." Could I still get to my contact info? I didn't know anyone's phone number by heart.

"Well, that's done. You're there. That's all that matters. So, is her house just as you remembered? It's strange, isn't it, how much our perceptions can alter our memories? The house probably seems much smaller than you thought it was as a child. Since you were smaller, the house seemed bigger..."

Honestly, I zoned out a little. I'd already heard Mom's theories on perception versus reality many times. I knew she was trying to cope with her worry by burying it under cold, theoretical questions.

Still, I only had four dollars to my name. I needed help. "Mom," I interrupted. "Can I ask a favor?"

"Oh, of course, dear. I'm sorry. I lost track."

"No, it's fine." I felt like I was standing in that checkout line all over again, everyone watching while I counted out pennies. Gah! I did not want to do this! "Mom, I need some help. Justin closed down my credit and debit cards. Would you be able to loan me some money—just until I get a job and can pay you back?"

"Oh, honey. I can't believe he did that! Did you call your lawyer? He doesn't have the right to do that!" She sighed, anger fading. "I could send my graduate students over to beat him for you. Shall I do that, dear? One of them is quite large."

I gave a wheezy laugh. "Thanks, Mom, but I don't think we need more people arrested."

"Some of these boys are very big and strong. They could follow him, wait until he's alone and then jump him. Who would ever suspect a couple of archeology grad students? It's a perfect crime!"

I laughed. It felt good. "That'd be a pretty quick line to draw, Mom. Grad student to adviser to me."

"Oh, you." She chuckled. "I thought it was a good plan." Sighing, she said, "Of course I'll send you money. Is a check okay? Or should I wire the money to you directly?"

Hmm, good question. "How about a check, Mom? I'll need to go into town and open a checking account, anyway."

"Okay, dear. I'm writing it as we speak. I'll have one of my students run over to the post office for me. I have a class starting in a few minutes." She paused. "I love you, sweetie. Hang tough. You'll make it through this. You're made of much stronger stuff than me. You'll be just fine. I promise."

My throat constricted at her absolute faith in me. I wasn't sure I shared her confidence, but it helped me sit a little straighter. I didn't even realize how crushing the pressure was until it had eased some. "Thanks, Mom. I love you, too."

I hung up and looked down at Chaucer, who was lying on the floor in front of me. "Okay, buddy. It's time to hunt us some critters!" I hopped down, and pulled the traps and peanut butter out of a bag on the counter. "Everybody likes peanut butter, right?"

It'd be my luck to end up with a house full of pests who suffered from nut allergies.

CHAPTER NINE

Aiden

FUCKING BEAR. I turned away from the diner window. I was not going to watch him flirt with Katie. Especially since I'd already witnessed him getting her to laugh.

The door opened behind me. "What the hell was that? You are the world's shittiest wingman! I have a gorgeous redhead—and you know how I feel about redheads—standing here, with the greatest dog I've ever met, and you can't be bothered to tell her I'm not an ax murderer? What good is having a cop friend if he can't reassure beautiful women to take a chance on me?" He paused and studied me for a second, his eyes narrowing. "I've been playing poker with you for ten years. I know that face. Are you interested in her?"

I wanted to punch that grin off his face. "Don't be stupid. Of course not."

Bear dropped his hands from his waist, staring at me in disbelief. "You can look at *that* woman, who by the way is very funny, and say of course you're not interested? Trust me, if there's anyone being stupid around here, it ain't me." He headed back to the kitchen and then stopped. "Seriously, Aiden. Do you want me to back off? It's been a year and you haven't dated."

"I date."

"If we're using the word *date* the way prostitutes do, then sure."

I considered how hard I'd need to punch him to dump him on his ass. "I'm not interested in Katie Gallagher."

Bear just stared and then broke out the biggest shit-eating grin I've ever seen. "Good." He turned and went back to work.

I left Bear and walked toward the station, trying hard not to think about Katie and failing miserably. I'd been in love with her since that first summer she'd visited her grandmother. She'd been six years old, and she'd shone like she'd swallowed the sun. Her hair had been a curly fire floating around her head, and her light green eyes had glowed as though lit from within. Freckles dusted her nose and cheeks. I saw her across the church, sitting with her grandmother, and—even at five—I was a goner.

I'd scooted to the end of the pew and started to make my way to her when I felt my dad's massive mitt grab the back of my T-shirt, dragging me back to my place. She and her grandmother were sitting in a shaft of mottled light from the stained glass above them. I spent the rest of Mass staring at her.

After the service, my parents had stopped to talk with Nellie so I studied Katie up close. She looked exactly like a fairy should. She wore a white sundress, butterflies fluttering all over it with a matching butterfly headband, pulling her corkscrew curls back from her face. I remember trying to peek behind her, looking for her wings.

In the summers that had followed, my obsession with Katie Gallagher grew. She was the one against whom all others were measured and found wanting. The summer she turned fifteen everything changed. I'd finally built up the courage to ask her out, and before the words could leave my mouth, she walked off, laughing about my being a little kid. It crushed me. And then she left, never spent another summer with us. The last thing she ever said was "Him? Come on. He's a little kid." It took me a couple of years before I gathered the courage to ask another girl out. Then years later, Alice came along and finally cured me of romantic love.

These days I dated. I had fun. But I didn't involve my heart or my trust anymore.

I'd just sat down at my desk when Heather's voice crackled through the intercom. "Chief, you have a call on line two."

"Chief Cavanaugh."

"Hello, this is Justin Cady. I'm told you interviewed my wife, Katherine Cady."

"Yes."

Silence filled the line. He waited for me to elaborate. As I wasn't going to do that, I let the silence stretch.

He cleared his throat. "Can you give me the phone number of our house up there? I can't find it in any of the paperwork."

I knew Nellie's number by heart. "I'm sorry, sir. I can't give out that kind of information over the phone. Why don't you contact your wife?"

He grunted. "Have you seen what she did to my car? I'm trying to avoid the psycho."

"Then why would you—"

"It's for my lawyer. He needs to get an appraiser out there."

"Appraiser?" This was not good. It would really hurt Pops to have Nellie's house sold.

"We're divorcing. Obviously. That house is the only thing of value my wife has. Real estate prices are good up there, but I've never seen what kind of condition the place is in."

Because he'd never visited. Interesting. I tapped my pen on my open notebook. "I see."

He paused. "What?"

I shook my head, pointlessly. "Nothing. You and your wife can do whatever you choose with the house. I'll just be sorry to see more changes. I knew Nellie Gallagher. Quite well."

"Oh, then you can tell me what I need to know."

I made a noncommittal hum. "I'll let your lawyer fill you in. House appraisal isn't in my skill set."

"Which leads me back to the phone number."

"And me back to advising you to contact your wife."

"Ex."

"Mmm-hmm."

"Have you at least seen the car? Is it as bad as I remember?" There was a whine in his voice I empathized with. Half the car was a beauty.

"Probably worse. It doesn't take long for exposed metal to rust up here."

I heard a strangled scream. "Fine. Screw her! She'll see what I can do when *I'm* motivated."

"I'd also advise you not to threaten someone while talking to a cop."

"Not a threat, a promise."

CHAPTER TEN

Kate

BEAR ARRIVED EXACTLY at seven. Chaucer barked once to alert me and then stood by the door, tail wagging. But I was busy panicking. What the hell was I thinking, agreeing to go on a date? "No men" was the first item on my to-do list. My divorce wasn't final yet. I had already proven to have poor decision-making skills. What was I doing? It had been over ten years since I'd been out on a date, out with a man other than Justin. Granted, Bear seemed nice, was wicked hot and Chaucer loved him, but I couldn't shake this nervous, unsettled feeling, two parts great and three parts wrong. Maybe I could call in sick. Through the door. Just shout "I'm sick!"

After I'd left my ex, and it was just Chaucer and me alone in a car for days on end, I began looking back over my marriage without the blinders of mistakenly placed faith. All the furtive looks and smiles I caught directed at other women, the late-night business dinners and client meetings took on new meaning. He hadn't been tirelessly working to build his new business for us. He'd never stopped dating. Once I saw it, I couldn't believe I'd been blind for so long. I'd wanted so much to love someone who could love me back that I hadn't looked closely enough at the man declaring his devotion.

I'd accepted degradation and humiliation for the promise of affection. It was a hard thing to learn about myself. Consequently, I now had no faith in my ability to make good, sound, non-needy choices.

The knock came a moment later. I straightened my spine and reminded myself it was just dinner. I wasn't making the same mistake again. Chaucer gave an impatient woof. A big, strong body rub was waiting for him on the other side of the door, and I was taking too damn long to open it.

I put my hand on Chaucer's head, reminding him to stay, and then opened the door. Bear stood, smiling at both of us. He wore dark blue jeans with a white button-down under a navy sweater. He extended a hand for Chaucer who looked up at me, waiting to be released. I gave him the hand movement, and he barreled out, actually jumping up on Bear, Chaucer's paws at Bear's shoulders. I ran after him, apologies flying out of my mouth, but Bear just laughed.

"Oh, my God, I can't believe he just did that! I'm so sorry!" I was trying to pull Chaucer down, but he wasn't having any of it. "He knows never to jump. I can't believe he didn't knock you down the stairs. That's 140 pounds of excited dog you just took to the chest."

Bear was in the process of giving a very happy Newfoundland a full body rub. I thought Chaucer's tail was going to wag right off his body. "It's fine. I'm big. I can take it." Bear gave him one last head scratch and then pushed my dog down. "Well, that was a nice greeting. You know, if you wanted to throw yourself at me, I'd catch you, too."

I didn't invite him in and felt rude for not doing so, but friends don't let friends enter demon-possessed houses.

"I hope you're hungry," he said. "I called the Chart Room—a little restaurant up the coast, right on the water—and asked if they were still serving on the deck. It's late in the season for outdoor dining, but they said they'd do it for us if we wanted to take Chaucer, too. So, would you rather be inside, warm and toasty, but with the pooch left at home, or outside in the cold wind with the dog?"

My mind went blank. "You would do that for us? Sit in the cold and wind just so Chaucer could come, too?" Thoughtful, gorgeous dog lover with dimples, the man was too good to be true. And, it meant my baby wouldn't be locked in with vicious, nasty beasties. "Not that he deserves it after jumping on you, but I vote for cold and windy."

He nodded and grinned. "My kind of woman. Okay, you're going to need a heavy coat. Has he eaten yet?"

"He'll lie to you, but he's been fed." I looked down at my pearl gray trousers and blazer, my ivory top, all remnants of a previous life. "This, however, is the best I can do on warm coats." I grimaced. "Deal breaker?"

"No way. I have an extra coat you can use." Bear headed for his truck. "You'll drown in it, but it'll keep you warm."

Picking up my bag, I pulled out Chaucer's leash. He danced around me before sitting politely. "Okay, buddy, you can come." I leaned over and grabbed his big, bearlike head. "Best behavior. No jumping." He wriggled, licking my fingers.

"Was that a yes?" Bear asked.

"It most certainly was."

I locked up the house—no idea why—and got a good look at Bear's truck. There was a large open bed in back but no second row of seats in the cab. It was perfect for a contractor, but not so good for a dog, so I walked to my car. "Okay, looks like I'm driving, boys—saddle up."

Bear pulled two coats from the cab of his truck before heading to my car. Unfortunately, in trying to be a gentleman, helping me on with his coat and opening my door, he saw the trashed driver's side for the first time. I'll give it to him. He paused, assessed, glanced at my red face and made the valiant choice to ignore it. He was kind of perfect.

He directed us down through town and onto Highway 3. "It's just a couple of miles past Bar Harbor." He shifted in his seat, trying to find a comfortable spot that didn't have the glove box digging into his knees or his head cocked at an angle to fit under the roof.

"I think on the return trip you should sit in the back with Chaucer." I grimaced in sympathy. "I'm really sorry. I didn't realize this would be so cramped for you."

Bear shifted sideways, taking the pressure off his knees but still needing to bow his head. He sighed. "Not your fault. The world was not made for big people. You guys—" he motioned to my legs "—you can just shift your seat forward, and you're good. They don't make cars big enough that I can just shift a seat and fit. It's part of the reason I drive a pickup. It has the biggest cab on the market." He looked behind him at the bench seat Chaucer was on. "I think you're right, though. I will move back there. If I push the front seat forward, I'll at least have more leg room."

Chaucer popped up when Bear showed interest in him, leaning forward to rest his head next to

Bear's. Bear let his fingers sink into Chaucer's ruff, scratching behind his ears.

"It's up about a quarter of a mile on your right. See, right there. Good. Just park over to the side."

I pulled up to an unassuming white roadside café. In addition to the seating inside the restaurant, there were extensive decks in back. The decks were currently empty of tables and chairs, save for one, near the restaurant wall, with its own portable heater snugged up against it.

Bear noticed and nodded. "Perfect."

I got out and buttoned Bear's coat around me. He was right. It ought to keep me warm. The wool-lined garment hung to my knees. Bear took one look at me and burst out laughing.

"Yeah, yeah. I may look ridiculous, but I'm warm."

We walked to the entrance. Bear held the restaurant door open for me and Chaucer, but we didn't walk in. "I'm pretty sure they don't want him in their main dining area." I moved toward the walkway along the side of the building. "We'll go straight out to the table, if you want to let them know we're here?"

He nodded, absently pointing a finger at Chaucer. "Good point. Be out in a sec."

While Bear went to talk with the host, Chaucer and I wandered around the huge decked area. I leaned against a railing, suspended above the placid water. Chaucer sat next to me, leaning into me, warming that side of my body. The sun was setting, and it was glorious.

I felt, rather than heard, Bear approach. Like Chaucer, he was a wall of heat, only at my back instead of against my leg and hip. Bear didn't say anything, but I knew he was there. "It's gorgeous. Thank you for bringing us."

The low rumble of his voice sounded at my ear. "It *is* beautiful." His arms came up around me, leaning on the rail. He didn't touch me, but his body heat enveloped me. "Not trying to pen you in. You were shivering, even in that big coat. Just trying to help warm you up a little."

I turned and bumped into his broad chest. "Shall we sit down?"

"Absolutely." He put out his arm for me to take and then escorted me to the table that had been set up for us. He adjusted the flame on the heater and then inched it even closer to one of the chairs. He looked over at me and grinned, pulling the chair out. "Your seat."

I plopped in and felt the heat wash over me. He sat opposite me, with Chaucer opting for lying on my feet under the table. "The heater's practically on top of me. Are you warm enough? We should move it back to the center."

He gave a brief shake of his head, brushing off the topic. "I'm fine." He pointed out at the glowing sky. Reds and oranges were bleeding into pinks and indigos. "Every season the sky takes on a different face. Autumn, moving in to winter, the blues and purples take on a green hue." We watched the glowing sky for a few moments before he turned his attention back to me. "So, Kate, I didn't say this earlier, but I'm really sorry about your grandmother. I thought the world of her."

Petting Chaucer, I nodded slowly. "Me, too."

"I hear you're living in Nellie's house now." His warm brown eyes studied me.

"Yep, again."

"Well, if you need anything, run into any problems, you let me know. I've done quite a bit of work for Nellie over the years. Mostly handyman stuff, but I'll offer you the same service. If you have items on your honey-do list that are beyond your comfort level, let me know. I can always stop by and take care of them for you."

"That's awfully nice of you. I don't suppose you're an exterminator, too?"

"Sorry, no. Problem?"

"Nothing I can't handle." And by *nothing* I meant *everything*.

The waitress came for our orders. We both started off with the clam chowder to stave off the cold. It was only a few moments later that the bowls were placed before us. I breathed in the steamy goodness, anticipating my first real meal in weeks.

"Bear, it feels like I would have remembered

you if you'd been around when I visited as a kid. Did I miss you, or are you a transplant?"

He took a spoonful of soup and shook his head. "Rest assured, even if you hadn't noticed me, I definitely would have made myself known to you." He stirred his chowder. "I do have a weakness for redheaded women."

I looked down, busying myself with my soup, hoping the low light hid my blush.

"No. I grew up in Washington—the state, not the district. I met a girl in college and fell in love. She was from Bar Harbor. I came out to visit her and never wanted to go home." He tilted his head, a self-deprecating laugh at his lips. "The girl dumped me, but the town seemed to like me just fine, so I stayed."

"Her loss," I said softly.

Bear looked up at the seriousness of my tone. He reached over and rubbed my hand. "I'm fine, but thank you."

"How long have you lived here?"

The waitress came back, collected our soup bowls and placed the teriyaki tenderloin tips in front of me and the salmon in front of Bear.

We started to eat before Bear finally answered. He wiped his mouth. "I've been here for about ten years now."

The tenderloin was tangy and delicious. Chaucer lifted his head to sniff at the table. I pulled a rawhide from my bag and offered it to him.

He gently took it from my fingers and slumped back down under the table to gnaw on his bone.

Bear took a bite of his potatoes. "Can I just say that you have the greatest dog I've ever met? How did you two find each other?"

I extended my hand under the table and a moment later, I felt Chaucer's head push into my hand. I shifted back a little in my seat so he could rest his head in my lap. "There was a notice on the bulletin board at my ex-husband's club. A family had purchased him without doing their research. The daughter wanted a toy breed, and the wife wasn't too excited about dogs, period. I have no idea where they got him. I saw his little Newfy puppy face on that flyer and pulled it off the wall. I didn't want anyone else to see him. I ran outside, called the number and made an appointment to meet him that afternoon. I spent the rest of the day buying dog food and bowls, toys and a bed, a collar and a leash. I knew he was supposed to be mine. Through some weird twist of fate, he'd ended up in the wrong home, but I was going to fix that."

Bear had stopped eating, his focus on me. "And you did."

"Evening." We both looked up in the direction of the deep voice coming out of the dark. Aiden took a step forward, into the circle of light surrounding our table.

Bear placed his napkin on the table and pushed

back in his chair, so he could better see Aiden. "Fancy meeting you here, Chief." There was a tone I couldn't quite place, but Bear didn't appear to be happy about the interruption.

Aiden looked back and forth between the two of us, finally glancing down at the back end of a dark brown blob under the table. "At least I understand now why you're threatening this poor woman with pneumonia, Bear."

"Listen—" Bear began.

"This was my choice, and it's been lovely." I shifted my gaze to Bear. "Truly lovely. Thank you for bringing us here."

Bear gave a reluctant smile, some of the tension leaving his shoulders. "So, Chief, is dining al fresco illegal now?"

Aiden ignored Bear's little dig, reaching down to scratch the top of Chaucer's head, speaking directly to me. "Just driving by and saw your car. I wanted to apologize about before." He stuffed his hands in his pockets, as an uncomfortable silence surrounded us.

Bear's eyes narrowed, as he studied Aiden. He slowly shook his head, picking up his napkin and fork again. "Well, it sure was nice of you to visit, Chief, but our food's getting cold."

Bear's comment barely earned a glance from Aiden, who then gestured to me. "Go ahead and eat." He left, walking back around the side of the building. That was odd.

A moment later he came back, a knit hat in his hand. "I'm glad Bear loaned you a warm coat, but you need a hat, too."

I glanced at Bear who was staring openmouthedly at Aiden, his cooling dinner forgotten.

"California girl." I shrugged. "I forget about hats."

"Bear should have remembered." He leaned down and drew the hat on me, flipping up the extra knitted weave so it framed my face and covered my ears.

Bear threw his napkin down on the table, annoyance clear.

I hated to admit it, and I wouldn't aloud, but the hat helped. I gave Aiden a smile of thanks, and he nodded.

24) Buy warm hats.

Preferably the ones with the silly pom-pom balls on top.

"You lose heat out of the top of your head. Got to keep it covered if you're going to be taken out into frigid winds." He gave Bear a dark look and then shifted back to me. "Go ahead. Eat. I don't want you to have to be out in this cold for longer than necessary."

Bear smacked Aiden on the shoulder. Judging by Aiden's wince, I wouldn't term it friendly.

"Well, it's been a nice visit but we don't want to hold you up. I'm sure you have important things to do, being on duty right now and all."

Aiden ignored Bear, his eyes on me. "Please. Eat."

The waitress came out with a bowl of chowder, the host trailing with a chair. "Evening, Chief. We thought you might like to sit with your friends. Maybe have something to eat, too?"

Once the pair returned to the restaurant, Aiden continued to stand, looking uncomfortable.

"Have you eaten?" The big, embarrassed lug was killing me.

"Sit if you're going to sit," Bear said as he kicked the chair to the side in a half-hearted invitation.

"Go ahead, Aiden. Join us. Have some chowder. It's delicious," I said.

He looked between the two of us, sitting reluctantly. Bear, grumbling under his breath, returned to his meal.

The rest of dinner was strained, Aiden staying, even walking me to my car and opening my door for me. Once Chaucer and I were inside, Aiden and Bear had what looked to be a strained conversation. I'm a pretty good lip-reader, and I'm almost positive Bear called Aiden a cock-blocking asshole, but I couldn't be sure. Afterward, both men turned to me and smiled. Aiden walked back to his cruiser, and Bear circled around to the passenger door of my car.

He climbed in, buckled up and then we were off.

"I honestly have no idea what that just was. I'm sorry dinner got weird." He shook his head as though trying to clear it. "I don't think he's been on a real date since his fiancée ran out on him a year ago. Maybe he's forgotten how they work." He mumbled what sounded like *asshole*.

"Did you know her?" It was none of my business, but I was curious.

Bear nodded. "Yeah, Alice seemed nice enough."

"And?" That could not have been all he had to say on the subject.

He blew out a breath. "And I never liked her. It's easy to say that now, knowing what she did, but I didn't like her. She was sweet to Aiden, but she seemed, I don't know, open to the possibility of someone better. You know?"

I nodded, understanding exactly the kind of person he was describing.

"Aiden's my friend." He rolled his eyes. "Usually. Anyway, she kept touching me. You know, I'd make a joke and she'd laugh, grabbing my arm or running her hand down my back. Sure, she could just be a touchy person, but I noticed she didn't do it with everyone. Aiden? All the time. Me? Most of the time. Women or random dorky guys, not at all. When he learned that she'd dumped him for another guy, it crushed him. So, maybe I gave Aiden a little more leeway than I would someone else busting into my dinner date." He shrugged. "He's still an asshole, though."

I laughed and glanced over at Bear. He was gorgeous and sweet. What was he doing here with me? "Bear, why aren't you married?"

"Aunt Sarah?" He looked around in the back seat and then smirked. "Sorry, that's how most of my conversations with my aunt begin." He shifted in his seat. "Damn, I was supposed to sit in the back. I forgot." He looked longingly at the big bench seat Chaucer was stretched over. "The usual reasons. Haven't met, or convinced, the right one. Not yet, anyway."

When we arrived back at Gran's, Bear walked me to the door, stopping two steps down from the porch. I kept walking, pulling out my key before I realized he'd stopped. I turned to find him watching me.

"C'mere, Red."

When I stepped back toward him, I understood why he'd stopped. Two steps down put us at almost the same height. He grinned, holding out his arms, and I stepped right into them. A Bear hug was an amazing experience. It was just the right combination of warm affection, comfort and protection, without a skeezy side of cop-a-feel.

When he loosened his hold, I moved back. "Hmm, that was nice. You give a good hug, Bear."

"So I'm told. Would a good-night kiss be out of the question?"

Bear made me feel good about myself, about life in general—which was on my list—so I didn't think twice about leaning into him for a kiss. He framed my face with his massive hands. I felt the heat down to my bones. His kiss was soft and sweet. I enjoyed it, but it gave me no sexy-time tingles.

He broke the kiss, leaning his forehead against mine. "Damn," he breathed.

"Right?"

"Maybe we should try one more time, hit each other with the hottest kiss in our arsenals."

I couldn't help grinning. "Let's do this."

We flew into a passionate embrace, hands roamed, tongues met, but after a few short moments, we both started laughing.

Bear shook his head, rubbing his hands over his face. "Well, this is disappointing." He turned and dropped heavily to the porch.

"I'm pretty sure it's you, not me." I sat next to him, bumping his shoulder with my own.

He studied me and shook his head again. "Someone up there hates me. The hottest, most beautiful woman I've met in far too long and it's like kissing my sister. If I had one."

I shrugged, apologetically. "Maybe you're just not that good of a kisser?"

He put one of his huge hands on my knee and squeezed. "I'm sorry. What did you say?"

I giggled, squirming away from him.

"Okay, that's it. There's only one thing to do." He stood, grabbed me and threw me over his shoulder in a fireman's lift. "We need to have sex and make sure."

I laughed like a loon as he bounced me up and down. He grabbed my ass, steadying me. "Careful, don't fall."

I pounded on his back, trying to speak through the laughter. Chaucer barked once and then sat himself in front of the door, blocking Bear.

Bear lifted me easily and placed me back on my feet. "Saved by the dog. All right. I'll accept defeat, but I reserve the right to kiss you at will in the hopes that we eventually spark."

I wiped away tears, my stomach hurting from laughing so hard. "I accept those terms but reserve the right to slap you if I find myself annoyed by the intrusion."

He nodded. "And I accept *those* terms."

After Bear left, I dragged myself upstairs to change into my warmest sweats. I wished I'd felt something when we kissed. He was kind and funny, sexy and sweet. Why couldn't I be attracted to him? And why did Aiden bringing me a hat to keep me warm give me the squishy feels? *Gah! Officer Grumpy cleans out animal traps and I'm smitten. Bear kisses me and nothing.* Sometimes, life truly sucked ass.

I AWOKE WITH a start, the phone echoing through the empty house. Chaucer put his nose against my forehead. "Dude, I hear it. Keep your cold, wet body parts to yourself!" I'd slept in the one chair left in the living room. Neck throbbing, I straightened, shaking out the hand currently being attacked by pins and needles, and ran to get the phone.

"Hello."

"Katherine."

I froze. My skin crawled.

"Katherine, are you there?"

"What do you want, Justin?"

"Many things. Fortunately, none of them involve you. First, though, I want my car. Before it starts to rust."

Of course. The car. "How am I supposed to do that? You closed my banking accounts."

"*My* banking accounts. I'm the one who makes the money. You're the one who spends it."

"No-fault state. And I worked my ass—"

"Your considerable ass."

"—off, cooking, cleaning, organizing your

social calendar, hosting dinner parties and charity events."

"True. You made a better personal assistant than a wife. I'm rather enjoying not having you always silently moping in the background."

Was that true? Did I act like that? I thought about our ten years together, but couldn't pinpoint a time or event that caused a shift. He'd always relished complaining that something I'd done or said could have been executed better, corrected me to show me how I should have done it. After a while, it was easier to not say anything. He only ever listened to find fault, anyway. "Why are you really calling me?"

"I told you. I want my car back. If you were hoping for alimony or a settlement, you've got a wake-up call coming. So, here it is. You're getting nothing from me. Nothing. I'm very good at what I do, Katherine. Your lawyer will never find my money, and it *is* mine. I want my car and then I'll wash my hands of you. Well, almost. I have another gift coming your way soon." Click.

My head throbbed. Justin. Threats. Infestations. Starvation. Unemployment. Gran. At the thought of Gran, a band seemed to squeeze my chest. I couldn't handle it coming at me from every direction all at once. Chaucer leaned into me and then plopped his butt down on my foot. The band began to release. "You're right. One thing at a time. We need to get you fed."

I moved to the pantry and opened the door. Movement made me squeal and slam it shut. Chaucer barked, sniffing in the crack under the door.

Glancing at the phone, I wondered if this fell into the category of a 911 call. It totally should, but I doubted the cops would see it that way. Frick! Chaucer started clawing at the floor, trying to dig under to get at whatever was in the pantry.

I'd put a trap in there yesterday after I fed him, worried Chaucer's food would attract critters. If a trapped animal was the price of being right, I'd rather be wrong. Chaucer barked and whined.

"I know!" I stamped a socked foot. Now what? I forgot to bring my hazmat suit and industrial-grade gloves with me.

Buy a hazmat suit! Lead lined.

I slowly opened the door again, body blocking Chaucer who desperately wanted in. "Sit." He sat, but his body strained around me, trying to see the predator stealing his food. Two angry eyes glared at me.

I may or may not have screamed. Those eyes had to have been a foot off the floor. I slammed the door. Pounding on the door caused me to jump, falling over Chaucer. My head cracked on the floor, but still I scrambled to get farther away from whatever was in the pantry that could pound on doors. Tears sprang to my eyes, but I stood up and stalked back to the pantry. I smacked the flat of my hand against the door over and over. "No more! Get out and stay out!"

When the pounding started again, I realized it was the front door, not the pantry. *Oh.*

"Katie? Are you all right? Open up!"

Sure. Why not be Aiden? He's clearly what the situation was lacking. I needed another man who thought I was a worthless idiot.

Chaucer ran to the door, giving a happy bark. I stumbled behind him, my head pounding while my brains leaked out. I wiped at the tears on my face and took a deep breath.

Pound. Pound. Pound. "Katie?"

"Yeah, yeah, I'm coming," I mumbled. I opened the door to find tall, dark and dickish with his hands on his hips, apparently pissed off I hadn't moved faster.

"Why did you scream? And what took you so long to answer the door?"

See? "I'm having a prob—wait! Yes." I grabbed his arm and pulled him inside. I circled behind and pushed him toward the kitchen. He didn't move. I kept pushing, but had no traction on the slick wooden floors. My feet slid out from under me. I was not going down twice inside three minutes. I grabbed his waist and held on, finally able to right myself.

"Can you please take your hands off me, Katie?"

Pointing around him toward the kitchen, I said, "Protect and serve. Get in the kitchen and protect us from whatever huge snarling beast is in there, and then serve us by getting rid of it."

I had no idea what he was thinking. His large back was better at looming than conveying thoughts. Tentatively, I reached a hand out and tried one more shove. His hand whipped back and grabbed mine, pulling me around to stand in front of him.

"Hey! You're the cop. You have the gun." I scampered around behind him again and shoved with both hands. Nothing.

"Woman, if you push me one more time, I'm arresting you."

"If you'd just move, I wouldn't have to push."

Chaucer scratched at the pantry door again.

"Please, can you help us?" I whined. I kind of hated him for making me whine.

He moved forward. "Was that so difficult?" He stopped by Chaucer, patting the dog's head and then pushing him aside.

I stood in the kitchen doorway, ready to make a break for it. "So, I have to beg before you'll do the decent thing? You're all the same," I mumbled.

He shook his head and pulled his flashlight from his belt.

"Don't forget your gun! Whatever's in there is huge."

He opened the door a crack, his foot braced against it, opening farther. He shone the light through the divide, turned back to me, rolled his eyes and flung the door open.

"Careful!" I half hid around the doorsill.

Aiden crouched down. "Hey," he murmured. "You're okay. I'll get you out of there."

I leaned forward, trying to see around him.

He stood, carrying something toward the back door. "You want to open the door, so I can let the vicious beast out?"

I ran forward to do as he'd asked and looked in his arms. A baby raccoon. It looked at me and hissed as he carried it past.

I closed the door and leaned against it. The band was back, squeezing my chest. Damn. The door opened, smacking into the back of my already-throbbing head. I stood a moment, absorbing the pain.

"You need to take two steps forward, so I can open the door enough to enter."

I ignored the sarcasm, shuffling forward to sit, dropping my head to the table. I'd hurt a baby raccoon. My husband, the man who pledged to love me forever, thought I was a sad piece of crap, one he couldn't scrape off the bottom of his shoe fast enough. The house was infested. My body hurt from sleeping in that chair. I couldn't afford an exterminator, let alone a bed. And Gran was dead.

I flinched when a big, warm hand settled on

the back of my head. "Ouch. Did I do that with the door?"

The heat from his hand felt nice. "No. I bounced it off the floor when I saw the raccoon's eyes glowing in the dark." I put my arms up on the table, cushioning my head. "It was all me." I looked up at him. "Is the raccoon okay? The trap didn't hurt him, did it?"

He pulled out a chair and sat next to me. "He'll be fine. His limp looks minor. It sure didn't slow him down any. For now it makes him look like a tough guy."

I dropped my head back to my arms. "At least I've helped his street cred."

I should write a letter of apology to the raccoon family. Maybe leave my trash uncovered for them. Wait, would that bring bears?

"Does Maine have bears?"

Silence.

I lifted my head, waiting for an answer.

Confusion and concern lined his face. "I feel like you should come with subtitles."

"You're the one withholding local wildlife facts." I put my head back down.

"Black bears, yes." At my gasp, he continued, "But none around here. Acadia National Park sometimes has bears or moose, but they don't wander down this close to town." He paused. "Can I get you some aspirin?" His voice was a gentle rumble.

"Sure. Do you have any?" I sat up and stiffened my spine. "I'll be fine. Thanks."

He watched me for a moment, nodding thoughtfully. "Are there other traps you need me to check while I'm here?"

Blinking, I thought of the other traps and having to do all of this again. "Please." I stood and swayed a moment, grabbing the chair for balance.

He reached out but didn't touch me. "Do you have someplace you can lie down?"

"Sure." The back seat of the car as soon as you leave.

He sighed. "Where are the other traps?"

Chaucer sniffed all around the pantry, paying close attention to his bag of food.

I gestured to the other side of the kitchen. "Under the sink, downstairs bath, closet under the stairs, upstairs bedrooms, bathroom and linen closet."

He lifted his eyebrows, staring at me.

"What?" Chaucer wandered back to me and leaned against my leg. "There are strange animals living all over the place in here." I put one hand on Chaucer's head. "I need them gone. They have the whole forest to live in. They don't need Gran's house, too."

After he went to clean out the other traps, I grabbed Chaucer's bowls to fill them. I hesitated to open the back door for his visit to the newly appointed little boys' room by the tree line—what if that raccoon ran back in? I looked out the window in the door, searching for any shady woodland creatures looking to storm the joint.

Chaucer whined, wanting to get out. I put my hand on his head, scanning the yard one more time before I opened the door.

"Anything out there?"

I jumped at Aiden's voice. When I turned, I found him grinning. "What the bleep? Will you not be happy until I seize?"

He shouldered me out of the way and opened the back door. Chaucer ran past us. "It's not my fault you're jumpy—" he grinned wider "—and apparently frightened of trees and bushes."

I almost tripped him. Almost. I was afraid he'd drop whatever animal was squirming in the bag he was holding. "It's not the bushes and the trees, you dillhole! It's all the freaking animals that live in them!" I stepped out onto the porch and glared at the yard. "Listen up! This is my house. Not yours! I'll stay in here, if you stay out there. You can have the whole yard. That forest over there. The gard—wait, no. Not Gran's garden. Stay out of that. Otherwise, the world is yours. Just stay the frick out of my house!" I turned back to the door, and then remembered. "Oh, and if you have relatives currently staying in my house, can you pass on the word to get out?" I took another step. "Without actually entering my house, of course.

Just, you know, use your predator alarm systems. I watch nature shows. I know you guys can do that stuff. Thump your tails on a log or something. Just get 'em out!" I paused, waiting for a squirrel to give me the high sign that my message was received. Nothing. Furry little bastards.

Aiden came around the side of the house. "Communing with nature?"

I side-eyed the yard as I followed him in. "Something like that."

After he cleared out the critters, reset the traps and left, I sat at the kitchen table and stared at Chaucer. He blinked at me. "You're right. That was weird. Why was Aiden here in the first place?" I shook it off, hoping whatever it was might bring him back to clean out more traps soon.

The quickest that Mom's check would get here was a few days. I had four dollars to my name. I needed a job. First, though, I needed a shower.

I cautiously made my way through the house, stopping frequently, checking for sounds. When I made it to the upstairs master bedroom, I ducked my head in quickly, not wanting to be too easy of a target. Nothing. I eased into the room and looked around. Aiden seemed to have been carrying out some bigger animals from the second floor, but I wasn't positive. It was kind of a don't-ask-don't-tell arrangement. There could be a family of marmosets up here for all I knew. Or skunks. Maybe bobcats. Do they have bobcats in Maine? Not the point. Fricking marmosets were probably laughing their asses off, watching me tiptoe through the house.

No more!

I stomped across the bedroom and into the bathroom before slamming the door. I leaned my ear silently against the door, listening for marmoset chatter. I heard a whine and hopped back from the door. Had I hurt their feelings? A scratch at the door made me take another step back.

"You'll protect me, right, Chaucer?" And then I realized that my baby wasn't in the bathroom with me. I opened the door, and he trotted right in. "You gotta stay with me, buddy. We're traveling behind enemy lines here." I assessed my pup's abilities. "Unless you were on a reconnaissance mission…" I leaned forward and kissed his head. He gave me a sweet doggy grin before rolling to the floor to wait me out.

I turned on the shower and peeled off the clothes I was wearing. I'd left my suitcase up here, figuring this is where I'd be dressing. Hopping from foot to foot, icy tiles leeching away precious body heat, I decided a carpet was needed in here. Slippers would be good, too. Some of those big, wooly jobs.

I leaned into the shower to test the temperature. Gran, or perhaps Mr. Cavanaugh, had kept up with repairs because the water quickly became hot. It felt heavenly. It pounded into my tight, sore muscles. I used supermarket shampoo and conditioner I'd purchased on the road, nothing salon tested to straighten curly hair. And I wasn't going to blow it straight, either. Screw Justin and his hatred of curls. You know what I hated? Cheating bastards.

I'd canceled my last hair-straightening appointment, the result of a combination of being distraught and a fairly pathetic attempt at rebellion, considering my friend Christine, who I'd been staying with at the time, couldn't care less what I did with my hair.

After getting dressed and toweling off, I made my way through the house in my stampiest walk—screw those snickering marmosets! Chaucer assumed we were playing, and kept darting forward, lunging at my feet.

"Come on, buddy. Lots to do today. Mommy needs to figure out how to pay for your food." Screw Justin, too! I didn't need him. I had Gran's house, and I was going to find a great job to support us.

CHAPTER ELEVEN

Aiden

THANK GOD, I had that duffel bag in the trunk. She would have stroked out if she'd seen the opossum I pulled out of the bedroom closet. I'd need to stop at the hardware store and pick up long, thick work gloves. I wasn't interested in contracting rabies.

I'd also need to go up every morning until the traps were empty. I should've called Harv, the exterminator, but she appeared to be living lean. I was not going to think about that pantry, empty except for a huge bag of dog food. She was taking care of the dog, but who was taking care of her? I shut that thought down. Not my problem.

Driving down Main Street, toward the station, I saw Chuck's food truck back where it shouldn't be. We'd received yet another complaint about it from the woman who ran the cupcake shop near Agamont Park. They didn't sell the same type of food, but regardless, the food truck wasn't allowed to park and do business within two hundred feet of a food-based business. Trudy, the cupcake lady, and Chuck, the food truck guy, had been arguing and measuring for years. I sent Mikey to answer a call yesterday, but he'd come back saying the truck had moved before he got there.

I pulled up behind the truck and got out.

Trudy rushed out of the cupcake shop. "Chief! Are you finally going to do something about that idiot? He knows he can't park—"

"I can park anywhere I damn well please, and you know it!" His muffled voice issued from the open panel of the truck.

Trudy marched over to the open but empty panel. "Don't you cuss at me! You know you need to park seven more spaces away from my shop!"

I wasn't positive, but it sounded like Chuck had told her to get an effing life. Trying to head off another blowup, I stepped in front of Trudy and turned her back to her shop. "Let me handle this. I'll be in to pick up a cupcake in just a minute."

"Humph. That man does this on purpose! I don't know how his wife puts up with him. She's a saint!" She marched back into her shop, bell dinging over the door.

Stepping up to the open panel and customer counter, I peered into the dark recesses of the truck and saw nothing. "Chuck? Are you in there?"

He staggered to his feet, looking rough. "'Ey, yeah, I'm here. Just avoiding that one."

"Everything okay?" He smelled like stale beer, but that could have been from last night.

Shuffling items on the prep table, he avoided my face. "I'm not breaking the law." Gesturing wildly around the kitchen, he said, "Does it look like I'm cooking in here?" He reached down, twisted something open and tipped his head back, downing a whole bottle of water. A drawer slid open and slammed. "I can't find the damn aspirin."

"If you're not planning to cook, why did you open the customer panel?" He looked as though he'd slept in the truck last night.

He gestured at the ceiling, eyes still down. It sounded as though he was going through every drawer he could find. "I needed the light from outside to find the aspirin. Bulb blew and I don't have a spare. I need to see, don't I?" He glanced out of the truck, toward the cupcake shop. "Then that one comes tearing out, yelling to wake the dead." He shook his head, finally looking at me. "Then you show up."

"Have you been home, Chuck? You don't appear to be in any condition to be driving this behemoth and cooking on that grill. Maybe we should give Myra a call to pick you up."

Making a derisive sound, he turned away and walked to the front of the truck. "Good luck with that. She's been at her sister's for weeks." The engine started. I jogged around the front of the truck cab, knocking on the closed windows. He stared ahead, pointedly ignoring me. When he reached for the gearshift, I pulled my badge out of my pocket and tapped that against the window instead.

"Turn off the engine and open the damn window, Chuck."

A long-suffering sigh was emitted before he leaned forward to turn off the ignition. He took another moment before opening the window. "What?"

"You know what? You smell like the floor of a bar. Your eyes are bloodshot and light sensitive. I need to know that you're okay to drive."

He grumbled as he opened the door and slid out. "I ain't drunk. And excuse me for not lookin' as pretty as you."

If Myra had left him, I understood the drinking. I kept my face blank, and pulled the Breathalyzer from the back of my belt. "Take a deep breath and blow for seven seconds."

He coughed at the end, but the readout was almost clear. He wasn't inebriated—at least not anymore. "Okay," I said, as I placed the machine back in its holder. "You're clear." I nodded my head toward the back of the truck. "You should close that back panel, though, before you drive anywhere."

"I'll risk it," he grumbled, as he started up the engine.

I stepped back, but needn't have worried as he rolled forward exactly seven parking spaces, before cutting the engine again.

Walking back to my cruiser, I saw Trudy duck her head out of the shop. Damn. I forgot I said I'd buy a cupcake. I changed direction and followed her into the store.

"That man! He is going to be the death of me." She waved her hand, shooing away thoughts of Chuck. "Now, Chief, what would you like?" She walked behind the display case. "The white chocolate raspberry turned out especially well today. Or the chocolate ganache—it's one of my most popular."

I studied the perfectly iced, pastel-colored desserts, and remembered that I didn't have much of a sweet tooth. Trudy looked so pleased, though, I could hardly walk out empty-handed.

"I'll get a dozen. Mix 'em up any way you want."

Her eyes got big, but she quickly folded up sheets of cardboard, creating small bakery boxes. I didn't understand why she didn't just use one big box. It'd be a hell of a lot easier to carry than little ones sliding all over the place. My gaze wandered to the menu board behind her. What the shit? Cupcakes were $4.50 each? No wonder she was so happy.

Driving back to the station, I thought about Katie's empty pantry. No. Not my problem.

Still…in the end, I left three of the bakery boxes in my car, taking the other three into the station. *Sap.*

"Morning, Chief."

I walked to my office, nodding at Heather, the coffeepot foremost in my thoughts. Damn, I would have to apologize to Bear today. I grabbed a cup of coffee and sat at my desk. I'd get through some paperwork first. I was not looking forward to that conversation.

An hour later, I finally found my balls and called him.

He picked up after one ring. "Hey, if it isn't my friendly neighborhood cock blocker."

He was not going to make this easy. "Yeah, about that. Where are you?"

"In bed with Katie. Shh, I don't want to wake her. Poor thing, I really worked her over."

In the silence following that statement, my stomach turned. I knew he was screwing with me, but my body reacted just the same. Bear laughed, and I decided I'd need to kill him before I apologized.

"I'm at the diner. Why?" His voice had a strange echo.

I wanted to get this over with. "Just needed to apologize and I'd rather do it in person."

Bear laughed. "Good. Get over here and grovel. Bring my cock a present. He likes porn." He hung up.

I put on my jacket, grabbed my phone and hat, and made my way back through the station. Nancy was in, chatting with Heather. I almost turned and went out the back door but something she said caught my attention.

"…arrested?" Her voice was gleeful with the prospect of someone being arrested.

"No, not arrested, Nancy, and you know I can't talk about that kind of thing."

It was Heather's voice that had first caused me to stop. She'd sounded annoyed, even in hushed tones and across the station, which was unusual for her.

"You don't have to say anything. I've already been hearing stories. I think her husband must have thrown her out." She leaned into Heather, who shifted away. "LaraBeth told me that she had two cards confiscated at the market. I don't know if they were stolen or in default, but they weren't just declined. They were taken from her."

"Oh, now, I don't know anything about that, and I wouldn't want to speculate. She seemed real nice when she was here. Her dog was real well behaved." Heather shuffled papers around on her desk.

Nancy leaned down farther. "I also hear she's been dating, still married but dating." She tilted her head, knowingly. "Probably why her husband threw her out. She always was a wild one. I'm not the least bit surprised to learn she hasn't changed a bit, always the center of attention, always flirting—"

I cleared my throat and Heather jumped. "Chief! What did I say about sneaking up on me?"

"Didn't sneak," I said, patting Heather's shoulder, staring at Nancy.

"Chief, it's so good to see you. I was just telling Heather how I needed to steal you away for lunch. You're looking too thin." She put her hand on my arm and leaned in, smiling.

I brushed her hand off. Why had I never seen the meanness before? Did I have my head so far up my ass I didn't know that the woman throwing herself at me on a daily basis was a stone-cold bitch? Where the hell had my instincts gone?

"That didn't sound like what you were talking about."

Nancy waved her hand and gave a breathy laugh. "Oh, that was nothing, just some girl talk. So, how about lunch?"

"What it sounded like was you trying to spread rumors, trying to convince Heather to divulge confidential information, in short, trying to stir up trouble. Katie Gallagher is none of your business, Nancy. She's a friend of mine. I'd think it would behoove you to show her welcome, not gossip about things you don't understand."

Nancy's smile was sharp, predatory. "Oh, I

think I understand just fine." She looked me over lazily. "A *friend*, is she?"

I stared at Nancy as I spoke. "Heather, we're not going to be needing Nancy's help around here anymore. Unless she reports a crime or commits one, she has no reason to be in this building. Is that clear?"

"Yes, Chief," Heather answered.

"Wait just a minute. You're making a mistake. I have been helping you for a year. Now she's back and I'm out?" Nancy's voice had become strident.

"Nope. It's got nothing to do with Katie. It has everything to do with my realizing exactly who it is that's been coming in and out of this station. If I can't trust you, I can't have you here. It's as simple as that."

"Well—"

I held up my hand. "Stop. Not interested." I pointed. "There's the door, Nancy." I stared at her, waiting. She sputtered a moment before giving up. Good to know my hard stare still worked. A moment later she spun, her heels clicking on the floor as she made her way out.

I shook my head. "Heather, I'm running up the block to talk with Bear. If you need me, call."

She wore a secret smile that was all Bear's. "Tell him I said hello."

I said I would, and then rolled my eyes as I walked out. *Fucking Bear.*

A few minutes later I walked into the diner and headed back to the kitchen. The door to the cold storage room was open, so I ducked my head in. Sure enough, Bear was standing on a ladder, his head through an opened panel in the ceiling.

"Bear."

His voice was muffled. "Just a minute. I've almost got it."

I leaned against the wall and waited. He came down the ladder a couple of minutes later, wiping his hands off on a rag before stuffing the grease-stained cloth into his back pocket.

I motioned up. "What's the problem?"

"Not sure, yet. Motor's working fine. Now I need to check each of the cooling units to see if there's a short." He looked me over. "I don't see a bouquet of porn."

I took a deep breath. "I'm sorry I was such an asshole last night." I shook my head. "I don't know what the hell that was."

"Don't you? I never thought you were stupid, Aiden." He just stood there and waited for me to explain myself. Bastard.

I shrugged. "It was just residual adolescent crap. I had a huge crush on her when I was a kid. She's back now, and my brain is responding to her like it used to. It's stupid and doesn't mean anything. I haven't seen her in fifteen years, and it's not like we were ever friends or anything."

I shook my head, trying to dislodge the image of her looking so sorrowful over that baby raccoon. "Seriously, it was just a weird chemical reaction, and it's out of my system now." Except that it wasn't. The small room was making me claustrophobic, so I walked back out to the main kitchen.

Bear followed me, leaning against the cold storage door frame. Nodding slowly, he studied me. "I see. So, you're not interested in her anymore, is that right?"

I shook my head. "No, not interested. Not interested in dating. Period." If I said it enough times, maybe it would be true.

Bear grinned. "So, if I was to continue seeing her, you wouldn't have a problem with that?"

I shook my head again.

Bear stepped forward and put out his hand to shake. I took it. "Well, that makes me really happy, because I got to tell you, Aiden, that is one fine woman. You know how redheaded women get my engine revving. And her ass!"

My hand jerked involuntarily.

"Ow!" He pulled out of the handshake.

"Sorry."

Bear shook out his hand. "No problem. Listen, I'm really glad this isn't going to be a problem for you because I am in serious lust."

"You know she's still married, right?"

"I can work with that. She's in the process of

a divorce, so I'm in the clear, ethically speaking. Hell, this works to my advantage. If he's been an asshole, she'll be more receptive to kindness and compliments. I can work with that, too. I kissed her good-night, and she all but melted in my arms. Trust me, I'll be hitting that very soon."

I don't know what happened. I wasn't thinking. One minute, I was standing there, listening to Bear, and the next, my fist was in his face. I never made a conscious decision to punch him. My fist was working on its own.

Bear staggered back a couple of steps, *tough bastard*, rubbing his jaw. "What the—"

"Leave her alone." Enraged, it took all my self-control not to punch him again.

"What is with you? I'm supposed to keep my hands off her just because you had a crush on her when you were ten? Screw that. You don't date. I do. And I cannot wait to sink into that one."

I was very close to beating him. I couldn't remember the last time I felt this angry. I shook out my arms and turned my back on him, leaving before I did something that'd get me arrested. "Don't talk about her like that. And leave her alone!"

"Yeah, that's not going to happen, but thanks for stopping by, Chief."

As I slammed the front door, I heard him laughing. Bastard.

It was a testament to how much Katie messed

with my head that it wasn't until I made it back to my office and slammed the door that I realized Bear had just been baiting me. Damn. I had it bad. And Bear knew.

I tried to put Bear, Katie and that punch out of my mind so I could work, but I kept hitting a wall, a Katie-shaped wall. The attraction was still there, but that was all it was. I barely knew Katie, then or now.

I needed to get my head screwed back on right. I wouldn't go down that road again. All I had to do was think about those people who'd come to town for the wedding, staring at me with sympathetic eyes, to put it back in perspective. No more damn rings and caterers, designer dresses and reception halls. It was bullshit, and I'd already been burned once. Katie wasn't mine and never would be. If it wasn't Bear, it would be someone else, and as much as I hated to admit it, Bear was a good man who would treat her well.

Until I could think about dating a woman without breaking out in a cold sweat, I had no business starting anything. Maybe someday I'd be ready for another woman in my life, but it wasn't now. Of course, by the time I was ready, Katie would probably be married to Bear with a couple of kids. The thought made my chest ache.

CHAPTER TWELVE

Kate

I WALKED UP and down Main, looking for a job. Any job. It was the off-season for Bar Harbor. Every place I tried told me to come back in the late spring, when they'll be hiring and training for summer. How the hell would I survive for seven months with no job?

Mom's check arrived by FedEx's one-day delivery, thank goodness. I cashed it immediately. I'd planned on opening a bank account with it, but I wanted to be able to do that with Gallagher as my last name, not Cady. The woman at the bank was kind enough to tell me where I had to go to file the paperwork for my name change. I also figured it would be good to contact my lawyer again—maybe she could expedite the process.

My salivary glands went nuts when I stepped into a cupcake shop. Oh, my goodness, everything looked gorgeous and delicious! My stomach rumbled, and I slapped a hand over it.

Just then a woman walked out of the back

room. "Afternoon, hon. What can I get for you? The white chocolate raspberry are amazing today."

My stomach rumbled again, louder.

She laughed. "I heard that. Which one looks good to you, and would you like a drink to go with it?"

My face flamed. "Sorry. Honestly, they all look delicious, but I'm here for a job. Are you hiring?"

Her smile dropped. "Oh. Sorry. This time of year it's too slow to afford more help. I can handle things myself. Try again in late May. I usually hire a part-time helper then."

Nodding, I said, "I understand. Thanks, anyway."

As I turned, she said, "Are you sure you don't still want one?"

"Thank you, but I'm not hungry," I lied, as I stepped out the door.

I stood on the sidewalk and took in the gorgeous park and harbor. The trees were aflame in red and gold. I may starve, but I'd do it in picturesque surroundings. There was that.

I was just about to dash across the street, to try my luck with the shops on that side, when someone yelled.

"Yo, Red. You wanna dog?"

I spun, trying to figure out where the voice was coming from. A man was leaning out of a food truck, his arms braced on the counter, watching me.

I walked over and stood before his counter. "Actually, I wanna job."

He shrugged. "Buy a dog and we'll talk about a job."

Squinting, I took in his blotchy face and blood-shot eyes. "Really? Or are you just trying to sell me a hot dog?"

He laughed, before taking a large gulp of water. "Oh, I'm definitely trying to sell the dog, but that doesn't mean I don't have a job, too."

I went up on tiptoe and tried to see inside. "It's clean in there, isn't it?"

"Not as clean as it's going to be once you get to work. Now, do you want that dog?"

"How much?" I was calculating how long the money I had would need to last.

"Five bucks."

Stepping back, I looked around. "What is this, a baseball stadium? Five bucks for a hot dog is robbery. No wonder I'm the only person standing here."

I turned to leave, but he held up his hand. "For that five bucks, you get a dog, a drink and a possible job. Seems like a good deal to me."

He had a point. As if on cue, my stomach rumbled again. He sniggered, pointing. "Gotcha! Now, whaddaya want on it?"

I gave up the five bucks and ordered a dog with

chili, cheese and jalapeños. When he handed it to me, I was hit with the overpowering stench of sour, stale booze. Either he bathed in it, or it was seeping from his pores. Given his rough appearance and bloodshot eyes, I was going with the latter.

I had to stop myself from inhaling the hot dog. I opened my mouth to take a bite and then thought better of it. "Do I want to know how many days you've been reheating this chili?"

"No," he said, before taking another gulp of water.

My mouth was watering. E. coli be damned. I took a huge bite, closed my eyes and stifled a moan. Truly, this was the food of the gods! I opened my eyes to study the man and his food truck. If I worked here, at least I'd be able to eat.

As if reading my mind, he said, "You can have one free dog per shift."

I took another juicy, spicy, smoky bite, wishing I had three more waiting for me. I swallowed and asked, "What would my job entail?"

He glanced around, confused. "What I just did. Weren't you paying attention?" He downed the rest of the water bottle. "I'm not really impressed with your attention to detail, kid."

"I'm a good cook. Would I be making anything besides hot dogs?" I ate the last bite, stuffed after so many days with little to eat. I was thinking about those warnings to starving people not to eat or drink too fast for fear of it coming right back up. I put my hand on my stomach again, willing the dog to stay right where it was.

He looked me over, speculation clear in his eyes. "You can cook, huh? Now, *that* is interesting. What kind of stuff—food-truck stuff—can you make?"

"Well." I crumpled the napkin in my hand and tossed it in the nearby garbage can. "I can make better chili than this from scratch. And if you grilled the jalapeños first, they'd taste better. I also do amazing grilled cheese sandwiches—"

"Sweet. That asshole Jimmy runs the grilled cheese truck. He's only around in the summer months, though. You'd have a couple of months to build a loyal following, so when he shows up, we can put him out of business." He smiled broadly, transforming his hangdog expression. "What else ya got?"

I shrugged. "Anything, really. I can make cheesesteaks, burgers, corn dogs. Whatever."

There was a gleam in his eye when he said, "You're hired, kid."

My heart leaped, but wariness followed close behind. "How much will you pay me, and what are my hours?"

"Enough, to my way of thinking, but probably not to yours. And as many as I need. Jeez, you ask a lot of questions." He wiped down his prep area. "So, you want the job or what?"

I needed a job to survive and I could make this work. It'd be like my own personal, tiny restaurant. Thinking about the dark recesses of the food truck, I amended that description to a tiny, filthy, possibly rat-infested restaurant. I'd be a fool not to say yes.

"You need to give me an actual dollar amount and a general idea about my hours before I can agree." Standing my ground, I looked him in the eye and waited.

"Fine. Fine. But I'll fire your ass if you do a lousy job."

"Agreed."

"Seven bucks an hour, and you'll be working the lunch shift—ten thirty to about two thirty. But weekends will be longer hours. And if you can make something people want to eat for breakfast, something that pays for itself and you, you can open earlier and sell that, too."

"You do know that seven bucks an hour is below minimum wage, right?"

He grumbled a few choice words. "It's my damn truck. I get to decide what to pay people, not those worthless politicians." He paused for a second, studying me. "This is all under the table, too. I'm not paying for any insurance or withholdings or any of that crap. You work an hour. I hand you seven bucks. Deal or not?"

I thought about the quickly dwindling bag of dog food in the pantry. "Deal."

"Good." He opened and closed a drawer, then held up a key. Tossing it to me, he said, "I don't want to deal with you today. My head is killing me as it is. Get here tomorrow at nine and you can clean up before you begin cooking." He turned his back and walked toward the front of the truck.

"Wait! Why the key? Won't you be here to train me?"

"I've got a second truck I take to Bangor. There ain't enough people in the Harbor this time of year to make much of a profit." His voice was muffled as he continued, "You can cook, right? Figure it out." The engine rumbled to life.

I ran to the front of the truck, but my new boss was already looking the other way and pulling out onto the road. "I don't even know your name," I shouted at the back of the moving food truck. "And your service panel is open!"

Great. If a drunk hires you, are you really hired?

I trudged back up the other side of the street on my way to my car, but stopped at the window of a clothing boutique. The periwinkle, watered silk cocktail dress on display called to me. It was ethereal and lovely. It felt emblematic of a better, more serene life.

A light tinkling sound came from overhead as I entered. Mesmerized by the play of light on the iridescent silk, I slid a finger down the skirt.

"Would you like me to find your size?"

I spun to find a tall, stunning, dark-haired woman waiting for my response. "Oh, no. Thank you. I just—well, it's beautiful."

She brushed nonexistent dust off the back of the dress. "It certainly is. And it's done its job, bringing you in."

The shop was deceptively large. It appeared quite small and narrow from the street, but it was long, allowing for different sections within the store. There were light, feminine dresses near the window, but I spied jeans and sweaters, coats and gloves, even shoes farther in.

I noticed the woman looking me over. She smiled and said, "I thought that was you. Welcome back, Katie. I was wondering when you'd stop by."

I stared a minute, not able to place her. "I'm sorry." I shook my head, embarrassed.

"It's Maureen Cavanaugh-Howard. Mo." She grinned. "My grandfather dated your grandmother."

"Oh, of course, you're Aiden's sister."

The bell on the door tinkled again, and we both turned. Speaking of Aiden, that brunette who liked to touch his arm walked in.

"Hi, Nancy. How are you today?" Maureen gestured toward me. "Do you remember Katie Gallagher? She spent summers here growing up.

She was the one who tossed out condoms at the Fourth of July parade all those years ago."

Snickering, I remembered. I'd been fifteen, and the local paper had just published an article on the rise of STDs, especially among teens. I was fulfilling my civic duty.

"Gran had never been so angry with me." I smiled, recalling her thirty-minute lecture on my inappropriate behavior. That poor woman did her best to keep me in line.

"Is that why you stopped visiting?" Mo asked.

"No, my dad died two months later." And my wild streak died with him. An era of fear and uncertainty took over.

Mo took my hand and squeezed. "I'm sorry. I didn't realize." She turned to that Nancy woman. "Did you two know each other?"

I stared blankly at her. "I don't—"

"Sure. We know each other. Your friend Daisy's little sister was my best friend. We hung out at the lake with you sometimes."

"Oh, of course, yes. It's so good to see you." I think she could tell I was lying. Her expression turned flinty.

"Maureen, I'm here to look for a gift for my mother. I'm just going to browse around." She gave me a brittle smile before wandering to the back of the store.

Maureen, like her brother, was gorgeous. I shook my head. "What is it with you Cavanaughs? I just about fell off my chair when I realized that skinny, knobbly-kneed Aiden had turned into tall, dark and angry. And you, just beautiful." I rolled my eyes. "I remember you used to move so fast, it was hard for my eyes to keep up, running, swimming, diving, arm wrestling." I shook my head, marveling again at the woman.

She laughed, a joyous, inclusive laugh that said all was right in the world. "I forgot about that. I kicked everyone's butt arm wrestling. I may have been skinny, but I was strong." She brought up her arm and flexed.

"Do all Cavanaughs grow into stunners? Because I've got to tell you, speaking as a mere mortal, it's starting to piss me off."

She laughed again. "Aw, you've made my day. I was feeling a little crabby and out of sorts today, and now I don't feel anything but tickled." She looked over my clothes, not judging, just assessing. "So, are you shopping today or getting the lay of the land? Pops told us you were back, so I hoped I'd see you soon."

"Are your parents still living in Bar Harbor?" Mr. Cavanaugh hadn't mentioned his son and daughter-in-law.

Mo pushed her long, dark hair over her shoulder. "No. By us, I meant my husband, Gary, and our son, Patrick. Wait…" She pulled a phone out of the pocket of her tweed slacks. "Here he is.

That's my little Paddy." She turned the phone around to me.

I reached for the cell, my insides twisting. "Oh, Mo, he's so beautiful. He looks just like you." My finger traced his chubby cheek and dark, wavy hair. "He has your eyes." I looked up to return the phone. "Congratulations." My longing must have been obvious because she gave me a surreptitious squeeze on my arm before pocketing the device.

She walked farther into the shop, drawing me with her. "My parents, however, have said a fond farewell to frozen winters. My older brother Caleb—do you remember him?"

I nodded.

"He and his family live in San Diego. Mom and Dad have a little bungalow near them. Usually they don't go until November, but Mom's arthritis was really bothering her this year, so they went early. They tried to stay all winter last year, after Alice—" She cut herself off, flicking her hand as though that was enough of that topic. "They wanted to be here for Aiden, but Mom was in pain, so he sent them West."

Mo walked to a nearby display table. "This would be gorgeous on you." She held up a thick, intricately woven, turtleneck sweater in emerald green. "Not many can wear green without looking sallow. On you, it would be stunning. Come on, you'll try it on." She gathered items for me as we made our way to the fitting rooms. "You've been living in California, right?"

I nodded, looking everywhere at once. "Yes, but I can't affor—" I gestured toward the front of the store. "It was just the dress. I'm not actually shopping for anything," I ended lamely. "But if you're hiring, I could really use a job."

She dropped the clothes she was carrying onto the counter and strode to the back of the store, waving me to keep up. "I'm not hiring, unfortunately. The Harbor does all its business in the spring and summer. Fall and winter, it's just the year-round residents. We can easily maintain our shops on our own. I wish I could offer you a cocktail instead of cold-weather clothes on sale."

"Clothing stores should totally have liquor licenses," I said, following in her wake.

"Preaching to the choir, sister." She looked at my thin wool trousers and sweater set. "Maine winters are frigid. Do you have a good warm coat?"

I shook my head. "Just this," I said, indicating the unzipped jacket I was wearing. "It's one of Gran's old parkas."

Mo smiled. "I'm thinking you're going to want to update that look." She led me to the back, to the outerwear racks. She pulled a long, black suede coat with lamb's wool lining off the hanger and held it up to me. "This is very warm and would look incredible on you, very dramatic."

I ran my fingers up and down the soft suede. Justin's voice tried to impinge, telling me black was too much for me, but I mentally shut him down and grabbed the coat from Mo. I slid into it and felt the warmth down to my toes. Mo shuffled me to the mirror and stepped back. It looked wonderful, my hair standing out like a flame against the night sky. There was no hiding, no blending in with a coat like this. I felt uncomfortably visible.

Feeling the price tag dangling over my hand, I lifted it up to read—$775. I sucked in a breath and held the tag out to Mo. "It's gorgeous, but I can't afford a coat like this."

She glanced down at the tag. "No, that's not the price. Here." She pulled the coat off me. She turned it over to show me a large tear at the bottom. It had been repaired, but was still noticeable.

"I sold it to a tourist last year. She brought it back that same day, wanting a refund. When I told her I couldn't refund a coat she'd ripped, she threw a hissy fit and stormed out. I held the coat behind the counter for months, assuming she'd come to her senses and want it back." She rolled her eyes. "I waited one whole year and then got the repair done. It's too small for me, but would be perfect for you. I'll just charge you the price of the repair, okay? Forty-five dollars."

I heard a gasp and turned to find that Nancy woman watching us avidly.

"I know. Right? Unfortunately, we're both too tall for this coat, but Katie is tiny enough to make it work." She turned back to me. "What do you say? It's a sign. I just put it on the rack yesterday. It was meant for you."

"I say I'd be crazy not to buy it."

Nancy mumbled something, but I ignored it.

"Actually, I just got a job at a food truck. I need a super warm hoodie or something, too. Something I can throw in the wash every day. Anything like that? Preferably with a huge tear?"

Mo laughed, walking us back to the counter to drop off the coat. "Are you working for Chuck?"

I shrugged. "No idea. He didn't tell me his name. He threw me a key, told me to start at nine tomorrow and drove off. I can cook, but I've never tried to do it in a truck before."

She straightened a sweater on a display. "Chuck's a good guy, but he has some problems—"

"He's a drunk," Nancy interrupted.

Mo turned her back to Nancy, talking just to me. "Yes, that's one of them. He's not a bad guy, though."

"Honestly! Do you know what he said to me at the Reef last Saturday night?" Nancy stepped forward, shoehorning into the conversation.

Imperceptibly, Mo's eyes rolled. She turned to

Nancy, saying, "I'm sure it was awful. He can be quite belligerent when he's had too much." She turned back to me. "But I've known Chuck all my life. He's just a little rough around the edges. And he and his wife are having some problems."

"Rough?" Nancy scoffed.

Mo walked away, ducking down into the recesses of the store. "I know every piece I have in here, Katie. There's a forest green hoodie down here somewhere. It's a large, as I recall, but it's cotton blended with one of those warm fibers they use in subzero sleeping bags… Here it is! It's a one of a kind, from two years ago, so it got shoved to the back."

She stood, holding it up for me. "Hmm, a little big, but it'll keep you warm."

I dodged racks, making my way to her. It was crumpled, even hanging up by its shoulders, but the color was beautiful. "Are you sure that's only a large? It looks really big."

Mo checked the collar and smiled. "That's because it's a men's extra large." She looked at the price tag and then up at Nancy who was following us back. Mo whispered, "It's been back here for two years. Seventy-five percent off puts it at around thirty dollars." She grimaced. "I know you didn't want to buy anything today, but that truck is freezing. Aiden worked in it in high school. Oh!" She looked around and grabbed a pair of thermal fingerless gloves. "Trust me.

You'll need these, too. They're thin, so they'll fit under those clear, plastic food-service gloves."

Mentally, I did the math. I'd be lucky to get out of here for less than a hundred dollars. I needed the warm clothes, and she was giving me a huge deal. I nodded. "Thank you. I'll take all three."

I followed her back to the cash register. "If I made a Belgian-waffle pocket, stuffed with eggs, sausage and cheese, would you buy that for breakfast?"

Mo looked at me strangely. "Interesting topic change."

Blood rushed to my cheeks again. "Sorry, I was just thinking about breakfast foods I could sell out of the truck." I glanced around, checking for Nancy's whereabouts. I lowered my voice. "Chuck said if I could find something people wanted to eat for breakfast and I sold enough to cover the expenses, I could get more hours."

"Sounds delicious, but if I ate that every day, I'd need a whole new wardrobe." She rang up the coat, hoodie and gloves. She grimaced. "That'll be $92.65."

I waved away her concern. "You found amazing deals for me. I can't thank you enough." Opening my wallet, I pulled out one of the crisp hundred-dollar bills I'd just received from the bank.

"You're going to do just great here, Katie. I can feel it."

I thought of my empty refrigerator and the animals living in my house. "I hope so."

CHAPTER THIRTEEN

Aiden

"HARV, IT'S AIDEN…Oh, yeah, just fine. You?…
Listen, you know the Gallagher place off Old
Farm Road?…Yeah, that's it. When we moved
Nellie out, we didn't check windows…Exactly.
They've made it their home. Her granddaughter
is trying to live there…I don't know the story,
but she's living there…Raccoon, opossums, mar-
tens, mice…I haven't seen one of those yet…
Well, that gives me something to look forward
to, doesn't it?…

"That's why I'm calling. How much would
you charge to come take a look and give an
estimate?…Free, she can afford. Tomorrow
afternoon?…I'll run up and talk to her, see if
she agrees. Plan on coming. I'll call you if for
some reason tomorrow isn't good for her…Yeah,
I appreciate it."

She was sleeping in a chair or in her car, afraid
to be in her own house. It wasn't right. I was just
upholding my duties as an officer of the law.
Serve and protect. It was no different than when

Mrs. Jameson ran out to the sidewalk and pulled me in to get a heavy box off the top shelf in her shop's storage room, or when Cecil asked if I'd be on the planning committee for the new retirement home. No different.

As for the cupcakes, I bought too many. She's skinny as hell already. She could use the fat and sugar. I was doing this for Nellie. I loved Nellie, and Nellie had loved Katie. Civic duty was all it was.

Standing, I grabbed my hat, walked out of my office and through the station. "Heather, I'm going to be out for an hour or so. Call if you need me."

"Sure, Chief," she said, resuming her typing.

I checked to make sure the bakery boxes were still on the back seat and then took off. She was going to need furniture, too. She might not be able to find much in the Harbor. South Harbor had a secondhand shop. She might need to get off the island, though, hit Trenton.

Then again, she may end up reconciling with her husband, and all of this will have just been an adventure story. I rubbed my chest.

I was dropping off some food and trying to get her an exterminator. Nothing more. You can dislike and mistrust someone without wishing her ill. I didn't have to care about her to make sure she and her moose hadn't been attacked by wolves.

The image of her at her kitchen table, head down, upset with herself for hurting a baby raccoon came unbidden. Again. Still, this didn't mean anything.

Kate

DRIVING HOME, I watched russet leaves swirling in the wake of the cars driving up Main toward the Old Farm Road that led to Gran's. When I pulled up to the house, I was overwhelmed by a sense of home.

I opened the front door, and Chaucer bounded out, sniffing every inch of me. "Today was an adventure. I'll tell you that much." I walked through the entrance, my wariness returning immediately. "Did you scare off any critters while I was gone?"

Chaucer whined from the front porch, not following me in. Shit.

"What is it? What did you see?" I whispered. *Please, don't be a bat. Please, don't be a bat.*

He pranced on the porch, wanting to be right next to me, but not wanting to enter the house again. Double shit. Okay, enough of this crap. I was announcing my presence with authority. I hung the clothing bag on the doorknob, not wanting to leave it on the ground where rodents or snakes could take up residence. Snakes! How had I not thought of those before? "Please, tell me you didn't see a snake. I'm begging you, Chaucer. Tell me it was one of those heckling marmosets."

He just stared at me, shying away from the doorway and whining.

"Mommy's got this!" I ran into the kitchen, flung open the back door, grabbed two pots from the cupboard and proceeded to race around the house, screaming and banging the pots. No more, you little bastards! I tried not to think about the quick skittering movement I saw all around me. Chaucer howled, but I was exorcizing this joint, once and for all.

As I raced back down the stairs, I saw a huge man standing silhouetted in the door. I stopped screaming and tried to back up, forgetting where I was. I ended up on my ass, sliding down the stairs before falling in a heap at the bottom. He moved toward me, and I held up my pots in defense.

He wrenched the pots out of my hands and crouched down next to me. Aiden. Of course. "Have you run out of your meds, Katie?"

"Ha, ha." I tried to get up, but lost my balance. My ass was killing me. Damn, that really freaking hurt.

He pulled me up with one hand. The other was holding bakery boxes. Weird. Maybe I'd hit my head again. I reached out and poked his chest. Seemed real enough.

"Will you please stop poking me?"

I snatched my hand away and gave him my squinty, suspicious look. "Why are you here, and what is in those boxes?"

He angled his body, keeping the boxes out of my reach. "You first. Why are you racing around like a crazy person?"

I stamped a foot, frustration getting the better of me. "I'm trying to scare off whatever is in here that has Chaucer whining and unwilling to come back inside!"

He looked me up and down. "Maybe you're what's freaking him out."

"Pfft. He adores me. Don't cha, baby?" I picked up the pots, and glanced through the empty open door. "Chaucer?"

My dog stepped into the doorway, watched me warily for a moment and then ducked out of sight again.

"Well, sure, *now* I'm the one scaring him, but before it was something in here." I stomped and banged my way back to the kitchen. Leaving the pots on the counter, I shut the back door. Turning around, I found Aiden leaning against the door frame. "Tell me you don't have snakes around these parts."

He shrugged. "Some."

I walked over and smacked his arm. Hard. "What is the matter with you? The answer is always 'No. No snakes around here. Not for hundreds of miles.' Is that really so hard?"

"But that would be a lie." He shoved a finger in my face, backing me up. "And if you push, poke or smack me again, I will put you in cuffs."

"Jeez. You cops are such babies. Delicate, dainty flowers, each and every one of you." I ducked around the pissy cop and jogged to the front door. "Chaucer, baby! All clear. You can come in now."

He stepped in, looking around, his nose twitching. I went down on my knees to rub and hug him. "Mommy totally scared it off." He licked my ear, and then placed himself in front of me, growling down the hall toward the laundry room.

Aiden dropped the boxes on the dining table and went down the hall to investigate.

I whispered to Chaucer, "He's handy to have around. Shh, though. Don't tell him I said that."

"Can you go out to the cruiser and get the duffel bag in the back seat?" he called down the hall.

My stomach twisted. More fricking animals. I didn't consider myself fainthearted, but holy crap! There was only so much a person could take. I stomped down the front steps toward the cruiser. The back door was locked. How was I supposed to get the bag? There was a metal gate between the front and back seats, so I couldn't go that way.

I jogged back to the house and tiptoed down the hall to Aiden. He was blocking my view of the laundry room, but that was okay. I didn't want to see whatever he was looking at.

"Got it?"

"Nope. Door's locked," I whispered. No idea why, as he wasn't doing the same.

"Keys are on my belt."

He wasn't moving an inch, which was freaking me the hell out. What did he have pinned in there? My hand crept around his waist, not wanting to call attention to myself. I went into his front pocket, trying to find the keys. Empty.

"Well, groping is better than poking and slapping, but I said the keys were on my belt, not in my pocket." He pulled my paralyzed hand out of what I'd just realized was very close proximity to his personal business. He snapped the keys off his belt and put them in my hand. "Bag."

I hopped back and scampered out of the house to retrieve the bag. A moment later, I was reaching around to hand it to him.

He took the bag slowly and said, "Why don't you and Chaucer wait out on the porch?" When I paused, he said, "Go on, now."

He found us on the porch. I was sitting on the rail, wanting my feet up. "As long as I'm here. I'll check the traps again." He pulled one of the almost-forgotten boxes from behind his back. "Here. Take your mind off what I'm doing."

A moment later, I heard a loud squeal. I jumped off the porch and ran straight to his car.

Chaucer jumped in first, sitting in the passenger seat, while I sat on the driver's side. I closed and locked the doors, staring intently through the windshield, willing him to catch whatever in the heck had just made that sound.

An eternity later, he walked out the front door, scanning the yard. Spotting me leaning over the steering wheel, he stopped, picked up the pink box I'd dropped on the porch and strode to the car.

"You can come out now."

I glanced at him, but my attention was fixed on the front door. I'd been thinking of every animal that could have possibly made that squeal. It was a long and horrifying list.

"Katie, you can come out now."

I shook my head. No way was I going out there, where squealing animals roamed.

He knocked on the window. The box was open, and two banged-up but amazing cupcakes were pointed at me. "If you come out, you can have the cupcakes."

I might die a horrible death, but I'd get cupcakes first. Seemed like a good deal to me. I opened the door slowly, looking around before I stepped out. Chaucer bounded out after me. I reached for the cupcakes, but he pulled them away from me. My brows slammed down, and I readied my finger for poking.

"Trade. Give me my keys, and you can have

the cupcakes." He was moving toward the porch, and I reluctantly followed the retreating sweets.

"Do I want to know what made that horrible noise?"

"Probably not." He sat on the top step, patting the space beside him.

Did he really not understand that I needed to be up off the ground? Psycho.

"Katie, come sit next to me, and you can have the cupcakes." Exasperation and annoyance colored his tone.

"What kind are they?" I stepped closer, entranced by their crushed puffs of frosting, shimmering in the sun.

He looked in the box. "How the hell should I know? They're cupcakes. Does it matter?"

Rolling my eyes, I stepped forward and snatched the box from his hands. "Of course it matters, you dillhole." Mmm, dark chocolate ganache or snowy white frosting? Eenie, meenie, minie, mo…

"Katie?"

Hmm?

He had the strangest look on his face. "I cannot figure you out."

"Are we back to that again? I'm not insane, okay?" I sat on the step below him, figuring any animals hell-bent on carnage would attack him first, giving me time to run. I placed the cupcake box on my knees and selected the chocolate.

"Wait!" I jumped up and handed him the box. "Do not touch either cupcake, mister! I'll be right back."

"If you're getting milk, I want some, too."

Like I had any milk in the house. My stomach rumbled as I quickly washed my hands. I wasn't going to eat a finger food with dirty hands. A drink was a good idea, though. I filled a glass with water from the tap and then hurried back. I noticed another box on the dining room table and snagged it.

"Look what I found!" I held up the second box triumphantly.

He turned, watching me walk across the porch and down the stairs.

I sat, opening the second box. Pristine pastel pink- and blue-frosted cupcakes glistened in the box. They were almost too pretty to eat. Almost. My stomach rumbled again.

"Katie, are you eating?"

"Not yet. For a cop, you're not too observant." Pink or blue? Strawberry or blueberry? Cherry or blue raspberry?

He moved his legs, penning me between them, as he leaned forward and tapped me on the shoulder. "Katie?"

"Don't even think about it. These are mine. All mine." I tipped my head up to find him staring intently at me. "What? Do you have any idea how long it's been since I've had a cupcake?"

He shrugged. "A week? Two?"

"Pfft. Try ten years. These lovelies are going to put me into a sugar coma, and I'm going to enjoy every minute of it." Brown, white, pink or blue? Decisions, decisions. I could go lighter to darker. That way I'd be ending on a known, chocolate. Hmm, which to choose first?

Tapping on my shoulder again, he said, "Are you even listening to me?"

"Apparently not." Yes, white first. I reached into the box Aiden was now holding and carefully took out the dented white cupcake. "I'm so sorry I dropped you, my sweeting." I slowly began to peel the wrapping off the little minx.

"If you like these things so much, why haven't you had one in ten years?" He was studying me, and I didn't like it.

"Could you look over there?" I gestured vaguely to the yard. "You're making me uncomfortable. What we have needs to be shared in private. It's a secret love. Isn't it, my beautiful little cupcake?" I dropped the wrapper back into the box he was holding and stared at my naked lover. Mouth watering, I took a big bite, closing my eyes, flavors zinging my taste buds. I'm pretty sure I moaned. Whatever. I told him we wanted to be alone.

Aiden shifted, the boards creaking. "Why, Katie?"

My eyes popped open, and I found him right in

front of me. Damn, he was hot. Angry and short-tempered, sure, but really freaking hot. I wondered if he'd notice if I bit his jaw right there. Or his neck. Damn, his neck. Maybe a quick lick? No harm, no foul, no teeth marks. I swallowed. "What now?"

"Why haven't you had a cupcake in ten years?" His eyes were narrowed, like he thought I was lying.

"Please. I only got to have the bite of my wedding cake that they needed for pictures. Justin was very concerned about my not being bikini ready for our honeymoon. After that, it was all low-fat, no-carb, steamed, organic whatnot." Aiden's face was blank, so I went back to staring at my cupcake. I gave her a little lick. I'm almost positive I heard her giggle.

I flinched at what sounded like a growl. I leaned into Aiden and tried to see around him, through the open front door. "Did you hear that?" I whispered.

"What?" He asked in a normal voice.

"Shh!" I smacked his knee. "I heard a growl."

"What did I say about slapping, pushing and poking?" Still using his normal voice, as though he wanted to be eaten. Oh, well. Sometimes you had to let the stupid ones get taken out, so you could get away. I patted his knee. I'd miss him.

"There's nothing in there, at least nothing that growls."

"Huh. I thought for sure…" I turned my attention back to the coconut-vanilla dream in my hand. I took another big bite, savoring every morsel. Something flicked my nose, and my eyes flew open. I bolted up, standing on the bottom stair. Aiden was just sitting there. His finger in his mouth.

"Jumpy much?" He motioned to the cupcake in my hand. "That is good. Can I have a bite?"

I stepped down to the ground, moving away. "No."

"I bought them." He actually sounded offended that I wouldn't share.

"And you gave them to me. Ergo, ipso facto, they are mine." I slowly opened my mouth wide, intending to cram the rest in.

"Don't you do it!" He stood, and I bolted.

Running around the side of the house toward the ocean, I dodged a pine and hurdled a boulder. Clearly, evasive maneuvers were required. He was not getting my cupcake. I barely made it halfway to the cliff, when an arm came around my waist, snatching me out of air. I hung off his arm, shocked, and then I shoved the rest of the cupcake into my mouth, laughing too hard to swallow.

He spun me around and started licking the cupcake from around my mouth. I stilled, swallowing awkwardly. What? Holding my face between his hands, gaze intent, he leaned forward, licking and nibbling at my mouth. My eyes drifted shut, reveling in the feeling of his lips on mine, soft and warm. When he deepened the kiss, my arms snaked around his neck, and I pushed up on my toes. The heat from his hands sliding up and down my back seared.

He growled and grabbed my butt, crushing me against him. Parts I didn't even remember, that I wasn't sure were still in working order, jumped to attention. Damn, the man could kiss. I'd never been kissed like this before, not once.

Too soon, I was bumped and knocked off balance. I stared up into Aiden's dark, lust-filled eyes. What? Bump. I looked down to find Chaucer leaning into me. Pink frosting on his nose.

"Noooooooooooo!"

CHAPTER FOURTEEN

Aiden

I DIDN'T WANT to think about how much money it was going to cost to keep her in cupcakes. I flashed back to the monthly bills for Alice's designer dress, the caterer, the ballroom. I shut down all thoughts of Katie and cupcakes. Not again.

Still, watching her eat and moan… *Stop.* Her divorce wasn't even final. Her husband was planning to take the house. She probably wouldn't be living here in a couple of months.

God, she felt so good, pressed up against me. Those little sounds she made in the back of her throat. That shocked look on her face when I'd licked the frosting off her lips…

And what the hell was with her asshole husband, not letting her eat? I crushed the steering wheel in my hands.

It happened. I got it out of my system. It was done.

Hours later, after only a few reminders to get her the hell out of my head, I was driving back up Old Farm Road with dinner. I pulled up to Pops's house, my gaze drawn in the direction of her place.

Pops walked out onto his porch. "'Bout time. I'm weak with hunger."

Chuckling, I climbed the front steps, handing him the bag. "I thought we'd try the new vegan place."

He stopped in his tracks, staring at me.

"What? It just opened. And I heard it was good." I went inside, dropping my coat on the back of the couch. "Are we eating in here? I want to watch the game."

Pops was still standing on the porch. "Boy, you better be kidding."

I walked into his kitchen, leaving him outside. When I came back a few minutes later with a couple of beers, he was in the living room opening the boxes, finding burgers, fries, buffalo wings. I think I might have ordered nachos, too. I hadn't had time for lunch and was starving.

We sat side by side, watching football and eating silently. The silence had never seemed odd before. There was nothing to say, other than the occasional groan over a pathetic play, but after spending time listening to Katie chat away, the silence seemed strangely oppressive.

"So, how was your day, Pops?"

It took him a moment to turn to me, confusion clear on his face. "What?"

"Your day. How was it?" I wiped the barbecue sauce off my mouth.

"It was a day, same as all the rest." He turned back to the TV.

"What did you do?" I didn't know why I was pushing it. Maybe to prove to myself that I didn't need Katie to enjoy a conversation.

He stared at me. "Same thing I do every day. What's going on with you? Making jokes about food, wanting to chat during a game. Is something wrong?"

I shrugged. "Nah. Just checking in with you, Pops." I took a loaded bite of nachos off the plate.

"I'm fine. Now, pipe down. I want to listen to the game."

"Good talk." We watched the rest of the football game in silence.

By the end of the game, Pops was starting to nod off. "Time for bed."

He grumbled, shifting on the couch, pulling his feet up. "Change the station to the Packers game. I'll watch the end of that."

I draped a blanket over him, changed the station and said good-night. I think he spent most nights out here, letting the lights and chatter of the TV drive away memories, allowing him to sleep.

Cleaning up our garbage, I put the living room back in order. I'd ordered an extra burger we hadn't touched. I took it with me, intending to eat it for lunch tomorrow. When I saw lights through the trees at Nellie's place, I got in my car and detoured. All the lights in the house appeared to be on. What the hell was she doing?

Pulling up next to her beat-to-shit car, I scanned the house and yard, trying to discover what was with all the lights. Chaucer's head popped up in the car window. Not again. Damn it, she needed a bed and to not be afraid of her own house.

I walked around the car and looked in the window. She lay cocooned in blankets, curled up on the seat. I didn't want to scare her again, but I did want to make sure she ate more than a cupcake. Chaucer's wagging tail brushed back and forth over her face. Sleepily, she batted it away, missed and was hit in the face again. I choked back a laugh as she drowsily did battle with a wagging tail.

I left them to it, instead jogging up the stairs and into her brightly lit house. Putting the leftovers into her refrigerator, I tried to ignore the twist in my gut at seeing it empty. Not my problem. Good deed done for the day, I went home.

The following morning, I drove by the jewelry store, the ring box in my pocket, taunting me like the ball-less wonder I was. Fuck it. I parked and got out. My 'nads shriveled up as the bell chimed above my head.

"Morning, Chief!" Jen came around the

counter, her pregnant belly leading the way. "What can we do for you this morning?"

"Hey, Jen." I looked around for her mother. "Is Carol in?"

Jen rubbed her distended stomach. "Oh, sure. Hey, Ma!" Jen snickered. "She hates it when I do that."

Carol bustled out of a door in the back of the store. "Jennifer, what have I—oh, Chief, how lovely to see you." She came around the counter. Unlike Jen, who took after her father, Carol was a tiny woman, which for some reason made the whole situation worse. I felt like I needed to crouch in order to have a quiet talk.

"What can we do for you today?" Her eyes were bright with the anticipation of a sale.

There was no point in being coy. "I'd like to return this ring." I pulled out the damn box that had taken up permanent residence in my pocket for the last year.

"Oh." She patted my arm. "My dear boy, I still can't believe she did that to you." Glancing to her daughter, she said, "We couldn't get over it, could we, Jen?" Pity dripped from her words and shone in her eyes. She patted my arm again. "You're a catch, dear. You really are!"

And that was why the ring had sat in my pocket for a year. "Thanks, ma'am."

She took the box from my hands and opened it. "So beautiful. Custom setting." She walked back around the counter, talking to herself. "I remember, one carat canary diamond, WS2, quarter-carat trillions, platinum setting." She held up the loupe hanging around her neck to examine the ring. "Perfect."

The bell over the door rang, and we all turned to watch Nancy sail in. "Oh. Hello, Chief." She paused, turning away to study a display near the door, thank God.

Carol tapped my hand and tilted her head toward the very back of the store.

"Let me write you a check," she whispered, going back through the door she'd emerged from a few minutes earlier.

I leaned on the counter, my back to the store, wishing I were anywhere but here. A hand ran along my back. I flinched, stepping away. Nancy, of course. "Don't."

"Aiden." Her voice took on a wheedling tone. "I really am sorry. I guess I was just feeling a little jealous. Let me make you dinner tonight, some dessert—" she winked "—as a proper apology," she whispered.

Why wouldn't she just leave me alone? "No."

She leaned into me. "I remember a time when—"

Carol came out of the back room, a check extended. On seeing Nancy, she quickly dropped her hand and smiled. "Jen, could you show Nancy those darling earrings that just came in?"

Nancy looked back and forth between us. "What are you two up to?"

Carol glanced at me, before focusing on Nancy. "Could you give us a few minutes, dear? We're in the middle of something."

Nancy didn't move. I wanted out of here. Now. I held out my hand for the check. Carol passed it to me. I folded it without even looking, stuffing it into my back pocket. I nodded my thanks to Carol and left, Jen trying unsuccessfully not to watch me.

I needed to punch something. Hard. When I got back to the cruiser, my radio squawked. "Chief?"

I picked up the handset. "Cavanaugh."

"Hey, Chief. We just received another call. Cupcake versus food truck."

Perfect. Maybe I could punch Chuck. "Yeah, I got it."

I pulled up next to the food truck a few minutes later. Trudy, the cupcake lady, pushed opened her door and pointed at the truck. "He won't even respond to me. I can hear him banging around in there, but he won't answer me or move that damn truck!"

I held up a hand. "Got it." For once, the side panel wasn't opened. I pounded on the the truck. "Chuck! Open up."

I heard what sounded like a squeak and a chuff. "You know you can't be here." Nothing.

I pounded on the side of the truck again. *Bark.* What the hell? "Will you open this damn panel?" Nothing.

"Fine. Have it your way, Chuck. I'm writing the ticket right now." I pulled my citation book off my belt.

"Wait!" The voice was muffled but much higher than it should have been. The panel rose an inch. A plastic knife was pushed out.

"Is that supposed to be a threat?"

The knife tipped onto its side, and the panel door fell back down. "Damn it!" There was a grunt. Little fingers peeked out a moment before a metal bar took their place. The panel stayed open an inch and a half. "Please, don't write a ticket! I'll get fired."

I knew that voice. "Katie?"

"Um, who?" Another chuff and then a shush.

"Katie, do you have a dog in a food truck? Do you have any idea how many health codes that violates?"

Silence. "None?"

My head pounded painfully with the humiliation of the jewelry store. The check in my back pocket felt like it weighed ten pounds. Rubbing my forehead, I said, "What are you doing in there?"

"No hablas inglés."

"Damn it, Katie. I don't have the time or patience for this today."

Pause. "Why? What's wrong?"

I stared at the dirty, white side panel of the truck.

"I'm a good listener, Chief." *Chuff.* "See? Chaucer agrees. Um, you know, if he were here, which he totally isn't." She mumbled, "Shush. We're being stealthy. Remember?"

The tightness in my shoulders loosened. "I just returned the ring I bought for the fiancée who dumped me."

She made a sympathetic sound. "Ooh, that bites hard. Was everyone giving you their I'm-pretending-that-I'm-not-looking-at-you-but-we-all-know-that-I-am-and-that-I-totally-pity-you faces?"

I laughed and could finally take a breath. "Yeah. That was it exactly."

"Been there. At least you didn't have someone gleefully cut up your credit card while a line of people stared at you because you couldn't pay for your groceries" She paused, her voice was barely a whisper. "And then try to figure out how to pay for food for your boy—who is not in this truck, are you, baby?—with the cash in your wallet, knowing that's all you have to your name. Then having to call your mom to ask for a loan, at the age of thirty because you're such a loser."

My chest hurt. I leaned my head against the side of the truck and whispered, "Fuck 'em."

"Yeah, fuck 'em."

After a few moments of silence, I straightened up. "So, what are you doing in there, Katie?"

"Working. It's my first day." Her voice was teary. "And I don't know what to do. He told me to figure it out. I'm supposed to clean up in here and then cook and sell hot dogs for the lunch crowd. But there are no lights in here and I'm not strong enough to open that panel. There isn't enough light coming through the windshield to see anything back here. I couldn't leave Chaucer at home—something in there scares him. I can't lock him up with a scary monster for five hours, so I had to bring him with me, but now you're going to give me a ticket, and then he's going to—"

I pushed up the side panel and secured the rod to keep it open.

"Oh!" She looked back and forth. "That helps a ton. Thanks!" She turned around, looking at everything.

"Would you like a hand?"

Her smile could melt glaciers. "Yes, please."

I walked around to the back door. Locked. I knocked.

"Just a minute, please," she sing-songed. I heard scraping. "Hmm, no idea how to open this door. I don't think it opens."

"Safety violation."

"Damn it, are you going to help me or get

me fired?" Shuffling and grunting. "Yo, Aiden. Over here."

I walked back around the side of the truck to find Katie kneeling on the counter, leaning out the window. "I'll give you a hand and pull you in."

I stared at her for a beat as she reached out a hand. "Really?" I asked.

She reassessed the situation. "Good point. You could probably just climb up."

"Or I could go through the driver's door like I assume you did."

She brightened and clapped. "Yes, do that." She looked at her watch. "Hurry up. Lots to do!"

Rolling my eyes, I rounded the front of the truck and then crawled over the seat into the kitchen in back. The area was too small for the three of us. Chaucer nudged my hand so his head was directly under it, helping me to more easily pet him. I scratched his head. "Smart dog."

Katie beamed.

"He can't stay here." I watched her face fall. "Seriously, you cannot have an animal in a food truck."

Sliding off the counter, she began, "But I can't take him back—"

I held up my hand. "Let me think." Shit. "Is he as well behaved with other people as he is with you?"

Wariness had taken the place of disappointment. "Yeeees," she drew out.

"How about if he comes to the station with me, while you work here?"

She looked between the two of us, her brow clearing. "Really? You'd take him with you today?"

Crouching down, I took the dog's head in my hands. He stepped forward, pressing the top of his head into my chest. "Do you promise to be a good boy and mind me?"

"Yes!" Katie was grinning from ear to ear, bouncing on her toes.

"I was asking the dog." Chaucer continued leaning into me, so I gave him a full-body rub. "No peeing in the office, or barking at people."

"Never!"

"Still not talking to you." I scratched him behind his ears, and he leaned in more heavily. "Fine." Katie squealed, but I raised a finger. "Only today. You need to leave him at home tomorrow."

"But—"

"I'm calling Harv to go check out your house while you're here and Chaucer's with me." I stood.

Her brow furrowed. "Who's Harv and why would he need to check out my house?"

"Exterminator and because it's infested." She opened her mouth to speak, but I cut her off. "You can't keep sleeping in your car." Her face colored. "You need to sleep in a bed in your own damn house. You need to not be terrified to go *into* your own damn house. Enough, okay? I've recently come into some money." I patted the pocket holding the ten-pound check. "I'll pay for the extermination, and you'll pay me back eventually. Okay?"

Her eyes shone watery as she nodded slowly. "Are you sure?" Her voice cracked and she cleared her throat. "It might be a long *eventually*." She gestured around at the interior of the truck. "I'm only part-time. In a food truck."

"Don't worry about it," I said and pulled my phone out of my pocket to call Harv. Katie sat on the floor, Chaucer all but sitting in her lap, as she whispered to him. I explained the situation to Harv, that I needed him to call me with his estimate first, but then actually do the work today. I didn't want her to spend one more night sleeping in her car.

Was I being an idiot again? Trusting an unreliable woman. I almost hung up on Harv and walked away, but I knew I'd never be able to live with myself. I'd help. I might get paid back. I might not. What I was *not* doing was getting involved with her. It was one kiss, one amazingly erotic… No. One kiss and it was done. Romantic relationships were out. Still, that kiss…

Crackling in my ear. Shit. "Sorry, Harv. What did you say?" She was already screwing with my head. "Okay. Stop by Chuck's food truck. It's parked next to Agamont Park. Katie, the house owner, works there. She can give you the key… Yeah. Listen, send me the bill, okay?…Great. Thanks."

When I disconnected, Katie was watching me. "Okay." I clapped my hands together once. "Let me show you how everything works, and then I'll take Chaucer with me."

CHAPTER FIFTEEN

Kate

THAT CUPCAKE LADY seemed like kind of a dick. She came out, yelled at me to move the truck and stormed back into her shop. I won't hold her rude behavior against her innocent cupcakes, but jeez. Luckily, the road was more of a hill, sloping down to the water. Aiden said the truck had to be running for the grill to work, so I only needed to take off the emergency brake, let the truck roll for a bit and then put the brake back on. Easy peasy.

Don't believe anyone who tells you I almost took out a tree. I barely skinned it. And as a bonus, the customer window was now nicely shaded. Yes, the sun would have helped keep me warm, but whatevs. And aside from a few—okay, a lot—shivery memories of cupcake kisses, I'd mopped the floors, for what appeared to be the first time ever, cleaned the grill and micro-waves, inventoried the food, disposing of all the spoiled stuff and was grilling a dog for my first customer by eleven twenty. I totally had this in the bag!

"What would you like on it?" I rolled the dog on the grill and placed the bun on the toasting plate.

"Mustard, sauerkraut and relish." A guy with a huge camera hanging around his neck waited on the curb for his dog.

Shit. I'd thrown out the sauerkraut can because the expiration date was three years ago. What to do, what to do? "Is this your first visit to Bar Harbor?"

The man was taking a picture of the park, the harbor in the background. He didn't change his stance as he answered. "No. Come every year."

Is there anything back here that's sauerkraut-like? I foraged through the storage cabinet again. Pickled onions? Really? Who the hell asks for pickled onions? "I'm sorry, sir. I'm out of sauerkraut. Is there something else I could put on your dog for you? Pickled onions, perhaps?" I smiled big, really selling it.

He lowered the camera, confusion clear on his face. "How can you be out?" He checked his watch. "It's 11:22 a.m. How could you have already sold out of sauerkraut?"

"Not sold-out, just out. But I have chili, cheese, onions, jalapeños, pickles and the ever-popular pickled onions." Big smile.

He reddened, anger lining his face. "How

the hell are you running a hot dog truck without sauerkraut?"

I retreated a step, picking up a fork. "Well, what happened was—"

"Are you a moron? That's like trying to sell a hot dog without the dog." His bellowing made nearby birds take flight.

Stepping farther into the shadows of the truck, I glanced over to the truck cab. I'd never locked the doors. "I'm sorry, sir. It's my first day. I'm just trying to—"

"This is the problem in this country. Everyone has an excuse for incompetence. Let me guess. You're charging full price, aren't you?" He paced in front of the open window, hands flailing, spittle flying from his mouth. "You should give me that dog for free!"

The hand not holding the pointy fork fell to my side to tap my thigh. Damn. Why had Aiden taken Chaucer from me? "I'm sorry, sir. I don't think I can help you today." My head was pounding in time with my racing heart.

He strode off, muttering, "Stupid bitch."

I shook out my trembling hands and carefully continued chopping onions. I glanced up and down the street, comforting myself with the fact that he was nowhere in sight. Okay. That happened. I got crazy sauerkraut guy off the agenda right at the start. That meant clear sailing for the rest of the day.

A young woman and her son walked up to the truck. "Sorry about that."

I smiled to myself, realizing I was cocking my head like Chaucer. "Sorry?"

Holding her son's hand, she looked over her shoulder and scanned the park. "I heard that guy yelling at you. I called the cops." She shrugged, embarrassed. "You hear horrible stories—I was worried about you."

My stomach began to untwist. "Thank you so much for doing that." Gesturing down the street, I took a deep breath. "He left, but he was scaring the—" I looked down at her son "—heck out of me." I rubbed my hands together. "That means the dogs are on me!" I leaned over the counter. "Whaddaya say, little man. Do you want a hot dog?"

The mom laughed. "He'd love one, but I don't want you to get in trouble by giving away food. I heard you say it's your first day."

Moving the hot dog I was cooking for crazy guy from the warmer back to the grill, I shook my head. "I'm not giving it away." I looked back at the adorable boy in his baseball cap and red sneakers. "You helped your mom do a really nice thing for someone who was scared. My thank-you will come in the form of meat."

Looking back at his mom, I said, "I'm buying your lunch."

"Oh, my goodness. You don't need to do that."

She tugged on her son's hand. "Jeremy, say thank you to the nice lady."

"Sanks!"

His gap-toothed grin did me in. "What do you like on your hot dogs?"

"'Chup!"

Rolling the hot dog back and forth on the grill, I looked to mom for a translation.

"Ketchup."

I laughed. "Of course. I'm Katie, by the way. It's nice to meet you, Jeremy."

"I'm Sara," the mom said.

I nodded, placing a second hot dog on the grill. I put Jeremy's dog back in the warmer while I finished cooking his mom's. "What do you like on yours, Sara?"

"Oh, you don't need to buy me one, too." She waved her hand. "Really. It was nothing."

Shaking my head, I said, "Not nothing. You saw someone in trouble and you helped. That's never nothing." I met her eyes. "So, what'll ya have?"

She sighed. "Okay, I'll have a chili-cheese dog."

"Excellent choice!" Leaning over, I looked down at the adorable gap-toothed smile under the boy's Giants ball cap. "Jeremy, are you a fan of the Giants? They're from my hometown."

"Yeah?"

"You bet. So, who's your favorite Giant?" I asked as I stirred the chili.

He hopped, trying to get his head over the counter. "Posey!"

"I love Buster!" I ladled chili over the dog, before sprinkling cheese on top. I handed Sara her hot dog first, and then handed Jeremy his. "You two are my first customers, and you've both been lovely. Thank you so much."

Sara took a bite. "Mmm. Thank *you*."

After they strolled away, I realized someone was leaning against the side of the truck. I flinched before recognizing it was Aiden.

"Kind of jumpy." He looked over what he could see of me. "Are you okay?"

I shook my head. "It was nothing. I'm fine." Glancing around the park, I made note of other people walking nearby, and of crazy guy not being among them. I slowly let out a breath, feeling my body start to relax.

"If you're giving away hot dogs, I'll take one, too." His voice was light, but I watched him scan the street, his eyes hard.

Rolling a dog from the warmer onto the grill, I said, "Not giving away. Buying."

He shrugged, still looking everywhere but at me. "Same diff to me. Either way I get a free lunch."

"How do you figure?" I scooped onions onto the grill. He seemed like the kind of guy who'd like onions. "That nice woman and her son came to my rescue. What have you done for me?"

He turned his head, eyebrows raised. "Seriously? How about every time I've—"

I waved my spatula in the air to shut him up. "Fine. I'll buy." Shit. I was losing money by working. "How's my little buddy?"

He grinned and my stomach dropped. "I'm doing great. Thanks for asking."

A gust of laughter broke free. More of the tension I'd been holding drained away. "Not you, you ass. Chaucer. How's my dog?"

"Oh, him." Aiden leaned his back against the side of the truck, arms crossed in front of him, biceps straining against his shirt. Not that I was looking.

"Well?" My eyes were back on the grill, where they belonged.

"Hell, I don't know. I don't have time to worry about your damn dog. I put him in the cell in back. You can pick him up when you're done here."

I looked around for what I had that was big and long enough to hit him in the head with.

"Strange. I don't hear the spatula scraping across the grill anymore. Let me warn you, if you attempt to hit me with anything in that truck, I'll put you in a cell, too." When he turned his head to study me, I slowly lowered my raised arm. "Chop-chop. How long does it take to make a hot dog?"

I considered pulling the three-year-old sauerkraut out of the trash, but thought better of it. Instead, I dumped some jalapeños on the grill. I layered the jalapeños on the bun, before I added the hot dog and chili, thereby hiding them. I sprinkled cheese and onions on top, and then handed it to the ass.

"Mmm, looks good." He stared at me for a moment. "Don't I get a drink, too?"

I considered whether or not I could unscrew the water bottle cap and spit into it before handing it to him. He was watching me like a hawk, so probably not. Damn it. "Here," I said as I passed him the cold bottle.

"Good choice."

I wiped down the grill. "I don't know what you're talking about."

"You realize that every thought you have is written all over your face, right?"

Ignoring him, I turned my back and drank from my own water bottle. I was trying to keep my water consumption to a minimum. If I needed to pee, I'd have to sprint across the park. The restroom facilities were on the far side, past the huge open green, the fountain, the arbor. I crossed my legs, pressure building. I turned to watch Aiden eat his jalapeño-surprise hot dog in a few huge bites.

"Mmm, I love jalapeños. How'd you know?" He wiped his mouth, crumpled up his napkin and threw it in the trash.

Figures. "Can you do me a favor, Aiden?"

He spread his arms wide. "My being here is a favor. I'm the chief of police, and yet here I stand to make sure a sauerkraut psycho isn't harassing you. I have your dog in my station. I'm paying to have your house rid of an ungodly number of forest animals. What the hell more do you want, woman?"

"Can you just watch the truck while I run over to the bathroom?"

He stared at me for a moment, before pointing at the cupcake shop. "Trudy has a restroom."

"Strangely enough, she doesn't like me." I scrambled over the passenger seat in the truck cab and ran across the park toward the bathroom.

"Shocker," Aiden shouted after me.

Buttmunch.

When I strolled back, taking the leisurely, scenic route, I noticed a line of people waiting at the truck. Crap.

"Hey, Chief. You moonlighting in food service these days?" someone teased.

"I hope you've gotten better at this than you were in high school. I got the runs after you made me an undercooked hot dog," another man said.

"Cool story, bro."

When I climbed back into the truck, I didn't

find Aiden nervous and scrambling. He had multiple dogs cooking, was grilling the onions and pickles, had buns toasting and waters lined up on the counter ready to be handed out.

He turned to me. "Could you have walked any slower?"

"I sure could have. Would you like me to show you?" I turned as if to leave.

"Can you just start taking money, while I finish cooking?" He'd rolled up his sleeves, displaying strong, corded forearms. His shoulders were high and stiff, but his chatter with the customers was relaxed.

"Chief, who's your assistant?"

He ignored the question, barely giving me a glance.

Damn. He was really pissed off at me. I looked at the growing crowd of mostly middle-aged men and wondered where the hell they'd come from all of a sudden. Giving a half-hearted wave, I mumbled, "Kate."

Aiden tilted his wrist at me, his watch flashing in the sunlight breaking through the trees. "It's noon. This is what happens at noon." He handed me three loaded dogs for me to place in their paper boats.

"Are these for one person or three different people?" I tried to assess the group of men. I had no idea who was first.

Aiden shouted, "Line up." Which they did. He

gestured at the dogs. "The two onion and pickles go to Charlie, first in line. The chili and cheese goes to Mike, second."

"Got it." I raised my voice. "Good afternoon, gentlemen. Thank you for making the hot dog truck your choice for lunch today. We know you could have chosen many other restaurants, so we thank you for your patronage." I smiled broadly at one and all.

Aiden paused in his grilling, expression incredulous.

I shrugged. "It works for airlines."

Shaking his head, he handed me three more dogs. I kept waiting for him to hand me the spatula and duck out, but he stayed to get through the rush. At one point his radio crackled and asked for him. He told the woman to contact a cop named Sharon, and went back to cooking. Within ten minutes, we had the crowd cleared.

He wiped down the grill and utensils, then washed the rag in the sink. "I can't believe you don't have any sauerkraut."

I lined up waiting paper boats for the next group of people to arrive. "The can was three years old! I threw it out."

"It's sauerkraut. What the hell's going to happen to it? It's already pickled." Untying the apron, he stepped back from the grill.

"Wait, should I pull the can out of the garbage?" I probably should have opened the can to make sure it was a problem. I went still as he reached around me, wrapping the apron around my waist. He tied the strings in front. His chest pressed against my back as he looked over my shoulder. Hot breath on my neck.

When he finished, his fingers lightly trailed over my stomach, before coming to rest on my hips. "Feel like doing your own job now?"

The heat from his big, possessive hands, and the rumble of his deep voice scattered my thoughts. "What?"

His arms coiled around me, crushing me against his chest. I felt his lips on my neck. I *may* have sighed. If he tells you I moaned, he's a dirty, dirty liar. It was just a sigh. With some groany bits thrown in.

He let go of me. "Let's see if you can handle a half day's work." A moment later he was gone.

Wait, what? "Hey," I yelled at him as he sauntered past. "You can't just ruthlessly kiss me and then be a dick! Keep your lips to yourself, asswipe."

No men!

How hard was that to remember? And why did he always make me want to forget?

CHAPTER SIXTEEN

Aiden

HER MOAN ECHOED in my head. I raked my fingers through my hair. I needed to forget about her and her moan, or I would have to start walking around with my shirt untucked.

It was high time my dick and I had a heart-to-heart. Yes, she was adorable and wicked hot. No, she was not for me. I'd already fallen for one runner—I didn't need to add another to my life. I was doing a good deed with the extermination thing, that's all. Plus, it saved me from seeing her every day when I cleaned out traps. Katie was not going to worm her way in. No. I forced myself to remember Alice. The look on her face as she told me she loved me. The touches and giggles. The sighs in bed. All lies.

My phone chirped as I dropped back into my cruiser.

"Hey, Pops. What's up?"

"Do you know what that girl did?" he shouted.

I pulled the phone from my ear. What girl?

"No, I don't." Pops spent most of his time with his buddies, at home or at… Oh, shit.

"She threw away all of Nellie's furniture! I was just over there watering the garden, though I don't know why. She can do it herself, ungrateful brat!"

Shit, shit, shit. "If you were just watering, how did you know about the furniture?"

"I went to the side door and knocked, thought the dog might want to keep me company. But Katie didn't answer so I looked in the window by the door—"

"Peeping."

"—and saw the furniture was gone. What kind of person throws out her grandmother's beloved possessions like it's nothing? I was wrong about giving her a chance. She doesn't deserve one!"

"Let it go, Pops. It's not Nellie's house anymore. Katie can legally do whatever she wants." I watched another line form in front of the food truck, heard Katie greeting them like a flight attendant. Rolling my eyes, I focused on Pops. "And listen, you don't need to tend the garden anymore, either. Let Katie deal with her own responsibilities."

"She can forget about any more help from me." He paused. "Why would she do that, though?" The hurt in his voice killed me. "The furniture was in perfect condition. Nellie always took good care of her home, cleaning every day. She knew the value of things. Not like today's generation. Everything is disposable. Including people!"

I put him on speaker and drove away. "She's trying, Pops. Let her succeed or fail on her own. Okay?" I paused. "Chances are she'll be leaving soon, anyway." I swung around and drove back toward the station. Chaucer better still be sleeping under my desk. If he was chewing files, we'd have words.

"Leaving? She just got here."

"Yeah, but her husband's sending an appraiser. He's planning to sell the house." I pulled into the parking lot, grabbed my phone and walked into the station. My office door was now open—I'd shut it before I left—but Chaucer stood at the doorway, not trying to escape. I glanced over at a guilty-looking Heather who was stuffing something in her desk and putting her headset back on. Great. If Heather kept feeding him, he'd never want to leave.

"He can do that? Just sell the house out from under her?" Pops continued on the phone.

I put my hand out, and Chaucer stepped forward, sliding his head under it. I gave him a scratch as I walked past. "Yeah. He can, Pops. California is a community-property state. She inherited it while married to him." I heard a hiss and turned to look. I could see Heather through the doorway, motioning to Chaucer. He shifted his head, back and forth between us, one foot in the air, ready to go to her. I waved him away, and he trotted to her desk. "Katie doesn't have the money to buy him out. The only option is selling the place. It'll at least give her the money to get started somewhere else."

Silence. "Oh."

"Listen, Pops. I gotta get back to work. Don't worry about Katie. She's as good as gone."

I hung up and sat down hard. Damn. She was as good as gone.

CHAPTER SEVENTEEN

Kate

AFTER PICKING UP CHAUCER, who was not locked in a cell, I stopped and bought two big cans of sauerkraut on my way home. I was not dealing with that crap again tomorrow. When I pulled up to Gran's house, the exterminator's van was parked out front. Harvey had picked up the key from me, but I'd been so busy, I'd completely forgotten.

He stepped through the front door, as Chaucer and I got out of the car. "Heard you drive up. I'm done here. You had one heck of an infestation, miss." He scratched the back of his neck, and pulled out a notebook. "Let's see. I pulled a family of opossums from your attic—"

"Wait." I held up a hand, my voice pleading. "Don't tell me. I can't handle the truth."

He paused, nodded slowly and replaced his notebook in his back pocket. "Fine. I *only* found a small fawn. She was wobbling through the front room. I shooed her out, and now your house is completely clean."

"Aww, did you hear that, Chaucer?" I patted his head. "All those noises we heard were coming from a sweet, little fawn." I shook my head, smiling at Harvey. "I feel so silly for being worried." I walked up the steps and hugged Harvey. Hard.

He patted my back awkwardly. "It's okay, miss."

I looked through the open doorway with something akin to hope. "So, what do I owe you?"

"Oh, well." Harvey shuffled his feet. "The chief said he'd take care of it."

I rummaged through my handbag, pulling out a bank envelope with the money from Mom. "While I appreciate the offer, I'm paying." Thinking about the sheer number and variety of animals he rid the house of, I added, "You know, probably, assuming you didn't gouge me on the fawn-extraction fees."

He opened his mouth, but seemed unsure of what to say. I nodded my head, encouraging him to keep going with the ruse. He cleared his throat. "Fawn removal can be tricky. I charge $620 for expert fawn removal."

Feeling the hit to my pocketbook, and a corresponding light-headedness, I opened the envelope and began counting. So much for grocery shopping. "Food is overrated, Harvey." I tried to hand him his money. I did. I tried. He ended up having to pry it from my fingers.

As he walked down the steps, he threw over

his shoulder, "If you have any more problems, just let me know."

"What?" I glanced warily in the house. "I thought you said you dealt with my fawn infestation."

He turned, face stricken. "I just meant if any more fawns wander in, you could call me for help. I left the invoice on your dining table—oh, but it might be best if you didn't look too closely at that. My phone number is at the bottom." He started to walk back toward the house. "I can just fold up that invoice so you only see my name and number. How would that be?"

I wanted to tell him not to worry about it, but what came out instead was, "That'd be great!"

He jogged in and came back out a moment later. "All fixed. You have a nice evening, miss."

Waving, I called, "Thank you, kindly fawn wrangler."

He drove away and silence settled around us. Chaucer and I walked cautiously through the front door. I stilled, waiting for the telltale scratching, the almost subaudible squeaks. Nothing. I let out the breath I was holding. "It's really ours now."

After feeding Chaucer, I decided I should mop the floors and wash down the walls again. I'd been at it for three sweaty hours when Chaucer ran downstairs, barking. I followed and found Mr. Cavanaugh at the front door. Quickly closing the door behind me so as to block his view of the empty living room, I stepped out onto the porch.

"Good evening. How are you?" Chaucer wandered over to sniff at him.

He clenched his hands, a look of disgust on his face. "I'm mad is how I am."

"Oh, I see." I glanced around, confused. "Did I forget to do something with the garden? I'm—"

"You threw out all of Nellie's belongings!" Eyes sparking, face turning red, he looked like he wanted to punch me.

"What? No. I'd never do that." Chaucer stood in front of me, blocking the scary man from getting too close. My fingers shook as I sank them into his fur.

"Then let's just go in there and see. Open up that door!"

He lunged for the door handle, but I stood my ground. Consequently, I got knocked sideways and bounced off the door frame. Chaucer's deep growl caused Mr. Cavanaugh to reassess the situation.

Rage turned to resentment. "I didn't mean to push you." His focus shifted to Chaucer, whose low growl hadn't abated. Judging by the worried look on Mr. Cavanaugh's face, Chaucer may have thrown in some bared teeth to bring his point home.

I thought about all those sleepless nights in my car, afraid to enter the house, the scratching, the scurrying… I should have thrown open the door when he'd first arrived and shown him what happened when windows were left open for a couple of months, but I didn't—couldn't.

"I know you didn't mean to push me, Mr. Cavanaugh. I also know you're a good man who wouldn't willingly hurt a woman. Gran wouldn't have loved you if you had that in you."

All his anger drained away. He stood slumped and sad before me. Somehow, that was worse than his anger.

I screwed up my courage, pulling Chaucer closer to me, and lied. "It was ugly."

He looked up, confused. "What?"

"The furniture and stuff. This is my home now. I don't want it to look like an old lady's house. I mean, come on."

Shame ignited back into rage.

"Fresh start for me." I shrugged. "If you wanted her old stuff, you should have taken it."

"She left it for you! So you'd have a warm, safe, comfortable place to live, not that you deserve anything like that!" Righteous anger looked better on him than grief. "What kind of a heartless, self-centered woman are you?"

Was that a trick question? "The heartless and self-centered type?"

He took a step forward, ignoring Chaucer's louder growl. "That's what you do, isn't it? Make jokes. You break your grandmother's heart and you joke. You leave your husband and make jokes." He turned, gesturing to the battered BMW. "You destroy an expensive car and joke about it. Let your grandmother die without you. Don't go to the funeral and laugh it up. Now here you are, throwing out belongings she collected and cared for most of her life as though they were—*she* was—garbage. And you joke." Revulsion lined his face.

"Aiden was right about you, Katie. You're nothing but a cruel, shallow bit of nothing. When your husband comes to sell this house out from under you, I'll do a jig." He stormed off, while I stood frozen.

Buffeted by his words, back pressed against the front door, my knees gave out. I slid down, landing in an ungainly heap. *A cruel, shallow bit of nothing.* My chest ached and my mind roared.

Standing quickly, I dislodged Chaucer, who was trying to sit on my lap. I ran into the house and down the hall, just making it to the toilet before throwing up. Afterward, I lay curled up on the cold, freshly washed tiles and sobbed, missing my Gran and praying she didn't hate me, too.

CHAPTER EIGHTEEN

Aiden

A KNOCK SOUNDED on my open office door. Mark, a local contractor who does appraising as a side job, stood in the doorway. Damn. Her husband worked quickly.

"Hey, Chief. I got a call to do an appraisal on Nellie's place. The owner thought you might have a key if his wife wasn't there."

I tapped my pencil, pretending I didn't have a key to Nellie's place on the ring on my belt. "Nope. But Nellie's granddaughter drove home a few hours ago, so she should be there to let you in."

"Oh," He straightened and turned. "Good enough."

"So, he's really planning to sell the house out from under her?"

Mark stepped back. "Don't know. I was just called about a job." He shrugged. "Guy made it sound like it was a done deal. Are you saying the wife doesn't know?"

Shaking my head slowly, I sighed. "I don't think she does."

"Well, shit." Mark stared at the floor a moment. "I already took the job." He turned and left, grumbling.

I picked up the phone, to give Katie a heads-up, but then set the receiver back in the cradle. This was what I wanted. She needed to sell and move somewhere else. Pain radiated from my chest. A dick move? Sure. But I needed her far away from me. I didn't want to worry about her or feed her or check on her to make sure she was sleeping. I didn't want to *fucking* care. Not again.

My cell rang. Pops. "Hey—"

"I should have noticed. Should have seen what was going on."

Thumbing through the report on my desk, I paused. "What are we talking about, Pops?"

"Nellie's house, her things."

Crap. I'd told him to stay out of it.

"I went over there. Confronted her." Anger and grief poured through the phone line.

"Pops, I thought we agreed that you'd stop going over there." Damn, stubborn man.

"I wanted her to explain. I didn't mean to push her, though."

"Listen, Pops, anyone could have made the mistake—wait. Did you say you hit her?"

"Pushed, not hit. I was trying to—"

"Jesus. Pops! You're almost a foot taller and about eighty pounds heavier. What the hell?"

"It was an accident! I was trying to open the front door, but she wouldn't budge. I just kind of knocked her off balance, into the doorjamb. Damn it! That's not the point. She told me herself that she'd thrown away Nellie's things because they were old and ugly."

The pain in my chest intensified. "Let me see if I have this straight. You went to her house, yelled at her, tried to force your way in and shoved her when she didn't move. And after all that, she told you that she'd thrown away Nellie's things because they were ugly?" She'd kept her promise. Pops assaulted her, and still she kept her word to protect him from the truth.

"Exactly! She said she thought Nellie's things were ugly so she threw them away. Just like that! Seventy-five years of living, of being a good, kind woman, and it's all tossed because that spoiled brat didn't like the looks of it!"

Shit.

"You were right about her, and I told her so. She's nothing but a cruel, shallow bit of nothing! I don't even mind Nellie's house being sold as long as it doesn't go to her."

I couldn't rule out a heart attack at this point. I flexed my left arm, breathing deeply. "You told her I said she was shallow and nothing?"

"Damn right I did! You were on the money

with that one. I told her I'd do a little jig when her husband sold the house out from under her. And I will, too."

Heather walked in. "Chief, you have a call on line one."

I nodded and Heather left. "I've got a call, Pops. Do us both a favor and leave Katie alone. By rights, I should arrest you for assault and battery—"

"It was an accident."

"Accident or not, Pops, you shoved a woman who might be a hundred pounds soaking wet. You yelled at her and tried to force your way into her house. Stop acting like you're the victim here. It's just furniture!"

"But—"

"But nothing. I want you to think long and hard about what Nellie would say if she could have seen your little stunt today."

After I hung up on Pops and dealt with a call about a stolen car, I sat, staring out the window. After everything Katie had already dealt with today, an appraiser would be pulling up any minute to let her know she'd be losing her house, as well. I didn't know how to fix this. Or even if I wanted to.

CHAPTER NINETEEN

Kate

CHAUCER BARKED, RUNNING to the front door, as
a knock echoed in the cavernous house. Sure.
Why not? I got up from the bathroom floor and
studied my red puffy eyes, my blotchy cheeks.
Awesome. I splashed cold water on my face and
walked to the entry as another knock sounded.

"Chaucer, sit." I waited until he complied before opening the door. A stocky, muscular man
in jeans and a plaid flannel shirt stood on my
porch, a clipboard in his hand.

"Good afternoon, Mrs. Cady. My name is
Mark Rutherford." He smiled uneasily. "I'm a
local contractor and part-time appraiser. Your
husband hired me to determine the value of this
house before you put it on the market."

I closed my eyes and tried to control my breathing. Chaucer whimpered and leaned against me,
licking my hand. My stomach dropped out. Or
maybe it was my heart. Either way, a vital organ
was flopping on the porch like a fish out of water.

I blew out a breath and put up a finger. "Can you give me a moment to call my lawyer?"

He nodded and stepped back. "Sure. I'll just wait in my truck. Take your time."

I closed the door and walked to the kitchen. I had my lawyer's number on a notepad by the phone. My fingers shook as I dialed.

"Kate! It's about time you checked in. Your cell was turned off, and you haven't responded to my emails."

I gave her Gran's phone number. "Sorry. There's no Wi-Fi up here—"

"In Maine?"

I let out a breath. "No, I mean Gran's house."

"Well, I'm glad you called. I'm working with your husband's lawyer to try to hammer out a settlement. They're hardballing, pretending he's completely broke. Now I have to get auditors and investigators working on it. Unfortunately, that means I have no money for you right now. Are you surviving?"

"Yeah. My mom loaned me some money. Listen, though. I'm calling because there's an appraiser here. He says Justin's putting the house on the market. Can he do that? Just sell the house?"

Jean, my lawyer, cursed. "Yes. The rat bastard can, in fact, force a sale. I can stall it until we get his financials sorted, but unless you have the money to buy him out of his share, he can force the sale."

"Shit."

"Precisely. Let the nice appraiser do his job. We need to know how much it's worth anyway, so I can negotiate it as part of the distribution of assets." She paused. "You said the house was in bad shape, right? Dirty, animal infested?"

Fuck, fuck, fuckity fuck. "It was. I just paid an exterminator to clean it out, and I've been re-washing the walls and floors all afternoon. So it may be empty of furniture, but it actually looks pretty good right now."

"Our timing could have been better on that one. Nothing we can do. Let him in, and we'll see where we are. Just in case, though, try to make your peace with selling. We may not have a choice."

I hung up with Jean and made my way back to the front door. When I opened it, the appraiser stepped out of his truck.

"Am I good to go?" he asked, pulling a pen from his pocket and attaching it to the clipboard.

I nodded, sitting on the top step. "Yep. Go on in. I'll wait for you out here."

Chaucer sat with me, both of us staring at the trees, whipping to and fro in the fierce wind coming off the ocean. I shivered, but I refused to go inside and get a sweatshirt while that man was walking through Gran's house, determining what Justin could get for it. Justin, that sack of excrement who insulted and cheated on me for our whole marriage, was going to take this away from me, too.

Scooting closer, Chaucer broke the full force of the wind and warmed my side. I dug my fingers into his fur and hugged him tight. Yes, I know dogs don't particularly like being hugged, but I needed it. I may have even cried. Thankfully, dogs are good at keeping secrets.

Chaucer made a soft woof, his head coming up. I took a moment to wipe my face clean before I sat up. Police cruiser. Right. I'm a *shallow bit of nothing*. Wouldn't want to forget that.

Aiden stepped out and walked slowly toward us, as though afraid I would explode at any moment. I wished. I'd love to splatter the asshole with gray matter and burst organs. Try washing that out, you bastard.

"I hear you're having a rough day."

He actually looked concerned. Must be something they teach in the police academy, how to approach cornered and possibly vicious animals. Me, not Chaucer. Chaucer was a sweetie, through and through. Whereas I was a homeless, shallow bit of nothing who had just learned the truth about herself. Very dangerous.

"You're shivering. Don't you have a coat?"

I sat up straighter, willing my teeth not to chatter. "Is there a problem, Officer?"

He looked confused. And sexy. The bastard.

"Why are you here?" I put as much anger as I

could into my voice. I would not break down in front of him. "No more animals caught in traps. No need to keep wasting your time on nothing. Nothing to see here. *Nothing* at all." My voice caught on the third *nothing*. I cleared my throat and continued, "Move along."

Sighing, he ran his hands over his face. "Katie, when I said that, the nothing thing, it was your first day back. I didn't know you. I was angry about Alice, and I knew Pops would try to set us up."

I laughed. It was bitter sounding, even to my own ears. "No worries there. Your grandfather thinks I'm the Antichrist. Trust me, no one wants a loved one to date the Antichrist." I heard something in the house and turned.

"Why are you sitting out here in the freezing wind in only a T-shirt and shorts?"

I scooted closer, draping Chaucer's warm, furry legs over my knees. "It's refreshing out here. And last time I checked, being cold wasn't illegal. Bye now."

He walked back to his car. Good.

Unfortunately, he jogged back holding a big sweatshirt. "Put this on before you freeze to death."

"Nope. I'm good. Buh-bye." I shivered uncontrollably. Stupid Maine weather.

He walked closer and shoved the sweatshirt over my head.

I sputtered. "What the—dude, you cannot just force clothing on unsuspecting people! Go arrest yourself." Ah, warmth. I pulled the sweatshirt down over my bent knees. My entire body folded within the sweatshirt. "But before you fingerprint yourself, could you pull up the hoodie?"

Brushing stray curls from my face, he pulled the hood forward. Warm, calloused fingers brushed my jaw and tipped up my chin. "I'm sorry." He paused. "About a lot of things, actually." Scooting me over, he sat on my other side, adding another heat source and wind break.

He nudged my shoulder. "Thanks for keeping the secret." Tipping his head toward the front door, he continued, "About the open windows and the animals."

I nodded, shifting away from him, leaning into Chaucer.

"Why did you?"

"I promised you, didn't I?"

He leaned forward, his arms braced against his knees, and sighed. "Yes, you did." He stood abruptly, cursing. "I've got to go do something," he said, as he strode back to his cruiser.

"What about your sweatshirt?" I didn't want to give it up, but he already thought I was a cruel, shallow bit of nothing. I didn't need him to add thief to his assessment.

He waved away my question and drove off.

Score! New sweatshirt for me.

The front door opened and the Mark guy came out. "Ma'am, I have a preliminary number for you and your husband—"

"Ex."

"Right. If you could give me a day or so, though, I can give you the most accurate number. I need to check recent sales in this area."

I stood. "Take your time, the longer the better." The sweatshirt fell to my knees. "Actually, can you give me the ballpark number now?"

He looked over his notes. "I'd say at least a million and a half. I'll check sales on comparables and get back to you." He tipped his head and jogged off to his truck.

A million and a half? I couldn't afford groceries. How was I supposed to come up with half of that? I couldn't breathe.

I was going to lose Gran's house.

CHAPTER TWENTY

Aiden

I PULLED UP to Pops's house and turned off the engine. Damn it. I did not want to do this. I stepped out and mounted the stairs. When I knocked, Pops opened the door almost immediately. He looked confused and wary.

"Pops, I need to talk to you."

He opened the door wider, still watching me suspiciously. Maybe I shouldn't have yelled at him on the phone, but he'd knocked Katie around. The Katie bashing had to stop, me included.

I sat on the couch and waited for him to take his chair. "I need to tell you something, and I really don't want to."

His confusion deepened. "You can tell me anything. I thought you understood that."

"It's about Katie."

He bristled. "I don't want to talk about her."

I sat forward, not knowing how to begin. "I know." I took a deep breath. "The furniture? That was our fault, my fault really." He started to speak, but I cut him off. "Nellie had windows open in her house when we moved her out."

"So what?"

I shook my head, thinking about it. "I used to drive up there once every shift. Just to check on the house. Make sure no one broke in."

"Oh." He looked like he was waiting for a shoe to drop. "That was good of you."

I rubbed my hands down the thighs of my jeans. "But I never went *in* the house, Pops. After we moved Nellie to your place, I locked the doors and never went back in."

"Okay."

"See, it's my fault, Pops. I thought I was keeping an eye on her house, but I didn't check the windows before I locked up." He opened his mouth, but I had to get it out quickly. "Animals got in. A lot of them. By the time Katie arrived, the house had been abandoned to forest creatures for months. There was mud and feathers, smears and droppings everywhere. The furniture had become infested."

I heard Pops's shocked intake of breath, but couldn't stop. "Katie's been sleeping in her car. She's been washing down walls and mopping floors. She carried most of the furniture out all by herself. She's been terrified to go in, but it's her Gran's and she seems to feel it her moral obligation to fix it."

Pops's hands started to shake.

"She's had it rough. Her husband lied and cheated. Now he's trying to take Nellie's house away from her. The asshole wouldn't even let Katie eat. She's skin and bones. And when she left, he apparently canceled her credit cards and did something with their bank account so that she doesn't even have enough money to buy food. Her pantry and refrigerator are empty." I stood, needing to move. "She got a job working in Chuck's food truck, but I think that's so she can feed her dog."

"But she never said—"

"I asked her not to. I knew you'd be upset if you knew Nellie's house had been completely trashed." I ran my fingers through my hair. "Even with you yelling at her and pushing her around, she kept her promise and didn't tell you why."

Pops stood, too. "I won't be coddled and protected by you. You should've told me."

"Yeah." I dropped back onto the couch and scrubbed my hands over my face. "As we speak, she's sitting there, shivering in the wind, starving, while an appraiser does the preliminary work to take her house away from her. A house she's been killing herself to clean. And even though I said I'd pay for it, she spent the money her mom sent her to live on to pay for the exterminator."

I took the hands from my face and looked Pops

in the eye. "She wouldn't accept any help from me. She was sitting there, shivering in the cold, holding on to that dog, who seems to be the only one looking out for her, and refused to break. So, I'm sorry I kept it from you, Pops, but you have got to lay off her, okay?"

"What can be done? There's got to be a way to stop her husband." Pops was pacing, fired up. "What's that lawyer of hers doing?"

"Not enough."

CHAPTER TWENTY-ONE

Kate

AFTER A LONG, hot shower, I dressed in my coziest sweats and pulled on two pairs of socks, hoping the layering would keep me warm. I took the freshly laundered blankets from the dryer, draping one around my shoulders and carrying the other two in my arms. Delicious heat seeped into me. In the living room, I folded two into beds, one for me and one for Chaucer, and then used the sweatshirt Aiden had left me as a pillow.

Exhausted, I cocooned myself in the third blanket and had just lain down when Chaucer jumped up and barked at the door. A knock sounded a moment later. "Oh, come on. Do you understand how difficult it is to stand up now?" I struggled to extricate myself from the cozy, warm blankets. Another knock echoed in the room. "Keep your hair on," I shouted.

Chaucer was wagging his tail, so I opened the door. The porch was empty except for four grocery bags. I heard a car door slam and squinted out into the dark driveway. "Hello?"

Aiden jogged up the steps into the light pooling on the porch from the open door. "Delivery, ma'am." He pushed past me, two bags in his arms, and went straight down the hall and into the kitchen.

"Um." What the hell was that?

He emerged a moment later. "Can you get one of the bags? I'll grab the other three." He strode back out onto the porch. "Actually, I've got them. Just get the door." He picked up all four and brushed passed me on his way to the kitchen again.

Chaucer trotted after him, leaving me alone in the doorway, wind whipping my hair into my face. Shivering, I closed and locked it before cautiously making my way to the kitchen. I pushed open the door and found Aiden crouched down in front of my fridge, pulling food from the bags on the floor around him.

"I don't understand."

He glanced up before continuing to load my refrigerator. "I've had about as much as I can take." He stood. "Why don't you finish up here? I forgot something in the car." He walked out, and I stared at an unfathomable amount of food.

I looked in one of the bags and saw doggy jerky treats. My throat tightened.

Aiden walked back in a few minutes later with a forty-pound bag of dog food under his arm. He opened the pantry door and dropped it on the floor. When he turned, he found me standing where he'd left me. "I believe you were given a job." Grinning, he brushed me aside and finished unloading all the grocery bags.

I stood frozen, unable to make sense of what was happening. I reached up my sleeve and pinched myself. Yep. I totally felt that.

Aiden stood in front of me, eyebrows raised and said, "So, is this happening?" I pointed a hesitant finger at him.

Scowling, he said, "What did I tell you I'd do if you poked me again?"

I jabbed my finger into his hard chest. *Ow.*

He grabbed my finger and held on to it. "Is the rest of you as cold as this finger?"

"I was super warm and snuggly in my just-from-the-dryer blankets until you knocked."

He took both my hands and held them in his own, leaning down and breathing hot air onto my frigid fingers. He looked at me under his dark lashes. My stomach flipped and then growled. He grinned. "I brought dinner, too. Come on." He pulled me forward, handed me two plates from the cupboard, then spun me and pushed me toward the door. "I'll get glasses. Go."

I walked back to the living room in a daze. Next to the door was a sleeping bag and foam pad. Aiden walked up behind me and gave me a little push. He was carrying a wine bottle and two glasses. He placed them on the floor, picked

up the sleeping pad, rolled it out and then un-
rolled the sleeping bag on top of it.

He pointed. "Sit."

Plates still clutched in my hands, I dumbly followed his orders, dropping down onto the won-
derfully cushioned floor. He smirked as he took
the plates from me, before shaking out one of
my blankets and pulling it close around me like
a shawl. I was so tired, I could have dropped off
right then and there. The scent of meaty, cheesy
goodness was the only thing keeping my eyelids
from drooping.

"Here, sleepyhead. Stay awake long enough
to eat something."

He handed me a plate with a piece of pizza on
it. A moment later a glass of red wine was dangling before me. I snatched the glass and took
a big gulp. *Ah.* I put the glass down and picked
up the slice of pizza. The smell alone had my
mouth watering. I took a cheesy, spicy bite and
groaned. Not peanut butter! I inhaled the slice
and then went back to the wine.

"Do you want another piece?"

Another? "I want it very much, but I don't
think I could eat it."

He made a disgruntled sound.

"It's delicious. I'm just full."

He was sitting on the floor, leaning against
the wall nearby. "I'm not angry with you. I'm
angry that one piece of pizza fills you up. Your

stomach has shrunk to the size of a pea because you're not eating."

I huddled under the soft, warm blanket, my tummy blissfully full, and took another sip of wine. "I eat fine."

"What have you eaten today?"

My eyes drifted closed. His deep, grumbly voice was oddly soothing. "I had a peanut butter sandwich this morning."

"With what? There's no bread in your kitchen."

"The bread was implied. I imagined bread while I ate a spoonful of peanut butter." Mmm, delicious wine. Alcohol should be on the bottom of the food pyramid. It was definitely more important than meat or grains.

"Didn't you have a hot dog when you were at work? I know Chuck allows one free dog per shift."

"I gave *you* my free dog, Mr. You-Owe-Me-A-Free-Lunch."

"Damn it, Katie! You have to eat."

"Couldn't afford it. I only had ten dollars on me. I spent that on the nice mom and her son. He was so cute my heart hurt. I couldn't pay for yours, too, so it had to be mine." My voice sounded hollow and far away.

I felt myself start to tip. I had a moment to worry that I'd spill my wine and then it was gone. I snuggled down into my blanket, my head on

Aiden's sweatshirt. "I like your sweatshirt. You smell nice."

I think I heard him sigh. "What am I going to do with you?"

I liked it when he kissed me. Maybe he'd do that again.

"Okay."

Okay? Cool. He can read—oh, right. Stupid mouth was always getting me in trouble.

CHAPTER TWENTY-TWO

Aiden

SHE WAS OUT. I considered putting the rest of the pizza in the fridge, along with the wine, and then taking off, but I couldn't make myself leave. I brushed her hair back from her face. She sighed.

"I like kissing you, too," I whispered.

"Thank goodness. That would have been awkward."

I leaned forward and watched her. She was sound asleep and talking. I wished I were a better person. "What do you think of me?"

"Mean. Grumpy. Hot. Amazing kisser. Broody. Great ass. Ma'am."

I chuckled. "Great ass, huh?"

"Mmm-hmm. Damn."

Shaking my head, I tried another one. "Why did you really wreck your husband's car?" Her brow furrowed in her sleep, and I instantly regretted the question. It was wrong, prying into her subconscious this way. "Never mind. Go back to sleep."

"He stole Gran from me. Drove everyone

away." She curled tighter. "Never loved me. Cheated. Never smart enough. Pretty enough. Thin enough. Sexy enough. Never enough."

She was breaking my heart.

"Gran was sick and didn't tell me. She died. Without me. Didn't tell me. Ignored me. Smirked. Turned his back. On the phone. Golf club. Got his attention."

"Yeah, I bet you did. It's okay now. You're safe. You can sleep."

"Gran hates me."

I leaned over her and kissed her forehead. "No. Nellie loves you and always will."

Her brow cleared and her breathing slowed.

"Sweet dreams. Think about my hot ass."

"'Kay."

Lying down on the blanket next to her, I grinned. As I drifted off, Chaucer settled at our feet.

I awoke early the next morning. Katie was sound asleep, still cocooned in blankets. I took a moment to watch her sleep, to marvel at her soft radiant skin, the light dusting of tiny freckles over her nose and cheeks. I'd forgotten she had freckles. Her hair was curling again, not as tightly as when she was younger, but she was looking more like herself now.

Her dark lashes fluttered sleepily, and then I was staring into her glassy green eyes. I watched emotions flit across her face, cataloging them.

Confusion, fear, memory, confusion again and finally exasperation.

"Why are you staring at me?" Her voice was early morning creaky.

"Because I can."

"Stalker." She closed her eyes and went back to sleep.

Checking my watch, I groaned and got up, my body stiff from the floor. Chaucer got up with me. I walked him to the back door. Opening it, I waved him out. "Go ahead." Extraordinarily, he didn't run right out the door. He stared at me, looked back toward the living room where Katie was sleeping, and then stared at me again. He didn't want to leave me alone with her.

"Okay, I'll step out, too." I stood on the porch, in easy view, as he trotted out to a nearby bush and watered it.

"Chaucer, baby, where are you?"

We both heard Katie's voice from inside. Chaucer finished, hopped up onto the porch and tried to push the door open with the top of his head. I reached over him and turned the knob.

"Chaucer?" Katie's voice took on a hint of panic.

The dog hurtled through the kitchen and out of sight.

"Oh, there you are. You scared me." Her voice was coming closer. "Were you trying to figure out how to open the pantry door again? It's not going to happen, dude. No opposable thumbs. Make your peace with it."

I was leaning against the sink, laughing, when they walked in.

Katie's face went white at the sight of me, her eyes huge. She reached for Chaucer as she stepped back.

"It's just me. I was going to make some coffee, if that's okay."

"Aiden?" She took a deep breath and let it out. "Holy crap. Knock before you come in!" Shaking her head, she continued, "I finally rid the house of varmints hell-bent on eating my face, and I get human intruders. Doorbells. They exist for a reason." She checked the clock. "And why are you here so early?"

"I didn't mean to scare you. Like I said, looking for coffee." I watched her open the pantry door to fill Chaucer's bowls.

"No coffee. Sorry. I have some lovely tap water I can offer you, though." She reached up for a glass from a cupboard and handed it to me.

I accepted it, but then replaced it on the shelf where she'd taken it. "Actually, you do have coffee. I brought it last night."

Her brow furrowed. "Last—oh! I have food! Holy crap, how did I forget that?" She opened the fridge and clapped in delight. "So long, peanut butter! I'm dumping your ass." She took out a bottle of orange juice and placed it on the counter, before retrieving that same glass again. She looked me up and down, the fear gone. "Can I interest you in the delicious and refreshing juice of an orange?"

"As I don't see a coffeemaker in your kitchen, I'll gladly settle for juice."

She filled the glass in her hand and passed it to me, before reaching for another. Once she'd poured herself one, she stared at it for a moment, took a sip and closed her eyes in appreciation.

"Why do I feel like you've been in solitary confinement for ten years? Orange juice shouldn't be this big of a deal." I watched her slowly savor her drink, a corner of her mouth quirking up.

When she finished, she went to the sink and bodychecked me out of her way. I smiled, pleased she felt comfortable pushing me aside. She rinsed out her glass and then reached for mine.

"Solitary confinement." She smiled. "I like that description."

"It's just orange juice."

"Nothing is ever *just*. Yesterday, I didn't have orange juice. Today, I do. I'm grateful."

She smiled up at me and my chest hurt.

"Wait a minute. Why *did* you bring me groceries?"

I fought the urge to kiss her furrowed brow. "There's leftover pizza, too. And cereal in the pantry. There's also bacon and eggs in the fridge. What would you like for breakfast?"

She studied me for a moment and then grinned. "I'm choosing to be thankful and not suspicious. Bacon and eggs sounds amazing." She waved me away. "You sit. I'll cook."

"Deal." I sat at her table and watched her work. I should have been driving home to shower and change, but I stayed. Being with her settled something inside me.

Her phone rang. She looked at it warily, let it ring again and then straightened, walked across the kitchen and picked it up. "Hello?"

Her body relaxed. She leaned on the counter and chatted, answering questions. Whoever she was talking to, it wasn't the caller she was worried about.

"Um, he never told—oh! Try *Tesla*. See if that works. His passwords used to always be cars. I remember him saying that when we were dating. He's green with envy that another broker recently purchased a new Tesla." She rolled her eyes at whatever was said. "Yeah, he said his preliminary estimate is one and a half million." She paused. "What about our house there? Is there an estimate on it?" Her face hardened as she listened. "When did he do it? Conveniently timed, the rat bastard. Oh, check his mom's accounts. He's hidden money there before. He has power of attorney for her. Can they do that, follow the money?" She laughed. "Finally, being an asshole will bite him in the butt. Yeah, let me know. Okay. Thanks." She hung up.

"What was that?"

She hopped up on the counter. "Justin, my ex, is claiming that he mortgaged the house and lost all the money in a bad gambling decision. Of course, he didn't take out that loan until the day I left him. I don't know. My lawyer has auditors working on it. She says there's an account in my name that I have no knowledge of. I gave her a possible password to access it. He never told me any of this stuff directly, but I've picked up bits and pieces over the years. His mom is in a retirement community, and I know he's shuffled funds into her account in the past to avoid taxes or penalties or whatever. He's probably doing it again."

She hopped down and went back to making breakfast. "This is his area of expertise, money management. I hope her auditors are good."

Tapping the table, I tried to talk myself out of getting involved. "I know a guy. Reformed computer hacker. I worked with him a few times. Good guy. I can call him to see if he'd help."

"Why would he? For that matter, why would you?" She genuinely seemed befuddled by my kindness.

"Why wouldn't I?" Watching the play of emotion on her face, I realized that I could get used to this. Very easily and very happily.

She went back to cooking, but kept glancing

at me over her shoulder. "Last time I checked," she said to the frying pan, "you didn't like me. You keep kissing me, so you must at least be attracted, but you don't like me. So, why the food and the help?"

"I like you just fine. Quite a bit, actually."

She turned back to me. "Yeah?"

Nodding, I watched her lips part and her cheeks blaze.

She spun back around. "Oh."

Before I left Katie's place a little while later, my stomach full, I copied down her lawyer's number. I called Brian, the reformed hacker, as I drove home to shower and get ready for work. Brian's dad had screwed over his mom when he was little. I was sure he'd be more than happy to catch another man trying to cheat his wife. These kinds of cases rarely took him more than a couple of hours.

It's funny. As a society, we think our financial information is so secure, but all it takes is a computer genius like Brian and our lives are open for dissection.

After a quick chat, Brian promised to contact Katie's lawyer with what he found.

Feeling as though I was finally doing something positive, after a year of being a grumpy bastard, I got ready for work. Maybe I'd get a hot dog for lunch today.

Kate

BRIAN WAS A GENIUS! He sent my lawyer an email with all Justin's financial info, all his secret accounts and illegal deals. Apparently, it only took Brian one afternoon to find everything. Once Jean had that, Justin buckled like wet cardboard. Nary a week later, Gran's house was mine, and I had money in a bank account. All the legal stuff would still take time to go through, but agreements were made and funds were transferred. I was feeling positively optimistic!

I had my feet under me with the food truck. Customers were coming back and bringing friends. Aiden had been stopping by the truck every afternoon for lunch. I teased him about his questionable dietary habits, but a thrill raced through me every time I looked up and found him waiting for me.

Now that I had some money, I needed a bed, maybe a dresser. A phone! Another pair of jeans. The list spiraled out of control in my head. It was too much.

One thing at a time. I wanted a bed. I needed to focus on that one room. Bed, dresser, curtains, dog bed. Paint! *Yes, I could paint the room any color I wanted.* Once that was decided, I spent the afternoon daydreaming about beds and wall colors while I cooked and served hot dogs. It made for a lovely diversion.

"I'll take a dog."

I glanced up at the gravelly voice. Mr. Cavanaugh.

"Please," he added.

My hands trembled as I rolled a dog onto the grill. "Of course. What would you like on it?" It was the first time I'd seen him since he told me I was nothing and that he'd do a jig when I lost Gran's house. My stomach twisted.

"Katie, well, I want to say I'm sorry about pushing you like that."

I met his defiant eyes.

"I've never laid an angry hand on a woman in my life. I'm ashamed my temper got away from me." He blew out a breath. "I never should have said all those horrible things. They weren't true." He pulled on his earlobe. "I think I just wanted you to hurt as much as I did. If Nellie were here, she'd kick my behind for it. You're a good girl, and you deserve better than the hand you've been dealt. I've got no excuses. I was wrong, and I hope you see fit to forgive me in time."

Vision blurry, I tried to blink away the tears clinging to my lashes. He didn't hate me, didn't think I was rubbish.

"Oh, now, please don't cry." His voice shook. "I'm sorry."

I nodded, my throat constricted.

"What the hell, Pops? You said you were going to apologize."

At Aiden's voice, I jumped, quickly wiping at my face. The tears wouldn't stop, though. I crouched below the counter. I didn't want them to see me lose it.

The truck tilted, and then Aiden was there, pulling me up and crushing me in his arms. I pulled up my hoodie so I could hide.

He chuckled and ran one hand over my head; the other held me firmly against his chest. "We can still see you."

"He doesn't hate me."

"What did she say?" Mr. Cavanaugh asked.

"She said you don't hate her." Aiden held me closer, rubbing his hands up and down my back.

Sputtering, Mr. Cavanaugh finally said, "Well, of course I don't! I never... I didn't, Katie. I was an ass. I was missing my Nellie and taking it out on you. Please, don't cry."

I nodded my head against Aiden's chest, but the tears continued to flow.

"Okay. I've got you. Pops, can you get that?" The truck went dark. "Shh. Katie. You're killing me."

I tried to push away, to get my emotions under control, but Aiden held firm. I wiped at the tears again. "I'm okay. I'm sorry. I don't know where that came from."

Aiden brought his hands up, capturing my face, tipping it back so he could look at me. He kissed my eyelids. "You've been holding that in for weeks, probably longer. You've been terror-ized by giant rodents, harassed and cheated by your husband—"

"Ex."

"Thank goodness for that." I smiled. "You've been yelled at by a deranged, sauerkraut-loving tourist. You've been insulted and pushed by your gran's boyfriend. You've had no money. No food. You've been working in this truck, employed by a loudmouth drunk. You had your cupcakes sto-len by a dog. And let's not forget interrogated and almost arrested."

"When you put it that way." I gasped a laugh.

"That's better. I wouldn't want you to be cry-ing when I…" His mouth took mine, a soft, se-ductive possession. He pushed down my hood and plunged his hands into my hair, tilting my head, deepening the kiss.

My body went up in flames. I made soft, mewling sounds, as I got on my tiptoes, trying to get closer, wanting more. His hand dragged down my back, landing on my butt. He groaned, kneading me and pulling me closer.

He reached farther down, grabbed the backs of my thighs and picked me up. He plopped me down on the counter, my legs wrapped around his hips. He leaned in, his erection rubbing just right. I gasped. His lips were on my neck. I shiv-ered at the heat of his breath and the scratch of his stubble. His tongue teased sensitive skin, and my head fell back on a moan. His lips traveled down my throat, while his hands clutched my butt, setting a rhythm with his hip thrusts. I'd never wanted to be naked more in my entire life.

A loud bang sounded on the side of the truck. "Hey! Why is the window closed? It's still lunchtime!"

I collapsed back, panting and frustrated. Aiden leaned over me, breathing heavily.

"I'm gonna kill Chuck," he said under his breath.

"I told you. She was upset. Leave her alone. She'll open again when she's ready." Mr. Cavanaugh's gravelly voice tried to reason with my boss.

"The truck was rocking. That doesn't say crying to me."

"Oh, well." Poor, Mr. Cavanaugh. He sounded flustered as he uttered those two simple words.

"I'm okay now," I shouted. "I'll open in just a second."

Aiden bit my neck. "*I'm* not okay. I may not be able to walk properly for the rest of the day," he whispered.

I pushed him so I could stand up. I grabbed my pole and shoved the side panel up. The truck was flooded with light.

"I could have used another minute over here," Aiden grumbled.

"Had to be done," I said, pushing him toward

the front of the truck. "I'm trying to work. Go arrest people."

"This conversation is not over."

My body thrilled at his words.

When I looked out the window, Chuck was glaring, and Mr. Cavanaugh looked distinctly uncomfortable.

"I'm sorry, Mr. Cavanaugh. I burned your dog. I'll make you another one."

"What?" Chuck's face was getting red.

"It'll be my hot dog. I'm not giving anything away, don't worry." I tossed the burned dog in the trash and rolled another one out onto the grill.

"No. You're going to eat. Chuck, stop being an asshole," Aiden said and walked around behind Chuck, looking remarkably normal and relaxed. Whereas I felt like I had *I was just getting some* tattooed on my forehead. "She's working harder and selling more dogs than you ever have in the off months. Stop yelling at her."

"She's my employee. I'll treat her any way I want," Chuck sneered.

Aiden leaned in and took a sniff. "It's one o'clock. You're drunk at one o'clock?"

"That's none of your concern! I don't answer to you." He turned to me. "You're fired! I don't need this shit."

I stood stunned. I needed this job. It was literally the only job available in Bar Harbor during the off months. "I'm sorry, sir. He didn't mean anything. I can pay for Mr. Cavanaugh's lunch." I shoved my hand in my hoodie pocket and pulled out a five-dollar bill. "See? I'll pay for it."

"I said get out!"

"Chuck, don't take it out on her because you're pissed at me."

I turned off the grill, picked up my water bottle and scanned the truck. Nothing here was mine. I pulled the key from my pocket, climbed out of the truck and handed it back to Chuck. "Thank you for the opportunity."

Aiden's grumble echoed in my head.

I walked numbly toward my car. What was I going to do?

"Katie, wait." Aiden grabbed my arm. "Please, wait. Let Pops and I take you to lunch. We'll figure something out."

I shook my head. "I'm not hungry." Mr. Cavanaugh looked so concerned, I kissed his cheek. "Thank you for coming to see me, for saying what you did. It means the world to me."

"Katie, I know I've behaved horribly, but Nellie—no, it's not just Nellie. It's me. I want to be a part of your life, if I can. I want you to think of me like family. I know Nellie would have wanted that."

Family. It had been so long. My grandfather had died when I was little. Dad when I was fifteen, and Mom hadn't been the same afterward. She'd been more of an absentminded roommate than a mom. It had been Justin for ten years, and now not even him. I hugged Mr. Cavanaugh tightly and nodded. I had to get out of here before I broke down again. Waving to both men, I turned and walked to my car. Chaucer and I needed to put our heads together. I'd really been looking forward to sleeping in a bed. Damn.

CHAPTER TWENTY-THREE

Aiden

"COME ON, POPS. I'll buy you lunch, and we'll try to figure out how to fix what I just screwed up." I got her fired. She'd finally received some good news. The house was hers. And I went and got her fired.

"Wait until Chuck sobers up. He'll probably forget he did it." Pops pointed at a sandwich shop.

I veered for the door and held it open. "There's got to be a better place for her to work, anyway. The truck is freezing in the winter, and she has to deal with crazy customers daily." We sat at a table in the back. "Any place looking for a cook?"

Pops sank into his chair. "I can ask around. I feel like we're nothing but bad luck for that girl."

Propping my elbows on the table, I nodded my agreement. "She needs a job. She needs furniture. Walls need paint." I scrubbed my hands down my face. "Mo. Does she need help in her shop?"

Pops shook his head. "Nobody's hiring at this time of year."

"Crap." I stood to order our food. "Do you want your usual?"

Pops nodded, looking as dejected as I felt. We spent an hour brainstorming, texting friends, making phone calls. By the time I drove Pops home, we had a plan for one problem.

I PULLED UP to Katie's place at about six, my truck bed piled high with furniture. Chaucer came bounding down the stairs, while Katie stood in the doorway, watching. I hopped out and waved at the back of the truck.

"I come bearing gifts from yon Cavanaugh." I cricked my finger in invitation.

Descending slowly, she said, "What is all this?" She walked around the truck to stand beside me.

I breathed a sigh of relief. She was still talking to me. "My grandma redecorated twenty years ago. She and Pops put the extra furniture in the attic and the basement. Pops and I went through all of it this afternoon, picked the best pieces and polished them up."

I watched her looking at the dark wood dressers and tables, bed frames and chairs.

"These might not be your taste, but it'll give you someplace to sit or sleep until you can replace them with pieces you like."

Her smile could fuel a power plant.

"Really?" Her eyes twinkled.

It wasn't fair. How could anyone say no to her? When her smile dimmed, all I could think about was how to get it back. Shit. I was whipped.

"But, this should all go to you or your sister or your brother. Not me." She bit her lip, and my body twitched in response.

"None of us need furniture. Hell, I live in a tiny apartment downtown. Mo's house is fully furnished." I gestured to the ornate dark wood. "This isn't her style, anyway."

Katie stepped closer to the truck bed and ran her fingertips along a curved chair leg. "But it's all so beautiful. How could someone not fall in love?"

I watched her closely. "I don't know."

She flung herself at me, squeezing tightly. "Thank you!"

I let my eyes drift closed, absorbing the feel of her, the scent. When she let go, I hung on for one moment more. "So, I guess I'm unloading all of this?"

She clapped, bouncing on the balls of her feet. "Yes! Chop-chop."

"Okay, I'll haul them to the porch. You decide where you want them inside. This stuff weighs a ton, so no changing your mind a million times." I hopped up and handed a small end table to her. She carried it to the porch and came back for more.

While she took chairs and mirrors, I hauled

dressers and tables. The headboard and footboard were particularly heavy. I was not looking forward to dragging those upstairs. I should have asked Bear to help, but as I was trying to keep him far away from Katie, that seemed counterproductive.

A little after seven, just as the final piece of furniture was put in place, I got a call about a theft. It was a family friend who had asked for me, so instead of staying, having dinner and finishing that bottle of wine, I was leaving. Damn.

CHAPTER TWENTY-FOUR

Kate

FURNITURE HELPS TAKE the sting out of jobless-
ness. I was lying on my new dark walnut bed,
wrapped in blankets. I glanced over. Chaucer
was curled up on his blanket bed, head on his
paws, watching me. "Good morning, sweet boy.
We really have our own home now." It hadn't felt
like it before, sleeping in the car, propped sideways in a chair. But now, lying comfortably in a
bed, rested, the sky outside the windows bleeding orange in the coming sunrise, I had a deep
and satisfying feeling of home.

I was taking this room as my bedroom. I considered the smaller one across the hall, as it had
always been the one I stayed in when I visited,
but Gran's had the attached bathroom and large
windows looking out to Dorr Point, a view I
would never tire of.

Kicking off the blankets, I sat up. Chaucer rose
as well, coming over for his morning scratch and
hug. "It doesn't feel like Gran's room anymore.
Everything's different." I studied the off-white

walls and heart pine floors. "Let's paint. Paint doesn't cost too much. We'll make this room—this house—all our own." I stood. "But first, let's go get breakfast."

Chaucer raced out of the room and down the stairs. I wasn't going to fall back into the gloom. I didn't have a job, but I did have a beautiful home, one I no longer shared with snickering marmosets. I had a bed to sleep in and a bureau to hold my clothes. I had tables to set things on and chairs to sit in. I had some money in the bank, even after I returned Mom's loan.

I did not know what the hell was going on with Aiden, grumpy and dismissive one minute, kissing me the next. Regardless, this wasn't about him. It was about me, standing on my own, starting a new life.

As for the matter of being unemployed, I liked cooking, so I'd try to find a job that allowed me to cook. If it took me a few months to find a job, I'd survive. Gran's house was paid for, and I knew how to live lean.

I fed Chaucer and then opened the back door for him. While he went potty, I poured myself a bowl of cereal. As I didn't have a job, the day was my own. I grabbed a notepad and pen from Gran's junk drawer and began to write my to-do list for the day.

When Chaucer trotted back in, I closed the door before sitting back down. The nights and mornings up here were frigid. Chaucer sat by my side, resting his head on my lap. "So, here's what I'm thinking. I need bedding and a phone. I'd like a bathroom rug. Those tiles are flipping freezing. I also need Wi-Fi." I thought about the long, quiet nights. "Maybe a TV?" I scratched behind his ears. "Too extravagant? Maybe I should hit a used bookstore instead."

IT HAD BEEN a good day. I had accomplished a great deal, and I'd done it on my own. I'm sure the distracted teenage boy working in the phone store thought I was being indecisive, staring at the phones, hearing about all the options. The reality was that it had all become white noise, a kind of buzzing that vibrated through my brain. It was an old fear response to doing something wrong.

Strength isn't always apparent, or even noticed. I stood in that store, staring at the phones on the counter, and with Herculean effort I pushed the old self-doubt out of my head. Strangely, it was Aiden's shout of "insane!" that helped me shake off the specter of my ex's ever-present criticisms. I took a deep, clean breath and made a decision for myself. It was the first of many.

I stopped by Mo's boutique, mostly to say hello but also to look for jeans. In cleaning every inch of Gran's house, I'd found a couple of plastic totes in the back of the guest-room closet. They contained winter boots and sweaters, so now I really only needed some casual pants.

The bell above the door chimed, and Mo walked out of the back room. "Katie, you're back." She gave me a quick hug. "How's the hot dog life treating you?"

I rolled my eyes. "Not well. I was fired."

"Fired? Why would Chuck do that?" Mo looked outraged on my behalf. "People have been telling me what a great job you're doing."

It was surprising how much better that bit of praise made me feel. "Well, yesterday I needed a moment. I was a little emotional. So I closed the customer panel during lunchtime hours, just for a few minutes, but Chuck was upset. Aiden tried to defend me, but only made it worse. So, long story short, I'm out of a job."

Confusion colored Mo's expression. "Wait. What was Aiden doing there?"

What to say, what to say? "He brought your grandfather by so he could apologize."

Hands on hips, she pinned me with a glare. "What did Pops do that required an apology? An apology that made you upset enough to close the panel and then get fired!"

Now I wished I'd just waved and walked by. "It was nothing. I'll find another job."

"In the Harbor? At this time of year? No. You won't." She started pacing, her eyes sparking.

"I'm hearing all manner of gossip about those two and you. Aiden tried to arrest you?"

"What? Pfft, no way." I moved toward the door.

"He pounded on the food truck and threatened to write a health-code violation against you on your first day? He confiscated your dog? Forced you to give him free food?"

Where the hell was she getting her information? Was there a nanny cam in the truck?

"I hear your house was overrun with animals, absolutely unlivable, and did either of them offer you a room? No. Those bastards let you sleep in your car! Your husband cut off your bank accounts, and you've been living on peanut butter. Did they help? No!"

Holding up a hand, I tried to stem the stream of accusations. "Actually, Aiden brought me groceries a week ago." I nodded. "It was very kind of him."

"Kind? He's had a thing for you since he was a little kid. Yet he let you starve and sleep in a car for weeks before he finally did the easiest decent thing he could think of."

Leaning forward, I whispered, "Seriously, how do you know all of this?"

She strode to the window. "Katie," she said, voice resigned. "It's a small town. We all know each other's business. People heard you in the park, saw the blankets in your car, talked to the exterminator, chatted with the appraiser, were standing in line behind you in the store. Bits and pieces were pasted together until a picture emerged. Unfortunately, it's a picture that highlights the fact that my family is filled with heartless bastards."

"I wouldn't say *filled*. You've been great. You gave me some great deals." I smiled broadly to her back, hoping she'd turn, but she didn't.

"I sold you clothes from my shop at the marked price. I wasn't exactly doing charity work."

"Not true. You found me great clothes that I desperately needed at a price I could pay. And your grandfather just gave me a bunch of his old furniture."

Mo turned at that. "He did?"

Smiling, I continued, "He and Aiden went through the attic and basement, pulling pieces, cleaning and hauling them over. I slept in a bed last night! I cannot express strongly enough how wonderful that was."

She gave in to a reluctant grin. "Really? They did that?"

I nodded.

Closing her eyes, she hugged herself. "They've both been so bitter. Alice. Then your grandmother dying. Both of them haven't been themselves for too long." She studied me. "They brought you food and furniture? Argued with Chuck about firing you?" At my nod, she grinned and threw an arm around me. "Excellent! Now, what did you come in here for?"

RUSSET LEAVES SWIRLED in the wake of the cars driving up Main toward the old farm road that led to Gran's. I had the back windows open so Chaucer could hang out, enjoying the wind and scents bombarding him.

When we pulled up to the house, I couldn't help but think *home*. This was my home. "Come on, buddy. Let's get these bags inside." I opened the back door for Chaucer who jumped down and immediately began patrolling the area. Interesting. He'd never done that before. He'd sniffed. He'd meandered. He'd definitely sauntered, but he'd never patrolled. Newfoundlands were water-rescue dogs, not shepherds or guard dogs. Perhaps this was feeling like home to him as well, one that needed to be protected by the man of the house.

In addition to the television I'd purchased after leaving Mo's boutique, I'd also picked up some new bedding. I wanted to make Gran's house my own, starting with the bedroom.

The sheets I chose were a rich, buttery cream color. The warm down comforter was a vibrant teal, Van Gogh's flowering almond tree painted across the silk, delicate but brimming with life. Justin preferred subtle earth tones, nothing too bright or garish. I was desperate for color.

After the linens store, I stopped at the hardware store for paint and painting supplies. They even had a small coffeemaker on sale, so I bought that, too.

I considered the deep violet spot on the top of the paint can. It was a bold choice but a joyous one. How long did it take to paint a room? I wanted to sleep in my new bedding in a violet room tonight.

I brought in everything, weighed down, trudging up the stairs. It felt good. I was taking steps, making decisions. Chaucer got sick of following me up and down the stairs, though, choosing to flop onto his bed and watch the action instead.

Once all my purchases were inside, I made a quick call to the cable company to set up an appointment for service and then dragged furniture into the center of the bedroom so I could prepare to paint.

In addition to the deep violet, I'd also chosen a soft eggshell white for the baseboards and trim. The woman at the hardware store explained what to do. First up was taping off. After about forty-five minutes of climbing up and down a chair, taping off the ceiling and trim, my arms were sore, and I was seriously rethinking doing this on my own. But I took another look at the paint sample and decided I just needed a late lunch break before I began painting. I checked my watch, correcting that to an early dinner break.

"Come on, sweets. Let's get some grub." Chaucer was up like a shot and down the stairs before I had a chance to jump from the chair. Didn't have to ask him twice.

I'd just sat down to a leftover rice dish, when Chaucer stood alert and woofed toward the front of the house. A minute later a knock sounded. Chaucer and I padded through the house. I opened the door expecting Aiden or maybe Mr. Cavanaugh, but was instead confronted by a man in a cable uniform. His face had the slightly bloated look of a long-time alcoholic. Bruise-colored skin circled his eyes.

I took an involuntary step back. There was no logical reason for my sudden fear, but it was there and Chaucer sensed it, pushing into the doorway in front of me. It was the man's turn to take a step back, his eyes wary as they took in the sheer size and strength of my dog.

He smiled, and that was somehow worse.

"Ma'am." He pointed to the patch on his shirt identifying him as Joe and an employee of Comcast. "I'm from the cable company. You called for a hookup?" His eyes dragged over me.

"Yes. I did. They said someone would be out in a couple of days." I was more than willing to wait a few days for a different installer.

"That's right, but I was working nearby and had a cancellation, so they sent me over." There was a challenge in his eyes, one that said he was aware of how uncomfortable he made me.

I was sick of being afraid. I could take care of myself, and I had a big protective dog to help. "All right. Come in. I'll show you where I want the cable installed." I stepped back to let him through. Chaucer was still tense, but I was doing my best to appear relaxed and in charge.

Joe stepped in and looked around, his eyes scanning quickly. "Nice place," he mumbled as he walked through the living room toward the back of the house.

"We're going upstairs. I want the TV in the bedroom. I'm actually painting up there today, but I'm sure we can work around each other." Not to mention, I wasn't planning on leaving him unattended in my home.

I showed him the little flat screen I'd purchased earlier in the day, still in its box. I pointed to a long low bureau. "I'd like to set it up on top of that, so it's visible from the bed." I glanced over at the pile of drop cloths, paint trays, brushes, blue tape and rags that were currently burying my bed. "It's in the center of the room so I can paint, but it's normally against that wall." I pointed. "And the bureau is against this opposite one. Can the cable be installed in here?"

He looked around, and I shivered. Why hadn't I just said I was busy and couldn't do the installation now? I'd ignored the survival instinct telling me to slam and lock the front door. Or, perhaps I was being a narrow-minded, superficial bitch, equating a frightening visage with a black soul.

He didn't wait to see if I came to any conclusions about beauty image and preconceived notions of good and evil, instead hunkering down near the wall and the electrical outlet. "You're going to need wireless cable. We don't have a cable line to hook into way out here. I need to check to see if you can get a strong enough signal before I start."

I hadn't considered that, big-city girl that I was. "My grandmother had a TV. Wouldn't that mean that she had cable?"

He just stared at me a minute, his expression clearly stating that I was too stupid to live. "No." He turned back around to the device in his hand that had lights streaking up and down it. "It should work. The reception won't be as good as if you had the signal coming through a cable into the box, but it'll be a hell of a lot better than you'd get without it. And no drilled holes, which usually makes people happy." He checked his clipboard. "You also want internet, right?"

I nodded. "Yes, I do." Somehow I had ended up on the other side of the room. I'd been backing away from him without even realizing it. This shit had to stop.

"I'll install the internet hub right here, as well.

It's a small house. You should get a signal on a laptop pretty easy, probably even out on the porch."

He turned back to continue working, and I decided that I'd been reading evil intent into sagging, sallow features.

By the time I'd finished taping off the trim, he was done. He walked me through how everything worked, demonstrated the remote and gave me the instructions and passwords to get on the internet. He handed me the work order to sign.

I quickly walked him downstairs, wanting to have a locked door between us. He stopped, his eyes raking over me again.

I leaned forward and turned the knob, opening the door.

He opened his mouth to say something when we heard a voice call out from the back of the house.

"Katie? You home?"

Whatever Joe was going to say dried up as we heard the back door close. Joe's mouth snapped shut and he took off, pointedly not rushing.

Turning to meet Mr. Cavanaugh as he came out of the kitchen, I leaned against the closed door, trying to appear more comfortable and confident than I was.

"Say, the furniture looks nice in here, doesn't it?" He assessed the rooms, nodding, before approaching me cautiously. "I'm sorry, honey. I shouldn't have walked in like that. It was habit when Nellie was here. I'll try to remember to knock first. In fact, you should keep the door locked, so even if I forget, I still can't come in." He smiled tentatively, waiting to see what kind of reception he'd receive.

I stepped forward and gave him a big hug, which I think surprised him as much as it did me. I was so relieved to have Joe gone and this man in his place, not to mention grateful for my furnished home, that I threw myself at him. He gave me a tight squeeze and chuckled.

"Well, now. This is a surprise. I can't remember the last time I had a cute little redhead in my arms. I could get used to this. Forget what I said earlier. You leave that door unlocked for me."

There was something about being surrounded by a strong, protective male that helped me relax. I tucked my head under his chin, his strong arms encircling me. I allowed myself to sink into the hug.

"Are you trembling?" He leaned his head back trying to get a better look at me.

Muffled by his chest, I said, "Nope." I'd never understood young women who married septuagenarians. I'd assumed it was for money but maybe not. Maybe it was for this—strength and warmth and concern.

Another car pulled into the gravel drive, and

I flinched. Mr. Cavanaugh rubbed his hands up and down my back. "It's just Aiden."

I knew I'd have to step away in a second but not yet.

The steps slowed on the porch. A strange stillness enveloped us all, two on this side of the door, one on the other. The beveled glass panels in the front door didn't offer much privacy, but it wasn't the hug that needed to be hidden. It was my need for it. I felt movement behind me, and the front door quietly opened.

I stepped back, not looking at Aiden. "Thank you for all the beautiful furniture, Mr. Cavanaugh. It feels like home now. I'll just, um, go get some coffee started." As I left the room, I heard the low rumble of concerned male voices.

When the men walked into the kitchen a few minutes later, they were wary and observant. Aiden sat at the kitchen table and Mr. Cavanaugh came over to me. "Can I help with the coffee?" He put his arm casually around me, as though we did this all the time.

"Nope. Almost done. You guys want some dinner? I can throw something together." I still hadn't turned around, hadn't looked at Aiden. Did he always have to be around when I was falling apart?

"Sure. I love rice. We might need to heat it up, though," Aiden said.

I glanced over, looking at my abandoned meal.

"I forgot about that. The cable man interrupted my paint break." I gave Mr. Cavanaugh's hand at my shoulder a quick squeeze before I walked across the kitchen to check the refrigerator for dinner options.

He leaned against the counter, a smile playing over his lips. "Cable, huh? Does that mean you bought a TV today, too?"

Nodding, I started pulling items from the refrigerator. "Yep. I'm not letting a little thing like no job get me down. I'm going to do some home improvements while I look for work. I may need to go off the island to find a job, but I have a car."

Aiden shifted in his chair. "Wait. Paint break? What are you painting?"

Hunting through the fridge drawers, I found a chicken breast. I could whip up a skillet fry for dinner. "I got some new bedding and a gallon of paint. I'm starting in the bedroom." I checked Mr. Cavanaugh's reaction to that. "You don't think Gran would mind my changing things, do you?"

He was staring at the floor, lost in thought. At Aiden's quiet throat clearing, he looked up and beamed at me. "Sorry, just missing my Nellie. I think she'd be very happy that you were making her home all your own. It's what she wanted." His nod and smile were bittersweet as he took a seat at the table with Aiden.

Chicken, rice, broccoli, green bell peppers,

snow peas, carrots, garlic, soy sauce. I'd been shopping since Aiden had brought me some much-needed staples last week. I piled everything on the counter and then pulled down a skillet and got to work while the men discussed town news. It was all very normal, yet strangely foreign.

"Mmm, that smells good. What are you making us, and are you sure we can't help?" Mr. Cavanaugh's chair scraped against the floor, easing back, ready to lend a hand.

"I'm happy to have you both, Mr. Cavanaugh. Not that Chaucer isn't wonderful company, but it can get a little lonely around here." The skillet was sizzling, tangy aromas warming the kitchen. It *did* smell good. I could do this. I could take care of myself and maybe even a few other people.

"Call me Connor. Please."

I nodded, my heart swelling.

"You cook. We'll clean up," Aiden said, settling the discussion.

"Perfect. Looks like we're just about ready." I put out the plates and silverware. "What would you both like to drink? I think there's some beer and some wine in there."

"Now, I wouldn't say no to a beer," Connor said. Aiden hummed his agreement.

Once we were all settled and eating, I took a minute to sit back and watch the men at my table. Forty odd years separated them, but they were mirror images of each other, both tall and strong, gruffness hiding a well of compassion.

Aiden looked up. "Good dinner. So, do you want help painting?"

I intended to thank him for his offer but beg off. I liked the idea of doing it all myself...

Connor rubbed his hands together. "Oh, now that's an idea. I haven't painted in years." He obviously saw the look in my eyes and quickly headed off any argument by reminding me, "You're going to need our help. Little thing like you can't reach the tops of the walls. My back's not so good anymore, so if you paint the bottom half of the walls, we'll take the top." Then he looked to his grandson. "Aiden, Katie and I are going to sit right here and chat while you tape off the room." He winked at me and said conspiratorially, "I hate taping."

Aiden threw down his napkin. "Now, listen, old man, you're not sticking me—"

"I already taped the room," I cut in to stem the argument.

They both looked at me and smiled. "Well, then, what are we waiting for? Let's go paint your room," Aiden said.

CHAPTER TWENTY-FIVE

Aiden

She'd chosen a deep purple for the wall color. It was an unusual choice and yet fitting, the little flame-haired fairy slumbering in her violet bower.

Pops sat in a chair watching us, his hands clasped contentedly across his stomach, benevolently surveying his kingdom. He claimed we needed his expert supervision. He was actually too tired to keep painting, but Katie's face didn't register a second of disbelief or pity.

She kissed him on the cheek. "Thank you, Connor." She studied the half wall he'd just completed. "Yours looks wonderful. What am I doing wrong? Mine looks streaky and patchy."

A furrow developed between her brows. I had an urge to place my lips right there, to soothe that worry away. I turned back to painting. What was it about her? I knew I shouldn't care, knew it was a fool's errand, and yet I couldn't help myself.

"You're being too stingy with the paint, too hesitant with your roller. There's no place for fear in painting. It'll be written all over your walls. You need to paint like you live your life—with verve."

"Verve?" The furrow was back, her head cocked. "I don't have verve. What should the verveless do when they need to paint?"

Damn it, I was watching her again. She seemed so forlorn about her verveless state that I had to do something. "Someone without verve could never have started rumors about Joey Markum's penis and a vacuum hose," I said.

Pops goggled at her for a moment before he exploded. "Katherine Ann Gallagher! What do you know about Joey Markum's penis?" Pops pretended to be scandalized.

Katie's face was blank for a second before the memory came crashing back and she doubled over laughing. Giving up the fight, she plopped down on the floor, clutching her stomach and wheezing. I laughed myself, though it had more to do with Katie losing it rather than any memory.

Pops glanced at me. We shared a moment of perfect understanding. The memory of how bold and bodacious she'd been seemed to delight her almost as much as the rumor mongering itself.

Watching her laugh, my chest ached. I wanted to turn back to the wall, away from Katie, but I couldn't. The little fire fairy was melting my hard-won bitterness. I wasn't ready.

"I'm talking to you, young lady. What do you know about Joey Markum?" Pops was putting on his stern voice, but he couldn't hide the laughter in his eyes.

Katie was still on the floor gasping for breath while wiping tears from her eyes. "Oh, my God, I completely forgot about that!" She gave Pops such a brilliant smile that he found it impossible to maintain his mock condemnation.

"Well, as I'm the only person in this room who doesn't know the story, somebody better start talking fast." He looked to me to do it.

"She remembers. She can do it." I turned back to the wall, refusing to lose myself in her as I had all those years ago.

Pops settled in the chair. "All right, missy. Let's hear it."

She scooted back to lean up against her bed. "You know, I'm not sure how it began. Daisy and I—hey, does Daisy still live here?"

Pops shook his head. "No, Daisy moved away for college. She used to come back for holidays, but when her folks retired to—where was it, Aiden?—somewhere south, the whole family was gone for good. Her mom hated Maine winters." He shook his head again—still upset about their defection, or perhaps Daisy's mom's dislike of Maine winters.

"Oh, too bad. It would've been fun to see her," Katie said. "Anyway, Daisy and I were in the ice-cream shop, eating sundaes, when Joey Markum slouched in and took up roost on the counter stool right next to our table. He kept staring at us, making filthy comments under his breath about licking cherries, whipped cream, et cetera. Daisy laughed, and I remember I kicked her under the table. I didn't want her encouraging him. He was skeeving me out, big-time. Then Aiden walked in, and I was so relieved."

I turned around at that. "Relieved? Why?"

She looked up, a soft smile on her lips. "Because you were a hero, Aiden. When we were kids, you were a hero." She looked at Pops. "Did he ever tell you about that woman who used to run that little market on Cottage?" Pops looked at her blankly, so she continued, "I was in there one afternoon, in the back by the refrigerated cases, choosing a soda, when a boy came in. I wasn't paying attention at first, but then she started yelling about his stealing something. The boy looked confused. I remember he turned around, looking behind himself at one point, assuming she was yelling at someone else.

"There was something wrong with her. I think she got off on hurting children, anyone who couldn't defend themselves. I wanted to do something, but I was scared by the anger, the almost violence of it. Then Aiden walked in and stood between the woman and the other boy. She didn't even notice him. Her hand was already coming down to slap the boy, but Aiden took the hit." Katie shook her head in wonder. "He just stood there, a red handprint forming on his face, and stared her down."

Pops turned sharply to me. "She hit you?"

I gave a one-shouldered shrug. "It was a long time ago." My gaze shifted to Katie. "I can't believe you remember that."

"We were what, ten, eleven at the time? And you stared down that mean old cuss. She was easily a foot taller and probably had a hundred pounds on you, but you were so self-possessed. You had her stammering apologies. The other boy took off, but you just continued to take the measure of her.

"After that day, I watched more closely. You never hesitated to stand up to bullies, to protect those weaker than yourself." She smiled at Pops. "Like I said, a hero."

Pops cleared his throat and nodded. *Yes* was all he said.

"Anyway, Aiden walked into the ice-cream shop and sat down right beside Joey. As if to shield us. I felt safer immediately, able to deal with the situation. Except Joey stopped harassing us and began calling Aiden names. I couldn't just sit there while Aiden took the hit for me, so I made some comment to Daisy referring to a rumor I'd heard about Joey becoming amorous with a vacuum hose, the power button not work-

ing and EMTs needing to be called in to extricate an engorged, purpled body part." She smiled
broadly, quite proud of herself. "Or something
along those lines."

I took over the telling. "Joey glared at all the
snickering faces in the room and stormed out.
I was worried for a while that he might try to
retaliate—"

"Oh, damn," Katie interrupted. The humor lost,
her eyes wide. "Holy shit, that's who that was."

"Who what was? What's the matter, Katie
Ann?" Pops asked.

Katie was staring into space. Pops's voice
startled her into speaking. "Oh, um, that ridiculously creepy cable guy who was here earlier. He
looked at me like he was planning to eviscerate
me before raping my intestines… I told myself
I was imagining it, but damn, no wonder." She
looked between Pops and me. "He's not actually
a serial killer, right? Just a mild-mannered cable
guy with a face like death?"

Pops sat up, his jaw clenched. "Did he do
something? You were trembling like a leaf when
I got here."

I placed the roller in the paint pan, the wall
forgotten. Joey was a drunken waste of human
flesh, but he hadn't attacked a woman, not that I
knew of. "Tell me what happened, Katie."

She stood, waving away my concern, but she
couldn't hide the anxiety in her eyes. "It was

nothing. He was just giving off a deranged serial-killer vibe." She shuddered.

"You know, one of the first things we learn in the police academy is to trust our instincts. Time after time, when victims are interviewed, they talk about having a bad feeling, not being able to rationalize it and so putting it aside... right before they were attacked. When you feel something is wrong, you need to pay attention."

She let the roller hang by her side, listening. I got the impression she wasn't used to her concerns being taken seriously.

"Katie, I'd appreciate it if you did me a favor. If Joe Markum has to come back, make sure Pops is here with you. I know it's hard to believe, but there are a lot of people in this town who are afraid of Pops."

"Damn straight," Pops said. "And, well, they should be." He gave me an approving nod before returning his attention to Katie. "I can be here in five minutes, sooner if need be. You just give me a call." He winked. "It's no hardship to spend time with a pretty girl."

I picked up the roller from the tray. "In fact, I think I'll call Walt, his boss. People shouldn't be in fear in their own homes."

We finished the painting about an hour later. Pops stayed for most of it. When Katie caught his eyes drooping, she suggested he lie down on the bed for a quick rest. He looked sorely tempted but claimed he should get going as there was a football game he wanted to watch at home.

Katie glanced over at the newly installed television in the room. "You can—"

Pops cut her off. "When an old man says he needs to go home to watch a football game, he means that he needs to lie down on the couch, turn on the game as background noise and take a nap." He took in the room. "I like it. Nellie would have loved it. You're doing good." He squeezed Katie's arm and left.

We finished a short while later. After pulling the tape, we surveyed our work.

"Is it too much? Did I go overboard?" She nibbled her lower lip, self-doubt clear on her face.

I tried to pretend I wasn't tempted to soothe that lower lip with my mouth. "Nah, it's perfect."

She brightened. "You really think so?"

"Absolutely." I'd been watching her from the corner of my eye all day. I turned to study her directly now. Her hair was piled on top of her head, loose curls falling free. "Yes, I think it looks beautiful, and you look beautiful in it." I enjoyed the sudden flush rising up her throat.

CHAPTER TWENTY-SIX

Kate

WHEN I YAWNED, Aiden said it was time for him to go.

"Thank you for helping me paint my room." I walked him down the stairs.

"Seemed like the least I could do after I lost you your job."

He looked so dejected, I patted his arm. "Not your fault. That was all me."

At the bottom of the stairs, he drew me into his arms. I stilled at the touch of his lips on my neck. He ran his mouth up to my ear. He nibbled the fleshy lobe before his warm tongue soothed the gentle bites, and I went limp. His mouth was against my throat, one hand dragging down my back, the other, holding my hip in place. When he bit, my knees gave out. If he weren't holding me up, I would have fallen into a puddle on the floor.

He dipped his head, his mouth brushing across mine, whisper soft, his kiss an entreaty. I leaned forward, mindlessly searching for more. His hand wrapped around my neck to tilt my head back. His tongue slid like velvet against my own. I gripped his biceps, pulling myself closer.

He was just dragging his hand down my back, fingers beginning to knead my butt, when his phone chimed, echoing through the still room. He reluctantly let me go to check it. Aiden got himself back in control more quickly than I did. He ran his hand through his hair, turned from me and spoke into the phone. I was barely able to aim myself toward the couch before my legs gave up the pretense of holding me vertical.

My whole body was still vibrating, his phantom kisses alive on my skin. Part of my brain registered Aiden's low grumble as he spoke, but the rest was drowning in a swampy mire of lust, confusion, fear and let's not forget the lust.

Aiden ended his call, but stood staring at the door a moment too long.

"Everything okay?"

He shook his head, still not looking at me. "I don't know what the hell I'm doing. I swore I wouldn't do this again. And here I am." He reached for the doorknob. "I need to go." His back still to me.

"What happened?"

"Heather—my dispatcher—her husband walked out on her." He turned back, glaring. "Kindest woman you'll ever meet. Blindsided. I need to go. See what I can do to help. She was crying." He shook his head. "I know a little something about getting my ass dumped." He reached for the door again. "I can't do this, Katie. I don't know what I was thinking."

He stepped through the door, hesitating as though he wanted to come back. "Goodbye."

Oh, I guess not.

AFTER A FITFUL night's sleep, definitely not thinking about being dumped thirty seconds after being kissed senseless, I dozed in the soft, early-morning light, the sun diffused by the new sheer drapes. Snuggled in my feather bed, I opened my eyes to violet walls. Chaucer padded over and nudged my elbow with his cold, wet nose. "Quit it. I'm sleeping over here." It was no use, though. The damn dog could hear it when I opened my eyes. He wanted food and his morning constitutional. Faking sleep never worked. He just got more and more pushy until I got up. "Fine, fine, fine," I said as I threw back the covers. "But I'm coming back later for a nap."

He gave me his best inscrutable look and waited for me to slip on my sweats and slippers. "You're a damn annoying dog, you know that?" His response was a patient, long-suffering stare. As soon as I opened the bedroom door, he rushed out, bumping me off my stride. In his defense, he was almost twice my size, but would a little more delicacy be too much to ask?

When I got to the top of the stairs, his bushy tail was rounding the corner at the bottom on its way to the kitchen.

I'd found a wedding photo of Grandpa and Gran when I was cleaning a few weeks ago. I'd polished and hung it on the wall along the stairs so I could see it every day. I slowed now, as I often did, to say good morning.

They were married at Holy Redeemer, a beautiful stone church in town, the one we always attended when I visited. In the photo they're standing on the steps, just having emerged from the huge open double doors. They are surrounded by cheering friends and family whose arms are raised, rice flying, appearing to be caught in an unseasonable snowstorm. But even in the midst of that joy, your eye couldn't help but be drawn to the young, incandescent couple at its center, clutching one another's hands and running through the onslaught, ready to face whatever life threw at them, together.

My wedding photos were staged and elegant. We looked perfect but lacked what my grandparents had. There was no room for the chaos of love and life in the facade of a perfect wedding, a perfect marriage. Perfection was a cold and lifeless thing.

By the time I got to the kitchen, Chaucer was sitting by the pantry door, his food bowl clamped in his mouth, just in case I was confused about what should happen first.

"Man, you're a nag." I took his bowl and nudged him away so I could open the pantry door to fill his dish. He didn't even wait for the dish to hit the floor before he started inhaling the kibble. "Slow down! If you choke, I have no idea how to give a dog the Heimlich." I opened the back door for him. "Seriously, are you under the impression that if you eat it quickly enough, I'll just forget I've fed you and fill your bowl again? It's never going to happen, bud. Give up the dream."

I walked out onto the porch. The morning was chillier than yesterday, burnished leaves swirled in the wind, waves pounded the nearby cliff. Chaucer brushed past me on his way to the little boy's room in the forest.

I was just turning around to start the coffee-maker when I heard his deep, anxious bark. I jogged out to the porch again, looking for him, listening to the increasingly insistent howling. "Chaucer, where are you?" I ran out and found him crouched by the storm-cellar doors, growling, then whining as he scratched at the door. I went to him, weaving my fingers into his ruff. "What is it, baby? What's down there?"

It better not be another fawn. Just in case it was, I took out my phone and called the first person I thought of. It went straight to voice mail. "Hi, Connor. That growling and barking you're probably hearing is Chaucer, pawing at the cellar door. I could totally do this on my own, because I am not the least bit afraid of dark, cobweb-ridden, rodent-filled cellars. At all. I just thought you might be bored and interested in going down there first. I didn't want to cheat you out of a manly experience." I took a deep breath and braced myself. "Okay, I've probably stalled long enough. I'll keep you on the phone, so to speak, just so you don't miss a bit of the action. Here goes." I heaved the door open, and the biggest rat I'd even seen came running out, scampering over my slippers, heading for the trees. I screamed. I'm not proud, but, holy hell, that thing was huge!

"Sorry, sorry," I said into the phone. "I'm fine. Chaucer! Get back here! Right now, mister. That thing probably has rabies. At the very least, it's been irradiated. I mean, that rat must have been two feet long. What the hell is with Maine rats— oh, wait, was that an opossum? I've never seen one, only heard their squeaky conversations with those damn snarky marmosets. Huh. Okay, never mind." I hung up.

Two hours later, I was on my knees in the garden, weeding. Chaucer had flopped down under a nearby tree. Suddenly he sat up, giving a soft woof. When I looked around, I found Connor watching me, a tender expression on his face.

"Hello, honey. It sounded like you had a big morning. Any more irradiated rodents come looking for you?" He enjoyed a good laugh at my expense.

I rolled my eyes and stood, brushing off the knees of my jeans. "Whatever. How the heck am I supposed to know what an opossum looks like? For all you know, you do have radioactive varmints running around in these woods. You'll be sorry you mocked me when one bites you in the butt, and you mutate into some creepy rat man."

He continued chuckling while I put away the gardening tools. "Not that you deserve my hospitality, but would you like a drink, Connor?"

"I'd love one, thanks." His eyes twinkled.

He strolled up to the porch while I went in for refreshments. I filled a tray with two glasses of iced tea and a plate of cookies.

He looked surprised when I returned to him. "Mmm, what are these?"

"Pumpkin snickerdoodles. It seemed like a good idea. Let me know what you think."

He bit into one and his eyes fluttered closed. My pride swelled.

"Delicious! So, word is you went on a date with Bear a couple of weeks ago."

"I guess nothing's secret in this town." I took

a cookie and said, "I realize I barely know him, but I love that guy."

The smile fell off Connor's face. "Oh, is that so?"

"What?" Shit. Was he a serial killer after all?

Connor recovered himself. "Nothing. I just didn't expect you to fall for him so quickly."

I could feel my cheeks heat. "No, no. That's not what I meant. We had a great time, and he was totally fun. I just really like him is all." I took a cookie. "He seemed annoyed when Aiden showed up."

Connor choked a little on his iced tea. "Aiden showed up on your date?"

I shrugged. "Yeah. He said he saw my car in the parking lot of the Chart Room, so he came in to say hi. He ended up sitting down and eating with us." I jumped up. "Which reminds me."

I ran in the house and retrieved Aiden's hat from the table by the stairs. I didn't want to keep the hat of someone who didn't want to know me. I brought it back and handed it to Connor. "Could you return this to Aiden for me? He loaned me his hat."

Connor stared at me for a moment. "Aiden crashed your date, gave you a hat and invited himself to sit down and eat with you. Is that right?"

"I wouldn't call it a crash. He just happened to be there, and I asked him to have a seat."

He nodded, smiling. "Well, isn't that interesting." He slapped his thigh with the hat and stood. "Yes, it is. I've got to be getting on now. How about I take you to dinner tonight?"

"Oh, you don't need to do that. I could make something for us right here." I stood, too, feeling awkward, unsure of why he was leaving so soon.

"How long has it been since you've had fresh Maine lobster?"

Chaucer walked up and bumped my hip. My hand automatically went to his head. "Fifteen years, at least."

"See there, far too long. I'll come back around six. I'm not much for driving anymore, so do you think you could do the honors for our dinner date?"

"Of course."

He turned to leave, making his way down the stairs. "Good, good. I'll see you this evening then."

I turned to Chaucer. "Now, what do you suppose that was about?"

I brought the full tray back into the kitchen. I'd left Bear's card next to the phone. I thought about the crack in the plaster ceiling in the spare room. I went in this morning to consider paint colors and noticed it. I also had a leaky faucet in the downstairs bathroom.

I dialed and he picked up right away. "Good morning, beautiful!"

I stayed silent, trying to figure out if he thought I was someone else.

"Kate?" He sounded confused.

"Oh, you *did* mean me. Good morning to you, too." The easy compliment made me smile and relax.

"What can I do for you?" His voice had a strange echo.

"I was just wondering if you had time to do a couple of jobs for me. I'm slowly working on making Gran's place feel like my own, and I've found some problems, a cracked ceiling and a leaky faucet." I paused. "If that's not the kind of thing you do, could you recommend someone?"

"I asked Nellie to let me fix that ceiling two years ago. I did all kinds of handyman stuff for her, and I'll extend the service to you, too. Mainly I design and build things, but I'm pretty handy, as well."

"You're pretty handsy. I'll give you that."

He laughed. "Anything for the future mother of my children. We'll have four. Did I tell you?"

Why couldn't he be the one I wanted? He was sweet and funny and sexy as hell. Clearly, I had been an asshat in a previous life, and I was paying for it in this one. "Four? That means I'd have to have sex with you four times. I did not agree to that. Maybe if you were a better kisser..."

"A challenge, I like that. I'll be by this afternoon to look at your house and to lay one on you that'll have you rethinking your assessment of me. Personally, I'm good for four times a day, but if you can't keep up with me..."

I hung up on him, laughing. "Okay, Chaucer, let's go check the rest of the house and make a list for Bear. Your new best friend will be here soon."

I heard Bear's truck a couple of hours later. Chaucer stood by the door, tail wagging, waiting to get at him. I opened the door, and Chaucer was off like a shot but he stopped himself before he jumped.

Bear gave Chaucer a strong, full-body rub, and Chaucer fell to the porch in bliss. Bear stepped over my dog, grabbed me, dipped me and laid a huge kiss on me.

When he stood me back up, all I could say was wow.

With a huge, self-satisfied grin, he nodded. "That's right."

"No, I meant the dip. The dip was awesome. The kiss—" I grimaced "—meh."

He sighed. "I know. I worried when you said wow. Okay, let's fix stuff!" He clapped his hands together, walking into the house, Chaucer jumping up to follow.

I followed, as well. "You know, you look damn hot in that tool belt."

He turned to wink at me. "Why do you think I became a contractor? I make this look work."

I had six things to show him, and they turned out to be minor enough that he could easily get them all done in a day. When I asked how much it would cost, he laughed.

"I'll pass on Nellie's discount to you, especially as you let me kiss you whenever I feel like it."

I screwed up my face in distaste. "Feeling kind of whorish now. Getting kissed on a semiregular basis made me feel like a free spirit. If I'm getting compensated for it, I just feel dirty."

"I see. Does it bother you enough to pay full price?"

"Oh, hell, no. Maybe I'll try on dirty for a little while. Take it for a test spin, if you will."

"I knew I liked you." He stepped closer and picked me up. "Wrap your legs around my waist."

"Um. No." I was dangling in the air, trying not to laugh.

"You're not getting any lighter, woman. Put your legs around me."

I rolled my eyes. "Fine, you big whiner." I put my arms on his shoulders and wrapped my legs around his waist. His grip shifted to my ass. I lifted my eyebrows at that.

"I'm trying to more securely support your weight. I take no pleasure in this." He then squeezed my butt and pulled me up higher. Our naughty bits were nowhere near each other, thankfully. "Now that you're feeling dirty, I thought we could try this again. On three, we try out our dirtiest kisses. One. Two. Three."

His mouth crushed mine, his tongue invaded, wrestling with my own, as his hands continued to caress my butt. After a moment, during which I had the presence of mind to think that he was a darn good kisser, I called the experiment a failure. "Dude, you want to get your hands off my butt now?"

"But my hands love your ass. Don't make my hands give up their new favorite plaything. It's cruel."

I smacked his shoulder. "All right. Enough of this." I tried to hop down, but he wouldn't unhand me. Consequently, I was hanging two feet off the ground, my face still close to his, my butt still firmly in his hands.

He squinted at me, as though trying to figure out a puzzle. "Why isn't this working? You're hot, you're funny and I genuinely like you. Why aren't we losing our shit over each other?"

I thought of Aiden and shrugged. "Is there someone else you'd rather be dirty kissing?"

His gaze slid to the right. "Nah." He let me down. "Okay, I better get a few of these things done while I'm here. I'll finish up tomorrow or the next day. It depends on how my other jobs are going."

A few hours later, Bear had completed all but the ceiling, promising to be back soon to fix it.

He had only been gone a few minutes when I heard Connor return. "Katie, honey, are you here?"

I walked back to the kitchen. "Hi, Connor. You just missed Bear."

He stopped to pet Chaucer. "Oh, why was he here?"

"Doing some repairs for me. I'm sorry. I haven't had time to change for dinner. Can you give me a minute?"

He shooed me away. "Go, go. Chaucer and I are going to go sit out back, so take your time."

When I returned a few minutes later, Connor asked, "Are you hungry?"

My stomach answered for me.

"I may be going deaf but I heard that. Tiny thing like you, we need to keep your strength up." We moved back through the French doors into the dining room, and Connor stopped to make sure the door was secure before saying, "I promised lobster. Does that still sound good to you?"

I grabbed his arm. "Do you understand how much I've been looking forward to that lobster all day?"

He brought his big mitts in for a loud clap. "Now you're talking. This is prime lobster season, and Artie was telling me that they've been hauling in some big ones, the last few weeks in particular. Come on, my girl, let's get moving."

I looked down at a hopeful Chaucer. I scratched his head and let him down easy. "Sorry, buddy. I can't take you with me this time. You could sit in the car and wait for us, but that doesn't seem like much fun." I walked him back to the kitchen. "How about I leave you with a treat?" I pulled a bully stick from the pantry and handed it over. He had it trapped securely in his big jaw but gave me the downcast, poor-dog look, as well. I leaned over and kissed his massive, furry head. "I'll be back soon. I promise."

"Honey, what's this?" Connor's voice floated down the hall from the living room.

I found him holding a scrap of paper with a vacant property's address and the leasing agent's phone number. "Oh, just a silly thought." I was embarrassed and tried to retrieve the information.

Connor easily eluded my reach and pocketed the paper. "You can tell me all about this silly thought of yours over dinner."

When I pulled a long, belted sweater coat in aubergine from the closet under the stairs, Connor took it from me and held it open so I could slip it on. "Now, this is a good, warm sweater. Did you get it from Maureen?"

I spun, showing off the ensemble. "Yep." I pointed down. "And the boots!" I swiveled my foot around, still in love with the charcoal gray suede, wedge-heeled boots. They would be worth eating nothing but ramen for a year. Totally.

He chuckled, placing my hand in the crook of his elbow to escort me out. "You look pretty as a picture. Come on, let's eat."

As I drove, Connor directed me downtown to Galyn's on Main Street, a converted 1890s' boardinghouse for local fishermen. The architectural aspects of the historic building remained, but the rooms were now filled with dining tables.

Connor chatted with our host before we were seated at a table, right against the window looking out over Agamont Park and the pier. The view was breathtaking, the sky turning pink in the early evening, the water turning to a deep indigo.

He looked over his menu and then pulled his phone from his pocket. He looked down at the screen, smiled and then pocketed it again. "Well, I'm going for the Lazy Man's Lobster. Let them do all the work shelling it, so all I have to do is eat it." He looked at me, eyebrows raised over the menu top. "Traditional boiled, stuffed, Newburg, what are you in the mood for?"

The waiter dropped off some water and a basket of bread. I tore off a piece, while continuing to peruse the menu. I hadn't eaten anything besides a few snickerdoodles today, and I was starting to feel a little light-headed. "I think for my first Maine lobster in fifteen years, I will opt for the traditional boiled. It's a classic for a reason, right?"

The waiter, a young man with shaggy hair and a lip ring, returned a few minutes later. "Hey, Mr. Cavanaugh, have you and your date made your decisions yet?"

"Kenny, I want you to meet Miss Katie Gallagher. She's Nellie's granddaughter and is living in Nellie's house." I shook our waiter's hand. "Katie, this is Kenny Davis. Do you remember that little boy who—"

"Ah, come on, Mr. Cavanaugh. You don't need to remind her of that." Kenny looked pained, but amused at having his childhood discussed.

"Now, son, Katie's basically family." Connor turned back to me. "Do you remember that little boy who wore a New England Patriots football helmet everywhere he went?"

My eyes went wide as I took in our waiter with a new appreciation. "That was you?" I clapped. "You were awesome! I swear, you just made me giggle every time I saw you. How the heck did you see with that huge thing on your head all the time?" It had been an adult's helmet on a little boy. I'd always see his nose through the eyehole. I could never figure out how he didn't run into things constantly.

His cheeks turned a charming pink. "Yeah, see, mostly I just looked down and watched my feet. I could see a few steps ahead. Sometimes I bounced off poles and stuff, but I was wearing a helmet so it was cool. My parents usually held my hand and looked out for me." He shook his head. "I was convinced that if I wore the helmet every day, eventually the Patriots would have to let me on the team." He shuffled his feet and tapped his order pad against his leg. "I didn't realize that skinny guys who barely top five-ten don't get drafted into the NFL. My dad seemed huge at the time, so I figured I'd be huge one day, too."

Connor chuckled. "Well, now, by your dad's standards, you are."

Kenny smiled. "Yep, you're right. I got Dad beat, at least." He held his order pad up again. "Anyway, thanks for that little walk down memory lane, Mr. Cavanaugh." He looked to me first. "What can I get you, Miss Gallagher?"

"Please, call me Katie."

Once our orders had been placed, Connor looked down at his buzzing pocket. Excusing himself, he walked out to the porch to receive a call, and I settled back, relaxing into the moment. Connor walked in a moment later, stopped to speak with Kenny and was just sitting down when our drinks arrived.

"All right, Katie mine, tell me about this silly thought of yours." He took a sip of his beer and leaned back, focusing entirely on me. It was unnerving.

"Really, Connor, it was nothing." He continued to stare, so I elaborated. "It was just a stray thought." I blew out a breath and took the dive. "Chaucer and I were walking down Main, and I saw an empty storefront. When I stepped inside—that's where I met Bear—I could see it was a minuscule diner, barely enough room for eight or ten tables, but it was perfect. I just, I don't know, I fell in love, and I started to think about having my own little breakfast place, you know? Somewhere I could make pancakes, sausage and eggs, quiches and pastries or whatever. I'd only open for breakfast. I could do all the work myself. Although, I suppose I'd need to hire a server who could wait on people while I cooked. I could just see it all in my head, the decor and the menus."

I looked up at Connor and said, "It's just a silly pipe dream. I don't know anything about running a business. I love to cook, but I wouldn't know the first thing about starting a restaurant. People are much nicer about food they're given for free from someone they know. Food they have to pay for from a faceless person in the kitchen?" I shrugged. "Like I said, a fleeting thought. Anyway, how was your day? Watch any ball games?" I asked with a grin.

Connor, however, was not to be distracted. "How do you want to decorate it?"

I took another piece of bread and a large sip

of iced tea before nearly choking. "Wow, what did they put in this tea?"

Connor raised his eyebrows. "He asked if you wanted a Seafarer's iced tea, and you said yes." I looked at him blankly, so he continued, "It's a cocktail, like a Long Island iced tea only with more of a kick."

I fanned my face with my napkin. "Yeah, I'll say. You may need to call us a cab home." I took another tentative sip and felt the liquor work through me. I'd need more bread to sop up the alcohol.

Connor leaned back as Kenny brought us two appetizers, placing the dishes in the center of the table, plus an additional small plate in front of each of us. "To start out with, we have our famous lobster rolls, lobster in a cream sauce in puff pastry and our crab-stuffed mushrooms. I hope you enjoy." Kenny left and my stomach rumbled.

Connor flicked his hand toward the food. "Eat and explain your ideas for the diner." He popped a mushroom into his mouth.

I tried one of the lobster rolls, closed my eyes and moaned. Connor chuckled, my eyes popping open in embarrassment. "Sorry." I swallowed. "Really good." I took another sip of my cocktail. "Well, I was thinking about light walls. You know the creamy yellow of Italian plaster? With the word *pancake* in every language that has a pancake as part of their native cuisine—Gran and I looked it up once. There are a ton of different cultures that have something similar to what we call pancakes. Just in the US, there's *flapjacks*, *griddle cakes* and *hot cakes*. And I'm sure if we visited more remote, rural areas we'd find even more names for them. Anyway, I was thinking of those words written in kind of an unbroken chain, ringing the room at eye level—mine, not yours.

"And I'd have small, round, wrought iron café-style tables in the center of the room with a long red leather bench running down each of the side walls. Small square tables could be placed at intervals along the bench so if there was a big party, we could scoot all the tables together to make one long table. Otherwise, lots of eating areas for two to four people." I felt myself babbling but couldn't stop.

"There'd be a counter running along the service area in front of the kitchen so people could just eat at the counter, if they'd like. Take half that wall down, like Bear suggested. A large, sparkling chandelier hanging from the ceiling." I cleared my throat. "I know that sounds silly. I want it to feel warm and inviting, but special, too. I've always loved Parisian architecture, so I want it to have that feel. And, yes, there will be crepes." I paused to gauge Connor's reaction. He was smiling, but that could have been the smile you give a crazy person as you back slowly away. I ate a mushroom to cover my unease.

Connor wiped his mouth, the smile going with it. "Okay, now, let's get down to brass tacks. You want to open a diner. I want a tenant in my vacant property. How much do you think this venture will cost?"

I felt my face go slack. "Your property? But," I sputtered, "that wasn't your name in the window."

"Of course not, that's the agent's name and number. She fields all the inquiries and lets me know if anything sounds good. I've had a couple of potentials, but it's safe to say that you're the leading contender."

The empty plates were taken away. Connor leaned forward. "Sweetheart, I think this is a wonderful idea, and I'm more than happy to help you with—what are you calling this place?"

Nellie's Kitchen slipped out before I could stop myself. "But really, Connor, I'm not a good bet. My ex would be more than happy to tell you about all the projects I've started and left unfinished."

"I don't want to hear about him." Connor's easy smile disappeared. "He didn't know you, so his opinion means nothing to me." He took in my disbelieving look and continued, "If he truly knew you, he wouldn't be able to stop himself from cherishing you. My guess is he was too busy loving himself to give anyone else too much of a never mind, so I don't give two good—I don't care what he said about you. I know better. This is here and now, Katie, and I *know* you're the best bet. So, how much do you think it'll cost to open up this diner of yours?"

Dumbstruck, I was saved from answering by an interruption. I felt a large, warm body at my back, a frisson of awareness running up my spine. I knew who it was, even before he spoke. I didn't think I could deal with Officer Hot & Cold right now.

"Katie, it's nice to see you this evening." He circled the table and sat opposite me, with Connor at my left. "Pops, did you order me a beer, too?"

Kenny reappeared. "Chief, it's good to have you with us this evening. If we're all here now, I'll bring out your dinners," he said, before turning and disappearing once more down the hallway, presumably toward the kitchen.

I hate that my face is so easy to read. Aiden laughed. "Oh, didn't he tell you that I'd be joining you?" He took the napkin off the table and placed it on his knee. "I wanted to apologize for—well, too many things—most recently for being rude the other night. Buying you dinner seemed like a good way to do it. Pops is just tagging along for the free food." Connor nodded and ate another mushroom.

I felt my face flush. I hoped Connor didn't ask what Aiden was apologizing for. Gah! It was like accidentally watching an R-rated movie with your parents. *Oh, are people having sex? I hadn't noticed. I was just looking through this magazine right here.*

I waved my hand. "Please, forget about it." I gave him a significant look. "Really. Never speak of it again." I took another sip of my drink, while he chuckled at my discomfort.

"So." Aiden's eyes shifted back and forth between Connor and me. "What are we discussing tonight?"

"It's funny you should ask," Connor began, but I cut him off.

"This restaurant. Isn't it interesting that it used to be a boardinghouse for sailors?" Hey, I covered that up pretty well, for once.

"Yeah, that's what they say. And a speakeasy during prohibition. I think they also had an illegal gambling operation in the back at one point. This is a great place." Aiden took a drink from Connor's beer. "So, what were you two really talking about?" Aiden tried using his silent cop mojo to break me, but I wasn't going down. Connor, however, was apparently not the mojo-deflecting badass I was.

"You know my vacant property right up the street?" Connor asked him.

Aiden nodded. "Sure."

"Well, Katie and I were just discussing her renting it to open a breakfast diner." Connor was clearly tickled with the idea, and seemed to be waiting for Aiden to mirror his enthusiasm.

Aiden tilted his head and regarded me for a moment, before looking down at the table, nodding absently while his thumb rubbed back and forth across the white tablecloth.

Kenny reappeared with our food, breaking the tension. "Here we are. I hope you enjoy your meals. Please, let me know if there's anything I can get you. Chief, would you like something to drink?"

Aiden nodded again, without looking up from his plate. "Thanks, Kenny. I'll have whatever you've got on tap."

After a minute I felt the table jolt and saw Aiden wince. "What the hell was that for?" he demanded of Connor, who merely stared at him.

I tried to swallow the huge lump in my throat. I wasn't sure if it was disappointment or humiliation, but it didn't matter. I took a long drink.

"I know. It's stupid. I was just explaining to Connor that it would never work." I smiled too brightly around the table. "Well, doesn't this look delicious?"

Aiden shook his head disgustedly at Connor before turning back to me. "I don't think it's a stupid idea. I was just wondering how much weight I was going to gain, eating there every morning. I was also thinking about Kimberly, Jack's oldest girl. She could be your waitress. She's taking classes at the university, but maybe she could wait tables in the morning before going to class. Might work out better for her than trying to find a night job. Also, Bear could do the reno work. He knows the place well." He turned back to me. "Yeah, this could be real good, Katie. Start slowly, just doing breakfast, and then once you have everything down and a good staff in place, you can start doing lunch, too."

He nodded, picked up his fork and dug into his potatoes as though that was that. It had all been decided. Connor hid a grin behind his sip of beer, but nothing could hide the twinkle in his eyes. I felt like I'd been poleaxed. I took a deep breath and waited for an offhand comment that would highlight my flaws, but nothing came. Aiden and Connor were eating companionably, discussing the renovation.

I ignored their chatter, breaking into my bright red steamed lobster, dipping a glistening piece into the garlic butter. I let the feeling settle. Both of them seemed unreservedly convinced that I could do this, and do it well. I was floored and then horrified that my reaction to kindness and support was shock. In spite of that revelation, a huge grin pulled at my face.

Aiden glanced over. "Lobster good?"

A gasp of insane hilarity wanted to burst out,

but I locked it down. I nodded my head solemnly before responding. "Yep, very good lobster."

Connor reached under the table to give my knee a quick squeeze, all while continuing his discussion with Aiden. I took another drink and dug in to my most excellent meal.

CHAPTER TWENTY-SEVEN

Aiden

KATIE WAS A little tipsy, and it looked good on her. I'd told myself I would leave right after dinner. Instead, I found myself watching Katie. Again. Damn it. After dinner we'd moved to the lounge. Katie stood at the bar, chatting with Jane, our waitress, who had often hung out with her and Daisy when they were kids.

She scampered back and dropped into her chair. "Oh, my goodness, did you know that Jane married Michael? They have a set of twelve-year-old twins." She paused to look up at the ceiling, her fingers twitching. "Wait, I don't think the math on that works." She turned back around to look at Jane, a mischievous grin on her face. "Why, that little hussy. And with Michael." She leaned forward to take Pops and me into her confidence. "He was my first kiss," she whispered. "Ah, well, *c'est la vie.*" She leaned back. "So, who else got knocked up in high school?"

Pops stood, chuckling. "You'd have to ask this one," he said, pointing to me. "I prefer to believe everyone is pure as the driven snow when they get married." He winked at Katie. "Including his grandmother and myself."

"Thanks, Pops. That's a thought I really needed floating around in my head." I fake shuddered.

"Then my work here is done, and it's time for me to go home."

Katie immediately deflated. "Oh, Connor, don't go." She stood and wrapped her arms around him, her chin on his chest, looking up. I don't know how Pops could resist those bright green eyes. I couldn't imagine ever saying no to her if she looked at me that way. "I'll be your wingman" she said. "Get you hooked up tonight."

He leaned down and kissed her forehead, giving her a quick squeeze. He held her tight, his voice just a murmur in the crowd. "Katie, I have a feeling there isn't much you couldn't talk me into, but I'm an old man and tired, so I want to go home."

Blinking and looking thoroughly confused, Katie finally said, "Oh."

She reached under the table, picked up a tiny handbag and secured the strap across her body. "Okay, let's go."

Pops held on to one arm and shook his head. "No, you don't. You've had too many cocktails. Aiden—" he looked to me and I nodded "—is driving you home tonight. I don't want the proprietor of the newest eating establishment in Bar Harbor getting into any accidents, all right?"

She held up two fingers in a faulty Girl Scout salute. "I promise to be completely sober before I touch my car keys. I'm switching to water right now. Aiden can make me walk a straight line and touch my nose." She dropped her hand to the side, went up on tiptoe and kissed Pops on the cheek. "I'll be good. I promise."

"Ah, Katie, if I were only a younger man, I'd snatch you up and put you in my pocket." He turned and nodded at someone I couldn't see across the room. "Phil's going to run me home. He was here having dinner with his daughter and son-in-law," he explained.

Pops said his goodbyes and left. Katie immediately tensed up. I felt like a complete shit for having this effect on her. "Come on. Dance with me." Her eyes were big and bright, shining with confusion and not a little reticence.

"Oh, well, it's just that—"

I grabbed her hand and pulled her to the small dance floor. They were playing Patsy Cline's "Crazy," which seemed appropriate considering that's what Katie was driving me. She was so damn nervous and uncomfortable, I couldn't help but pull her in tight. I rubbed her back, trying to get her to settle, but she felt a little too good, so I stopped.

I cleared my throat. "Listen, I'm sorry I've

been sending mixed signals, kissing you and then taking off. I'm dealing with my own shit, and not very well. I didn't mean to drag you into it."

"Oh." She looked disappointed. "I see."

Did I explain that wrong? "I like you, Katie, and I'm sorry I've been such a dick. I've been thinking that maybe we should try to be friends." At her raised eyebrows, I continued, "Yes. I know most friends don't make out, but maybe we should. You know, kind of a friends-with-benefits deal."

When she reared back, I pulled her in close again. "I knew you wouldn't go for that." I sighed.

We were drawing some attention. I could feel all the town gossips trying to figure out what was going on. I didn't want to be grist for the mill, but the idea of letting her go and sitting back down definitely didn't appeal, either.

She glanced around the room, stiff in my arms. "We seem to have an audience, Aiden."

I slid my thumb back and forth, over her ribs. "Ignore them." It was an almost imperceptible move, but I watched her eyes dilate.

"What?" She said breathlessly.

I lowered my face closer to hers. "Having trouble concentrating?"

Her eyes were trained on my lips and then she blinked, her gaze turning calculating. "Not at all.

I think people might just be worried about your subpar dancing skills."

I groaned quietly, as I pulled her in closer, her chest pressed against my own. "Maybe. Or maybe people are just concerned I'll strain my neck, dancing with a pixie."

She leaned back, casting an assessing glance over her shoulder. "That's what they're saying, are they?" I could tell she was plotting. "Is this better for you then?" She asked as she stepped up on my shoes.

I'm sure she thought she was causing severe toe pain, but as I was wearing my steel-toed work shoes and she was no bigger than a minute, all she did was make me work a little harder to lift my legs. When I didn't grimace in pain, I felt her concentrate all her weight on the balls of her feet, resulting in a not unpleasant pressure and the unintended benefit of bringing her face closer to mine. She clung to me to keep her balance. My hands spread across her back, desperate to slide lower. She swayed toward me, my eyes starting to close in response to the kiss I was readying for. Instead, she blinked slowly and then jumped back off my feet.

"I'm going—" She floundered, gesturing vaguely. "Over there. I need to do something."

Eyes narrowed, I watched her and that almost kiss back away. "You have fun. Over there."

She spun and ran directly into Jane.

"Oof. Whoa, you okay there?" At Kate's nod, Jane continued, "Are you guys ready for another round?" Jane waited, blond hair tied up and serving tray at her hip.

"Oh, God, no." Katie glanced over at me and winced. "Water would be great, though. Thank you, Jane."

"Katie, it's karaoke night. Will you sing?" Jane asked.

I turned sharply to Katie. I didn't know she sang. Her fair, Irish skin did nothing to hide the blush coloring her cheeks, as she madly shook her head.

In the middle of Katie's panic attack, Jane noticed my surprise. "Aiden, haven't you ever heard Katie sing? Oh, you're in for a treat." Then she grabbed Katie's hand and pulled her toward the makeshift stage in the corner of the lounge.

With a hand firmly on Katie, Jane spoke into the mic. "Good evening, everyone. Welcome to Galyn's karaoke night. If you'd like to try your hand at it, speak with Greg at the bar. He can sign you up. Now, some of you might remember Nellie Gallagher's granddaughter, Katie, from when she'd visit here in the summers." She raised their joined hands up high. "Well, here she is, come back to live with us. You might recall that flaming, curly hair of hers, or perhaps you remember her sharp tongue. Others may still be in awe of her legendary parade-float scandals."

If possible, Katie's blush deepened. "But what I remember best about Katie is a voice that could make angels weep."

She squeezed Katie's hand. "Now, as a welcome-back present for *me*, Katie is going to sing for us tonight. Greg, play 'I Can't Make You Love Me.'" Jane turned to Katie. "It's my favorite, and you still owe me for covering for you when we were twelve," she said with a smile.

"Jane, not that one." Katie's whisper traveled through the microphone just as the first strains of the melody began.

Jane ducked out of the way, and Katie was left standing in front of a live microphone. The lights dimmed while the spotlight illuminated her. She took a breath, her spine straightening, and began to sing about need and loneliness and settling for touch rather than love.

The crowd slowly started taking notice. Most were still talking, but a wave of rapt attention gradually swelled toward the apple-crate stage. I'd never heard a more heartbreakingly haunting rendition of that song. To the rest of the patrons, drinking and chatting with friends, it was simply a surprisingly on-key performance. They didn't understand that Katie was baring her soul, exposing a yearning for love that seemed forever withheld.

It was too much, too intimate. I looked away from her, taking in the bar. All eyes were transfixed on Katie. I felt my atrophied heart lurch. I wanted nothing more than to turn off that damn song, pick up Katie and carry her away somewhere safe, somewhere quiet where I could hold her and love her the way I'd always imagined.

When she stopped singing, the bar erupted in cheers. Katie laughed and took a very theatrical bow. How did no one notice the glassy sheen of tears in her eyes?

When she popped back up, she leaned into the mic and said, "And that, Jane, is how it's done." She tapped her chin, eyes raised to the ceiling. "Now, I seem to remember a certain blonde waitress who spent many an evening when she was thirteen singing 'Kiss Me' to her hairbrush, while dancing in the mirror."

A bar towel flew at Katie's face, but she snatched it out of the air. "What? I thought that was what we were doing." She turned to the bar. "Greg, can you play Sixpence None the Richer for our scowling waitress? Payback's a bitch, sister. Get up here."

The crowd snickered at the battle, before returning to drinks and talk. Having successfully thrown the attention away from herself, Katie skirted the periphery of the room and quietly made for the door.

I stood to follow. Someone grabbed my arm, but I kept going. By the time I reached the street, she was gone.

I did the only thing I could—I followed her.

When I pulled up in front of her house, the lights were off. On the drive over, I'd tried to reason with myself, but my brain was a morass of conflicting impulses, incapable of coherent thought. I knew only one thing; I needed her.

As soon as I slammed the truck door and started walking up the steps, Chaucer's deep, menacing bark reverberated through the house. I reached for the bell, but the door opened before I made contact. Katie was standing in the dark, silhouetted in the doorway.

I intended to chide her for driving when she shouldn't have, to ask if she was all right. Instead, I stepped forward, took her in my arms and found her lips with my own. She gasped at the suddenness, and I took advantage, invading her mouth, sliding my tongue along her own. I put my hand at the back of her head and tilted so I'd have greater access to a mouth I needed like my next breath.

Kate

MY ARMS SLOWLY, tentatively crept around Aiden's waist. His strength enveloped me. My fingers dug into the muscles of his back. I craved him with a mindless need that overwhelmed me. I felt lost and yet finally found. He leaned over and gathered me up into his arms, kicked the door closed and took the stairs to my room, two at a time, without ever breaking the kiss.

He ducked under the low lintel into the bedroom. I didn't want him to put me down. As my feet hit the ground, I strained on tiptoe not to lose the connection, but when his lips traveled across my cheek to kiss and lick behind my ear, my knees weakened and a moan escaped.

His big, warm hands pressed me close before running under my sweater, spanning my back. A moment later, he pulled the sweater up and over my head, throwing it clear. He leaned back and looked down at me in my plain white bra and jeans. I felt suddenly shy, wanting to cover his eyes, not wanting to see disappointment there, wanting to pretend for just a bit longer that he desired me, just me.

He slid the backs of his fingers along my ribs, before lightly cupping my breast, his thumb gliding back and forth over the skin above my bra. My breathing became shallow and my heart tripped. Was I really going to do this? He met my eyes, his thumb slipping lower to rub circles around the hardening tip he'd found hidden beneath the prim white cotton. My legs buckled.

The chill I'd felt just moments ago disappeared under his heated gaze. "You are the most beautiful woman I've ever seen." He found his way under my bra, his roughened thumb rasping against me; a shiver ran through my body.

"Let me touch you, Katie," he said before leaning down to take my mouth once more.

In answer, I reached back, unhooked my bra and let it fall to the floor. I could feel his smile against my lips. I forced my hands in between us so that I could unbutton his shirt. I was distracted, though, as he deftly unbuttoned my jeans and dragged both hands down my body. My pants puddled at my feet, as he gripped my backside, pulling me up along the ridge of his straining jeans.

He walked me backward until I'd stepped free of my clothes, the back of my knees against the side of the bed. I tried again to unbutton his shirt, but then he simply pulled it over his head, still buttoned, and let it fall.

His chest was broad and muscled, a dusting of dark hair tapering to a thin line disappearing below the trim waist of his jeans. I ran my fingers over him as he had me. His skin was hot, shuddering at my touch. I traced the lines of his abdominal muscles, his breath hot at my neck before he grabbed my thighs, picking me up and coming down hard onto the bed with me.

He slid a leg between mine, rubbing me in a way that made me come up off the mattress. "Shh," he said before leaning forward and dipping his tongue into the hollow at the base of my throat. He dragged kisses down my body, stopping to swirl his tongue around my overly sensitive breasts.

I wanted him now, but he was having none of it. He seemed determined to fondle, kiss, lick and bite every inch of my body. I was panting and moaning, bowing off the bed by the time I was finally able to loosen his jeans and drag them down his body with my feet.

I wrapped my legs around him, cradling him between my thighs. He was right where I wanted him. I lifted my hips in invitation, and he groaned. I reached over and opened my nightstand drawer, revealing a large, multicolored assortment of foil-wrapped condoms. He raised his eyebrows in surprise.

"Okay, see, there's a really good reason I have—"

He shook his head and kissed me, reaching into the drawer. "Later." He ripped open the package, and I helped, maybe a little too well. Before long he was batting my hand away.

He braced himself on his forearms, trying not to crush me, then swooped down and took my mouth, one hand at my breast, his hips shifting, poised at the entrance. He leaned back and looked down at me, eyes dark and heavy lidded, before he slowly surged forward. My head fell back as my body struggled to accept him. It had been a while since I'd had sex, and I was coming to realize that Justin wasn't any better of a lover than he was a husband. When Aiden slid out and slammed home, all thoughts of Justin's deficiencies were forgotten, along with Justin.

My whole body felt like an exposed nerve, vibrating with too much pleasure. Once I found my release, Aiden followed me over. I lay trembling in his arms, never wanting to let go. Aiden shifted us, so his legs came up behind mine, his arm around my waist, my bottom nestled against his groin. I felt him kiss the back of my neck. "Sleep, sweet Kate, in your violet bower. I will attend you." I had little time to wonder over his words before I was out.

CHAPTER TWENTY-EIGHT

Aiden

I'D REACHED FOR her again and again throughout the night, overwhelmed every time that she was there, reaching back for me. I knew it was wrong, that I'd jumped into bed without a safety line. She hadn't agreed to my friends-with-benefits idea. She'd looked appalled at the suggestion on the dance floor. But it felt too good to regret anything now.

Snuggled up against me, her perfect ass warmed my cock, my hand wrapped around her, my thumb lazily circling a nipple, as I kissed her shoulder. She moaned sleepily, and I slid my hand down her stomach and between her legs. I knew she had finally woken up when she began to respond.

She let out a deep throaty breath that almost did me in. "Don't you ever rest?"

I lifted her leg and placed it on top of my own, repositioning her. "You go ahead and take a nap. I'll do all the work," I said as I slid in.

Her giggle was cut short on a groan. She

reached back, her small hand grabbing my ass, pulling me more firmly against her. I slid one arm under her so I could play with a nipple while my other hand continued to slide between her legs. Her breath was coming faster. I could feel her tighten around me before she exploded, taking me with her.

When I woke again, the room was light, and the other side of the bed was empty. Where did she go? Her bathroom door was open and the light was off. I slid out of bed, picked up the clothes I'd strewn around her room and dressed before continuing my search downstairs.

At the bottom of the stairs, I heard soft, happy singing coming from the kitchen. I followed the sound, stopping and leaning against the doorway, watching Katie sing and dance her way across the kitchen. Hot damn, she was making us pancakes.

"Smells great."

At my words she jumped, spinning around, a ladle clutched to her chest.

I walked in slowly. "Sorry. Didn't mean to scare you." I leaned in and kissed the tip of her nose. Her cheeks pinked, making me want to throw her over my shoulder and carry her back up to that purple room. I needed food, though, so I tabled that idea for later in favor of pancakes. "Those smell good. Pumpkin?"

"Pumpkin and chocolate chip." She smiled shyly, turning back around to the stove.

I intended to sit down and wait, happily watch her cook, but that shyness needed to be dealt with. I stepped up behind her, wrapping my arms around her waist, kissing her neck. "You're my new favorite way to wake up."

She tilted her head, giving me room to play. She was wearing a robe, and now that I had my hands on her, I could feel nothing underneath the robe. I'd need to take advantage of that. After breakfast, because those pancakes smelled great.

She pushed her butt back, trying to get me to stop crowding her so she could cook. It didn't have the desired effect. I'd intended to retreat, but then her soft, unrestrained ass was brushing against my crotch, and I was rethinking waiting.

"Sit, sit, sit. I'm cooking over here!" She swung an elbow, so I stepped back.

I poured a cup of coffee and sat down. Watching her too closely gave me ideas, so I looked out the back window instead. "Should we be concerned that Pops is walking this way?"

"What?" She squeaked, glancing down at herself and around the kitchen. She looked like she was getting ready to hide in the pantry closet.

I laughed as she went on tiptoe to look out the window. Panic turning to confusion. Confusion slowly turning to outrage. I laughed harder.

"That's not funny!" She stomped back to the

stove, grumbling, "Damn man." She flipped pancakes and then pointed to her pantry. "The cereal is in there. Go make yourself a bowl. No pancakes for you!"

I moved quietly across the room. I felt her jump when my arms slid around her again. I leaned forward and kissed her neck, nibbling up to her ear. My hands along her rib cage until each held an unrestrained breast. "I'm very sorry." I sucked her earlobe while pinching her nipples. I felt her jolt again. "Am I forgiven?"

She groaned, leaning into me. "What?"

I grinned against her neck, sliding a hand inside her robe. "Can I have some pancakes?"

"Hmm?" It took her a second before she stood straight and shook me off. "Damn it! Stop that. I'm cooking over here, and you just made me burn this batch." She used her spatula to pick up all three pancakes and drop them into the trash. "Those were yours."

I sat back down. "You have an evil streak."

She brought a plate to me a moment later. "Fine. You can eat."

"So gracious." I reached for the syrup, drizzling where I would normally drown, not wanting to cover up the taste of her food. She joined me a moment later with her own plate of pancakes. I slid the syrup bottle across the table to her. She stared at the bottle for a moment before giving a slight shake of her head and picking it up.

"What?" I took a bite of pancake, and sweet, tangy deliciousness exploded in my mouth. I might have groaned. It would have been appropriate.

She smiled, pleased with my reaction. "Nothing. I intended to pour the syrup into a gravy boat or something so I could heat it up. Gran would be annoyed with me for having a cold syrup bottle on the table."

It was hard to stop eating to respond, but I forced myself. "Eat. They're perfect." I watched her take a tentative, assessing bite of pancake. I grinned when her eyes lit up. "Right?"

We ate silently, each lost in thought. As I finished, though, my thoughts took a decidedly carnal turn. I watched her finish, slid back in my chair and crooked a finger. She stared at me, unimpressed. "I'm trying to thank you for breakfast, woman. Come over here."

"I can hear just fine from here." Her expression was blank, but her eyes were laughing at me.

I noisily slid the table to the side so there was nothing between us. "Damn it. Will you get over here, please?"

"I don't see why."

I leaned forward, grabbed the legs of her chair and slid her to me, pleased I had her closer to where I wanted her.

She crossed her arms. "What?"

I brushed her robe off one knee so I could

touch her skin, my fingers lightly trailing over and around her leg. I never took my eyes off her face, gauging her reactions. She took a deep, slow breath, continuing to feign disinterest. I brushed her robe off her other knee, both hands caressing her thighs. I watched her eyes dilate as my fingers explored under her robe.

She shifted in her chair, just a subtle adjustment, but one that widened the space between her legs. My thumbs brushed across her inner thighs, back and forth, until they found what they were looking for. Katie's arms lost their tension, dropping to her sides. My thumbs parted her, sliding up and down, slick. My fingers tightened around her thighs, pulling her forward so I could explore her more easily.

Her breathing had changed to shallow pants, her eyes sleepy as she watched me. I slid one thumb inside her while the other circled. She was gorgeous to watch, but I couldn't wait. I dropped to my knees, needing to taste her. My tongue explored. When I felt her clench, her orgasm rolling through her, I unzipped and pulled a condom from my back pocket.

She was so adorably spent, she barely noticed when I untied her robe and brushed it off her shoulders. I pulled her off the chair and brought her down on top of me. She climaxed again. I grabbed her ass, holding it to me as I pumped into her. She leaned back, her hands gripping my shoulders, as I took her breast in my mouth. She squirmed, moaning. My thumb circled between her legs again as our mating became more frantic.

When I felt her tighten and shake, I let go, groaning. God, she was perfect. Just so damn perfect. I held her to me, never wanting to let go, never wanting her anyplace than where she was right now.

After a few minutes, I tried to get up.

"What… Why?" She snuggled into me, her head on my shoulder. "Comfy."

"Shower." I kissed her cheek. "Do I need to carry you or can you move under your own steam?"

Her voice was soft and sleepy. "No steam. Steamless. Must carry."

My thigh muscles were already a little shaky, but I powered through and stood. Climbing the stairs was particularly interesting. But by the time we reached the top, she wasn't sleepy, and I had different ideas about the shower.

CHAPTER TWENTY-NINE

Kate

SHOWER SEX, WHO KNEW? My limited previous experience with the sport had been awkward and disappointing. I'd been too concerned with drowning to enjoy it. Perhaps the showerhead shouldn't have been pointed directly at my face. Whatever. Bygones. I was starting a new life, one with a man who made sure I was thoroughly clean, sliding his soapy hands all over me, although he did have some favorite spots. A man who made sure the nice, hot water was pulsating on our bodies, not directly up my nose. It's the little things.

Aiden took off at a run afterward. It was okay, though. I had plenty of stuff to do that didn't involve Aiden. Like right now, I was sitting on my porch, drinking a cup of coffee and thinking about last night. Technically, that did involve Aiden, but it wasn't necessary for him to be present for me to fantasize. I was fully capable of doing that on my own.

I heard leaves crunch and looked up. Connor was strolling through the trees toward me and Chaucer. "Shit, shit, shit, look innocent," I whispered to him. He stood, stretching, watching Connor approach. "I mean it. Don't rat me out, okay? There's a bully stick in your future if you pretend nothing happened last night." He turned his head and stared at me. "Or this morning."

"Good morning." Connor paused at the bottom of the steps. "Are you okay, Katie?"

I sat up straighter and folded my hands in my lap. "Of course. Why wouldn't I be?"

He slowly climbed the stairs, studying me. "Well, your voice is higher than usual, and you're looking everywhere but at me."

"What?" I popped up out of my chair. "Don't be silly. Just a nice, quiet, relaxing morning, just me and my dog, hanging out, not doing anything." I looked at my coffee cup, still avoiding eye contact. If it had been Gran standing there, she'd have taken one look at me and asked what I'd been doing to put that guilty look on my face.

"Can I get you a cup of coffee?" I hazarded a look in his direction. He appeared puzzled but not suspicious. Luckily, Connor didn't know me as well as Gran had.

"How much have you had this morning?" he asked.

My mind flashed on all the sex I'd had last night and this morning. "What?"

He pointed to my cup. "Coffee."

I reached for the lifeline and clung. "Oh, sorry, yeah. Too much, obviously! I'm a little wired right now." I picked up my cup and ducked in the side door. "Be right back."

I returned a few minutes later with coffee and a muffin for Connor. "In case you're hungry."

He picked up the muffin, seemingly surprised. "You make muffins, too?"

I shrugged. "I like to bake. They're apple."

He broke open the muffin and took a bite. "Mmm, delicious." He nodded, looking out over Gran's garden. "Did Aiden take care of you last night?"

I squeaked, "Uh…"

He focused on me again. "Aiden. Did he drive you home last night?"

I willed my pulse to slow. "Oh, right, no." His brow furrowed, so I quickly continued, "I switched to water and we stayed longer. I chatted with people and danced. Jane made me sing. It was a full night."

He grinned at the mention of singing. "Now I wish I'd stayed later. I'm sorry to have missed it." He winked. "Feel like taking a drive to a restaurant-supply store? I found one an hour or so northwest of here. How about we spend the day in Bangor?"

I sat up straighter. "I'd love to! Let me just go get changed into real people clothes." I was wearing yoga pants and a sweatshirt.

"Go ahead. I'll just finish my muffin." He shooed me away.

I returned ten minutes later with my curling hair piled in a loose bun, wearing jeans and a turtleneck with my new black coat. Chaucer stood and wagged his tail, expecting to be invited. I leaned over and gave him a hug and tummy scratch. "Sorry, little man. I can't take you. You'd be sitting in a car for hours." I walked him into the kitchen. "Come on. I'll get you a treat."

The drive from Bar Harbor to Bangor was lovely. The trees blazed with color, and the Saturday-morning traffic was light. Connor directed us downtown to a large warehouse in an industrial area.

"We're not buying anything," I assured him. "We're taking pictures, making notes, measuring. We're on a fact-finding mission only. Okay?"

He just smiled and nodded absently.

The warehouse was filled to bursting with furniture sets and fixtures, place settings and utensils, appliances and decor. The picture in my head of the diner changed with each new arrangement I saw, but we hadn't yet hit on the perfect one.

My phone buzzed. When I pulled it out of my pocket, I saw I had a text from Aiden. I glanced around to make sure Connor wasn't paying attention. He was talking with a salesperson, so I pulled up the message.

Do you want to meet me downtown for lunch?

Can't. On a date.

…

So far, so good. He's nice and handsome. Tall, broad shoulders, blue eyes. I can send you a pic.

…

I took a quick photo of Connor sitting in a booth, his hand brushing the fabric, and sent it to Aiden.

He took me to this fabulous place in Bangor.

So, you're saying that damn old man stole my girl and you'll be gone all day?

My heart fluttered. "My girl." I tried to shake it off. It probably was just a phrase, didn't mean more than that, but…

Your girl? Says who?

I believe I just did. Why is he petting a seat?

My heart beat faster. I could feel my face reddening.

We're at a restaurant supply warehouse, checking out things for the diner.

Hell, I was planning to take you to a place like that.

I smiled, warm and happy.

"Did you find one you liked?" Connor walked up next to me, to see what had me smiling.

"Oh, no. I was just thinking." I slipped the phone back into my coat pocket, as we continued down the aisle. "There are a lot of beautiful furniture sets, but they're just not right."

He stopped walking. "We could go grab some lunch and then come back with fresher brains and eyes."

"No. I'm okay. We only have a few more rows." Connor looked tired, so I changed the suggestion. "You know what? I'm just going to run up and down the last aisles. You sit here and I'll pick you up on the way back. Then we can go get that lunch."

He nodded. "I wouldn't say no to a rest." He sat down on the nearest banquette and waved me away.

When I turned a corner, I pulled my phone back out.

Kate? Call me when you're on your way back to BH.

Sorry. Connor snuck up on me. That man moves as silently as you do. I had to ditch my phone.

Why?

I didn't want him to see who I was texting.

Why?

I paused, not knowing how to answer that. Were we a couple? Or did he mean that friends texted, so what was the big deal? He called me his girl... What the hell were the rules for this kind of thing? My phone buzzed again.

Don't keep Pops out too late. He tires easily.

I won't. We're going to lunch in a few and then we'll drive back. Can we talk about the other stuff later?

Of course. Drive safely and let me know when you get home. I'd like to see you tonight.

I stood for a few moments, lost in thought, drowning in memories of Aiden. Shit. I was supposed to be checking out furniture. I looked up and saw it, the perfect set. It was exactly as I'd pictured it.

I raced back around the corner. "Connor, come look!"

I dragged him to see the set, and we both agreed that it suited my vision. Then we headed to grab something to eat.

After lunch, we visited Paul Bunyan's statue and took pictures. When Connor went to the restroom, I pulled out my phone again and texted the picture I'd taken of me with the giant to Aiden.

Look! Your taller, whiskered, ax-weilding twin!

I waited for a response until I saw Connor returning. I felt my phone buzz just as I was dropping it in my pocket. I made a half turn, blocking my phone arm. He'd sent me a pic. I couldn't wait until later so I turned a little farther, opening my messages and clicking on the photo. It was of Aiden standing in deep snow, laughing, and he had a beard. Damn, how could he still look so gorgeous with half of his face covered in hair? It was bullshit, that's what it was.

"Should we head back now?"

I turned, dropping my phone back into my pocket and nodding. "Yep. Let's hit the road."

CHAPTER THIRTY

Aiden

I CHECKED MY PHONE AGAIN. She'd seen the snow photo but hadn't responded. Maybe beards weren't a good look for me. I was working in her kitchen, Chaucer at my heels. He had been lying down watching me prepare food before he realized that, unlike Kate, I drop food all the time. Ever since that revelation, he'd been tripping me up, trying to get as close to the potential floor food as possible.

Yes. Technically, I was breaking and entering, but I wanted to make her dinner, and I honestly wasn't positive the appliances in my sad galley kitchen worked. Plus my apartment was kind of depressing. I hadn't noticed that before.

I'd stopped at the market and picked up steaks, potatoes and a bag of salad. Since I was hungry, I also picked up chips and salsa, cheese and crackers, and a package of thinly sliced Italian meats. As soon as I pulled the meat from the shopping bag, Chaucer sat down at my side, expectant. I knew I probably wasn't supposed to give him any, but how was I supposed to resist that face? "Just don't tell her, okay?"

I held out two pieces of meat, which Chaucer took slowly and gently from my fingers, then swallowed whole in one second flat. "Are there any doggy breath mints around here? We need to cover up your salami breath before Katie gets home."

I walked over to the pantry and stuck my head in. "*Organic* dog biscuits? Yeah, we're going to need to keep this salami thing under wraps, okay?" Chaucer sat near doggy-treat Valhalla, waiting to see if I'd do him a solid. I flipped a biscuit and watched him jump up and snap it out of the air. "I think I just figured out how we're going to kill time waiting for your mommy."

After finishing a quick run downtown to pick up a grill—who the hell doesn't own a grill?—Chaucer and I were hanging out on the porch, me sitting with my feet up on the rail, him running around, catching flying biscuits, when I heard a vehicle pull up. Chaucer tore off around the corner. No barking, so it must have been Katie.

I started jogging around the corner myself. But when I realized I was acting like her over-excited dog, I slowed to a stop and watched her get out of her car. My heart lurched. My woman was coming home, and I was here to meet her. This felt right. Hell, it felt perfect.

"What are you doing out here?" She looked at

the front door. "Holy crap, did I leave the back door open? And you stayed here, waiting for me?" She leaned over, hugging Chaucer. "You're the best boy ever! Hey, why do you smell like biscuits?" She stood up and looked around, spotting me leaning against the corner of the house. She stared at me for a moment, before a slow smile spread across her face. Thank God. That could have been awkward.

"Breaking into my house and bribing my dog, huh?" She walked up the steps toward me, and I waited, content to watch.

"Call a cop."

She stopped right in front of me, reached out and grabbed my T-shirt, yanking me toward her. "Help, police, help."

I leaned in, my lips hovering over hers. "What's the nature of your call?" I grinned. "Ma'am." I watched her eyes go from soft and hazy to sharp and annoyed. I swooped in to take her mouth before she could protest. I ran my hands beneath her coat, gliding over her hips and down to her perfect ass. I considered writing sonnets to the perfection of her ass as I grabbed the back of her legs and picked her up, hitching her around my waist.

I walked us back around the side of the house, stepping through the open dining room door and then kicking it closed. I'd intended to start cooking dinner when she arrived, but that wasn't happening, not for a while. I took the stairs to her room two at a time.

Kate

AFTERWARD, AIDEN AND I lay in bed, our legs tangled, our faces inches apart on the same pillow, as we breathed each other's air and whispered the contents of our hearts. I reached up and traced his lips with my fingertips.

"No secrets, okay?" Aiden said softly. "No hiding, not from ourselves, not from each other. Up-front and honest. I can't take more lies."

I felt myself drawing back. "I never lied to—"

He reached for my hand and pulled it to his chest. "Not you." He shook his head. "You've been remarkably honest. Alarmingly so, really."

I pushed against his chest. "Funny guy."

He pretended to bite my hand, but then kissed it instead. "I've been a miserable bastard for the past year." His hand settled possessively on my hip. "But then this crazy wind blew through town, clearing my head. You make me happy, Katie."

"Was it bad?" We were already wrapped around each other, but the look on his face made me want to hold him closer.

His eyes drifted toward the window. "Wedding, ring, tux, church, offer on a little house across town, the whole nine yards."

"Sounds perfect."

"Perfect." He popped the *p* sound, lengthening the word. "She dumped me the day before the wedding. Another richer, more powerful guy waited in the wings."

My body tensed, remembering what that kind of shame and betrayal felt like. "Who is this brain-dead skank, and where can I find her? I'm good with a golf club. Seriously, I could mess her up for you."

He grinned. "Settle down, tiger. I'm not putting a contract out on her, but thanks for the offer of assault." He shook his head, his hand on my back, pulling me imperceptibly closer. "If I'd married her, I wouldn't be here with you."

I nodded. "Good point." My body relaxed into the idea. "Good riddance to people who don't recognize what they have."

He pressed a soft kiss on my nose. "Hear, hear."

"Do you miss her?" I held my breath, afraid of the answer.

"I did. At first. But mostly, I was so damn angry. Eventually the anger took up so much space that I didn't have room for missing. I was full yet weirdly hollow. I felt like a clueless sap for believing she ever loved me. I refused to allow myself to miss her." His thumb brushed back and forth over my ribs.

I felt unaccountably blessed that we'd found

each other and were willing to try again. I needed to change the subject, though, to get that hurt out of his eyes. "Have you lived in Bar Harbor all these years?"

"Nah." His finger slid along my jaw and down my throat. "I went to college in Boston, then joined their police force. That was where I met Brian, our friendly neighborhood hacker."

I shivered at his touch. "Did you like it there?"

He nodded. "Mmm-hmm. I loved Boston, but Maureen was getting married, and Pops was getting older. Mom's arthritis was getting worse." He gave a small shrug. "My thoughts were more often in this town. It seemed stupid to stay there when the people I loved lived here."

"I bet they were happy to get you back."

He grinned. "That'd probably depend on which day you asked them."

I let my hand settle on his heart, content to feel it beat. "Police work here is probably different."

He let out a short chuff of amusement. "You could say that. Very few mob-related crimes or gun deaths in Bar Harbor. Unless you count accidental stray bullets during hunting season, and that hasn't resulted in a death in almost a decade." His hand spread on my hip, and he pulled me a few inches closer. "What about you? This is a bigger transition for the Cali girl with no family here." His hand slid up to my waist. "How are you doing?"

"First of all, it's always *California*, never *Cali*."

His hand slid over my hip and down my leg, pulling it more securely over his body. "I'll try to keep that in mind."

"See that you do." I felt myself blushing and thanked the darkness he wouldn't notice. "I'm doing well. Now."

He leaned in and kissed me. "I'm glad."

"I didn't know where else to go, what to do. After… Well, I just needed to get away, to find a home for Chaucer and me. I loved my summers here, and I needed to feel near Gran."

He pulled me even closer, his warm breath fanned across my chilled skin. I shivered, and he pulled the comforter around my shoulders. "I'm glad you came home."

I placed my hand on his scruffy cheek and then pulled his shoulder toward me. He rolled over on top of me, kissing me deep and long. He drew back and stared at me, while pulling open my nightstand drawer, indicating the vast collection of condoms. "Now you may explain."

My hands flew to my face, covering the top half. "Do I hafta?" I felt his lips touch my hands.

"Nope. It just seemed like an interesting story." He kissed my lips. "And secrets make me crazy, as you know. I obsess over the whys and hows. It makes me a good cop, but an annoying partner." He paused.

His girl, his partner. Did he mean it? I still wasn't looking at him, relying on that universal truth that if I couldn't see him, he couldn't see me. He kissed me, so I may have been misled about the effectiveness of this strategy.

He nuzzled my arm. "You have a latex deficiency and the doctor prescribed more condoms."

I smiled, but didn't say anything.

He ran lips along my other arm. "You planned to attend an orgy on your drive East, but weren't sure of the colors and sizes necessary to properly cover all your partners."

"That totally happened. I had to restock afterward."

"Please, tell me these are not the same condoms you threw off the Fourth of July float fifteen years ago. Because if so, we're in a lot of trouble."

"They're fresh!"

"Thank God. You lost a bet and—"

I slapped my hands over his mouth. We could see each other now. I moved one hand over his eyes and kept the other over his mouth. I felt him kiss my palm. I took a deep breath. "When I found out Justin had been cheating on me, I panicked. Aside from how incredibly crappy and betrayed I was feeling, I was also terrified he'd given me an STD. I made an appointment at a clinic to get screened."

I shook my head, recalling the experience. "It was fairly horrible. I'd never had to get tested before. I felt so dirty." I felt Aiden trying to say something, so I clamped my hand down tighter. "I know. I know. It's the mature, responsible thing to do, but that's the way I felt. Justin's the only person I've ever slept with—huh, I guess I can't say that anymore." I felt another palm kiss.

"Anyway, the doctor was totally nice and understanding. I was freaking out and told him everything, but he was gentle and calming. When I was leaving, he picked up the bowl of condoms they kept on the counter and tipped it into my purse. He said, 'Don't let embarrassment make you unsafe.'"

I let me hands drop, gauging his reaction. "I'm clean. I wouldn't have slept with you otherwise."

He leaned down and kissed me softly. "It sucks, doesn't it? I did the same thing when she left." He cringed. "But in the interest of full disclosure and no secrets, I went on a tear after she dumped me. I slept with quite a few women in a short amount of time. Not too proud of that, but there you go. And, yes, I've been tested since. Still clean."

He kissed my neck and said, "How long before you think we'll need to replenish the drawer?"

I glanced over at the pile of shiny wrappers. "Probably a week."

He laughed. "That's my girl."

CHAPTER THIRTY-ONE

Aiden

I woke in the gray light of predawn. Katie lay curled up next to me, her hair fanned out on the pillow. Just looking at her made my heart ache. Her hand rested by her cheek, fingers twitching as though reaching for something in a dream. I considered how I was going to wake her up this time. When she let out a soft, barely audible mewling sound, I hardened in reaction, slowly pulling the sheet down to expose a hip in need of kisses.

I couldn't get enough of her, couldn't touch enough, couldn't taste enough. I could do this. *I could.* For Katie, I could try again. For her, I'd do anything. I lov—no.

My heart raced and I started to sweat. Shit. I thought I'd protected myself against this. I didn't want to feel this way again. Never again. I didn't want to ever feel that kind of pain again. What the hell was I doing? When Alice betrayed and dumped me, I was hurt. Looking back on it, though, I think I was mostly humiliated. If

Katie were to leave me, I'd be done. There'd be nothing left of me.

I picked up my clothes in the dark and sneaked out like the pathetic human being I was. Hero? No. That wasn't me anymore.

Kate

I woke to the first hints of pink light filtering through the filmy sheers on the windows. I stretched and felt a twinge of soreness, spurring memories of the night before. Aiden and I couldn't get enough of each other. As soon as we settled down to sleep, one of us would kiss or stroke the other, playfulness turning quickly to mindless passion, lust turning to something much deeper. I got very little rest, but it was the most profoundly erotic night of my life.

I shifted, cautiously looking over my shoulder for Aiden. He wasn't there. Chaucer was snoring on the floor by the door, which meant Aiden wasn't downstairs making coffee either or Chaucer would be with him, trying to mooch food. I spied the nightstand and bureau. No notes. It was early Sunday morning. Where had he gone?

I slid my hand over to the other side of the bed. It was cold. Aiden had left a while ago. Grabbing my phone, I dialed his cell first. When I received no answer, I texted.

Morning! We never discussed terms of endearment. Are you good with Scooter Pie because I've always wanted a fella I could call Scooter Pie. Listen, Scooter Pie, you should have told me you needed to work today. I almost feel bad for keeping you up all night. Almost. How about if I bring you muffins this morning? What's your favorite kind?

When he didn't get back to me right away, I decided to take a quick shower and then start baking. If he was too busy to respond, he'd get what he got.

An hour later, I packed up a basket of chocolate chip and pecan muffins and headed into town. The little parking lot at the police station was mostly empty, but Aiden's truck was there. When I walked in, there was a new person at the front desk, an older woman.

"Hi, I'm Kate. I'm here to see Aiden. Is he available?"

She nodded, picking up the phone. "Let me check, dear. You can have a seat if you'd like."

When she hung up, she said, "I'm sorry, dear. He's in a meeting."

"I don't want to bother him. Could you just give him these?" I placed the basket on her desk. "They're still warm, so he should eat one soon." I waved over my shoulder on my way out. "Have a good one."

I left my car in the lot, wandering down Main Street, window-shopping and feeling very lucky in my new life. I grinned, thinking about Aiden's butt. He had an amazing butt, and I could totally grab it anytime I felt like it. Mostly. You know, not while he was on duty or anything.

I was considering the possibilities of other girlfriend perks when I realized I was standing in front of Mo's shop. She had a gorgeous, watercolor wraparound dress displayed in the window. I wondered if it would look good on me, if Aiden would like it.

I saw movement inside the darkened store. The silhouette of a woman waved. I waved back, hoping it was Mo and not a thief. That'd be awkward. It occurred to me, as I watched Mo walk toward the door, that I liked Aiden's family, too, and they liked me. The joy I was feeling, turned warm and fuzzy. A real family that loved each other and wanted to spend time together, I missed that so much.

Mo was just opening the door when I heard my name shouted. I turned to find Aiden jogging toward me. He'd said he wanted to be my fella, and he seemed to mean it.

I moved toward him. He stopped, but I kept going, walking into him, hugging him tightly. "Did you run all this way to thank me for the muffins?" I tilted my head back, my chin resting on his chest. "Did you like them?"

He looked aside, gripped my arms and pushed me away. His expression closed off.

"Are you allergic to pecans?" My head began to pound. "Am I not supposed to hug you when you're on duty? My hands were nowhere near your butt. Honest."

"I need to talk to you."

My stomach dropped. "Okay." I turned. Mo stood in the door, looking as confused as I felt.

"Go away," he said to his sister.

Mo ducked back in the shop and closed the door.

He dragged his hands through his hair. "I can't do this."

"Can't—which *this*? Eat muffins? Talk to me while you're at work? Hug me? What can't you do?"

He appeared shocked at my words. Shaking his head, he regrouped. "Us. The friends with bennies was a failure, and I'm not boyfriend material. I don't do love anymore. I can't, you know that."

"A failure?" I was a failure. Again. I'd fallen for a man who couldn't or wouldn't love me back. Again.

"Yes."

"I see." I wanted to slink away, to hide. I wanted to pack up my dog and hit the road. Again. Not this time, though. I was so angry, I fisted my hand and punched him right in the face. He blinked, unfazed. I was pretty sure I'd broken my whole hand, so the fact that he hadn't felt it just made him that much more of an asshole. "I can't believe I thought you were a hero." My hand throbbed painfully. "Boo-hoo, Aiden. Did you have your heart broken once? You think that gives you license to be an asshole the rest of your life? A coward, Aiden. That's what you are." I walked away, back to my car, my broken hand cradled to my chest.

Okay, it wasn't broken but it hurt like hell! I'd need to get ice on it as soon as possible. After the swelling went down, I planned to punch him again. With a bat. That would hurt my hand less.

When I got home, Chaucer whined and tried to lick my hand, sweet boy. I put ice in a waterproof bag, wrapped it around my hand with a dish towel. I didn't want to sit and think, so I took Chaucer for a walk along the cliffs, overlooking the surf.

I pulled Gran's rain parka close across my chest. I should have made a sling for my stupid hand. It would have been easier than carrying a homemade ice pack.

The bitter winds coming off the whitecaps seeped right through the fabric, chilling me to the bone. Dark storm clouds were moving to the south. Chaucer, however, was in his element. He stood at the bluff, his head up to the driving wind, looking like nothing so much as the figurehead on the prow of a ship. He was quivering in anticipation.

"Okay, boy, go!" I shouted over the wind. He didn't need any more encouragement than that. He crouched, tipping his weight back before cannoning off the ledge, dropping six feet toward the teeming water below. He surfaced a moment later, sounding a deep bark of joy.

Seagrass waved in the wind, tickling my legs through my jeans. I plopped down at the land's end and watched my baby swim in the ocean, rolling with the waves. Black clouds, heavy with rain, sped across the sky, blotting out the sun. A storm was coming. I could have called Chaucer, made him come to me so we could avoid the pelting rain, but I didn't. Instead, I sat in the deluge.

I loved Aiden, had poured out my heart to him, and he called it a failure. That's what he thought of me. A failure. If I'd been better, smarter, prettier, maybe I could have made him forget the one who broke his heart. But apparently, I couldn't even make him *want* to forget the hurt. A failure.

The storm battered me but I withstood, my anger and shame running in rivulets down my face and body, soaking into the ground.

When I stood on my front porch an hour later, chilled to the bone, my teeth chattering, what remained was the suffocating pain of rejection.

"KATIE, ARE YOU UP THERE?" The stairs creaked under Connor's weight.

I bolted upright in the cooling water. When we'd returned from the rain, I'd needed a hot bath to warm up. I looked down at my naked body. I didn't even have any bubbles left to hide beneath. "I'm in the bath." Panic was clear in my tone.

His voice came from the hall, right outside the open doors to my bedroom and bath. "Oh, sorry. I shouldn't have barged in. I just thought we could go over plans for the diner this morning. Maybe drive down to the property and do a walk-through. And then I thought when we were done we could have lunch in town, if you don't already have plans today."

Good things—my life was filled with good things, like this man right here. "I'd love to do that. Can you give me a couple of minutes to get dried and dressed?"

"Take your time. Chaucer and I will keep each other company." At the sound of his name, Chaucer stood and padded out of the bathroom. Funny, he must already know Connor's sounds and smells. He didn't even start at the sound of Connor's voice.

I wasn't feeling up to makeup or much grooming for that matter, finger-combing through the wet curls and calling it good. My hand still hurt, but the swelling had gone down, thankfully. I had a towel wrapped around me when I stepped into the bedroom from the attached bath. I could hear Connor's voice, but it was coming from downstairs. It sounded like he was talking to someone.

"Aiden, can you meet me for lunch today?… Good. I was thinking maybe Geddy's at about noon…Hmm…Yeah, Katie'll be with me…What's that?…Well, couldn't you rearrange it?…All right. Maybe another time."

I closed the door to the bedroom, not wanting to hear any more. We slept together and he chewed off his arm to get away. That's right. Katie Gallagher, the human equivalent of a bear trap. Screw everyone who thought I wasn't good enough, that I'd be acceptable if only I'd… Whatever! This was me. I was done apologizing for who I was. Don't like me? Get bent and move along. I had better things to do than worry over your disapproval.

I pulled out a pair of jeans, new but worn-looking. I was going to embrace my new life philosophy with comfy clothes. I pulled on a light green, long-sleeve thermal top and Grandpa's button-up fisherman's sweater. It was cream, hung down almost to my knees and had leather patches at the elbows. It was perfect.

I glanced at myself in the mirror. My face was clean. My freckles were more obvious, and my hair was pulling up into my natural corkscrew curls. Yep, I was ready to go.

Connor rounded the corner from the kitchen

and stood at the base of the stairs, a huge grin breaking across his face. "There's my little Katie Gallagher," he said as I stepped down to the floor. "Where have you been, my girl? I've sorely missed you."

I was unaccountably choked up by his greeting. I swallowed. "It's good to be home," I said as he leaned forward and brushed a kiss across my forehead.

He held out his elbow for me to take. I grabbed my bag and slapped my thigh, inviting Chaucer to join us before taking Connor's elbow, letting him lead me out the door and down the front steps.

We all got into my car, and I drove into town. Luckily, I found street parking just two doors down from the leased property. Chaucer jumped out and followed us. Connor pulled out his keys and then a small notebook from his shirt pocket, waving it at me. "We'll take notes on any changes you think the place needs. Where you want your new seating to go, et cetera."

The space smelled musty. "How long has it been vacant?" I asked.

"Oh, let's see. It freed up four or five months ago now. I've had a few people inquire, but the rent is expensive, and I'm picky. I don't rent to just anyone, you know." He winked.

Good point. "You know, Gran left me some money, but I don't know if I have enough to make

this happen. We might be getting ahead of ourselves." Businesses cost bank to start up. "How
much is the rent, anyway?" Shit, a prime location
on Main Street just two blocks from the pier in
Bar Harbor, Maine. There was no way I'd be able
to afford this place. It was probably five thousand or more a month, and then there were the
renovations to consider, licenses and permits...
My stomach started to cramp.

"Well—" he strolled to the window, looking
out "—this is a great property, excellent location,
the owner has kept it clean and safe. You'd only
need to make cosmetic changes. Let's see, taking all that into account, how about if I charge
you...one dollar a month?" He turned, taking in
my stunned expression before patting my shoulder as he walked past.

"Connor, you can't charge me one dollar.
That's ridiculous!"

"Too much? I did love your grandmother, but
I have a business to run, you know."

"No, that's not right. If you picked another
tenant you could be making five thousand times
that amount—"

"Probably. I guess it wouldn't make much
sense, me settling for only a dollar, then. Would
it? Strange, since apparently I'm going to." He
smiled and cut me off when I opened my mouth
to argue the gift was too great.

"Katie, honey, I'm an old man. I own my house

as well as a couple of other properties like this one. I don't need the rent money, or I wouldn't have left it empty for five months. I had a feeling I should wait, and it turned out I was right. I want to do this. I want to be a part of this new venture, and I'm asking if you'll let me. This is what I can do. I can't cook and I'm not much for waiting tables, but I can do this. All right?"

My throat burned. I crossed to him and buried my head in his chest, hugging him tightly. He held me, and I realized that I was wrong. Aiden wasn't home; this was. This man, this town was my home. I nodded, my head still against his shirt. "All right."

"Good." He patted my back. "Now, let's go look at the kitchen, see if we need to make any changes in there."

An hour later we were sitting in Geddy's, baskets of fish and chips on the polished wood table before us; a large group of noisy tourists in lobster bibs sat across the main room. It was lively and fun, servers joking with the customers as well as among themselves. Eclectic decorations lined the walls. I smiled at the flirty mermaid who watched over our table. The energy of the restaurant matched my own, as ideas for Nellie's Kitchen whizzed through my head, one barely taking hold before another pushed it aside.

"So, will the kitchen do or should we make some changes?"

"Connor, I know I've said this before, but I don't think you're listening. I have no idea what I'm doing. I've never done anything like this before. My opinion means nothing, less than nothing."

"Don't be silly. You've cooked for people before. This will just be on a larger scale." He stopped to think for a minute. "Maybe we should do a test run. Buy whatever ingredients you'll need for a few different breakfast items, and then you can cook for me and Aiden, maybe some of the kids from the police station who have some free time, so we can see how the kitchen works for you and what we need to do to make it better." He smiled at his ingenuity and took out his cell phone, beginning to text.

I mumbled. "This ought to be good."

"Hmm?" He looked up inquiringly.

I shook my head. "Nothing." I played with the remaining fries on my plate, making designs by swirling them through the ketchup. Aiden wouldn't agree to this, and I'd forgotten my bat at home. I needed to start carrying that thing around with me.

"How can he be busy all the time?" Connor grumbled as he replaced his phone in his pocket. "Never mind about that. Jack would love a free breakfast, and I could get a few more retired cronies who'll jump at the chance to have a pretty woman cook for them." His grin was infectious, and took some of the sting out of Aiden's continued rejection.

I excused myself, heading to the restroom. I needed to shake it off. Fuckers gonna fuck. Dicks gonna dick.

"Hello again, Kate. It's Cady now, isn't it? I heard you got married."

That Nancy woman came out of a stall. She looked perfect, as usual, but there was a meanness in her eyes that gave me pause. "Actually, Gallagher is fine."

She paused at the sink. "But I thought I heard you were married now." Her voice was sharp and insinuating.

I took a deep breath. This was life in a small town, everyone in your business. "I'm in the process of divorcing." I tilted my head, studying her. "I'm sorry, what was your name again?" Because fuck her.

Her smile was brittle. "Nancy Wilkins. Well, it's certainly been a while." She looked me up and down. "It must be hard, going through a divorce. The failure of love is tragic, isn't it?" Her tone was solicitous as she asked, "Having a hard time sleeping?"

"What?" I looked at my reflection in the mirror. Did I look haggard? I saw a brief smirk in my peripheral vision. "You know, it's funny, Nancy. I just don't remember you at all. I'm sure I saw you often as a child, but—" I shrugged, shaking my head "—some people I remember like it was yesterday, while others, nothing." I walked out of the restroom, back to Connor.

When he saw me, he tossed his napkin on the table and pulled out some money, leaving it under his plate. "Come on. We've got some groceries to buy, and how about we stop off at the hardware store and check out paint colors for the walls?"

Shake it off, Kate. "You bet. That sounds great."

My mind was buzzing when I dropped Connor off at his place. I had paint samples in my bag and catalogs of dishware and cookware. I couldn't wait to lay it all out on the table and geek out, choosing colors and designs. "Thanks, Connor." I grabbed and squeezed his hand. "You've turned a monumentally crappy day into one of my best days ever." I leaned forward and kissed his cheek. "I think you may be my fairy godfather."

He chuckled. "Pleasure's all mine." He hopped out and then leaned back in. "Do some thinking, and we can meet again tomorrow to plan." He waved. "Have a good evening, sweetheart."

A FEW DAYS LATER, I sat on the floor of the diner, Chaucer at my side, and gazed at the newly painted walls. "I love it! Don't you love it?" I studied the antique gold of the Italian plaster. It was perfect, just how I'd pictured it in my head. I pulled the dishware catalog into my lap, placed adhesive flags next to me and began to narrow down my top ten.

I heard the back door open. Chaucer stood and growled, low and soft. I wasn't expecting anyone and didn't realize the back door was unlocked. I would have assumed it was Connor or Bear except for Chaucer's reaction. I stood silently, braced for what was coming.

"Katherine." Justin stood in the doorway to the kitchen, his face strangely blank.

My body tensed, readying for the insult. Old habits were hard to break. I reached out to place my hand on Chaucer's head. The growling stopped immediately.

Justin followed my hand, his gaze resting on Chaucer. "Of course, the dog you keep. The husband you throw out." He studied me. "I see your priorities and common sense haven't improved during this little vacation of yours." He glanced down at the catalog and the notes I was making. A smirk lifted one side of his perfect mouth. "Oh, Katherine, really? Tell me someone didn't actually hire you to run a restaurant. That is—" he shook his head "—ridiculous. And pathetic."

He sauntered around the room, studying the layout. "Your lawyer contacted me. She gave me divorce papers to sign. What will you do if I refuse?" He turned to watch me. "Even if I were to sign the papers, it takes months to finalize an uncontested divorce. If you're thinking you can live off alimony—my money, Katherine—for the rest of your life, you'd better think again. I'd rather be unemployed and living on the streets than give you another dime." He smiled cruelly. "Whatever will you do?"

I laughed and shook my head. "God, you're like a villain in a soap opera. Why the hell did I let you tie me up in knots for so long?" I made a shooing motion with my hand. "Go. Twirl your mustache somewhere else."

He stepped toward me, anger lining his face.

I held up a staying hand. "Justin, you don't love me. I doubt you ever did. California is a no-fault state. We have no children—"

"Thank God," he interjected. "You're so stupid, Katherine. Why do you think you never got pregnant? I had that taken care of before we were even married. I did not want a fat wife running after snotty kids. No. That was not going to be my life."

I don't know what happened. He was sneering at me one minute, and then staggering back, blood dripping from his nose the next. I shook out my quickly swelling hand. Where the hell was my bat? "Strictly speaking, I don't think it's stupid to love and trust your husband, but, yes, I was stupid not to have seen the kind of man you are, not to have left you sooner."

Chaucer stepped in front of me, hackles raised, his deep growl vibrating through the floor. Justin stopped, wiping the blood from his lip, uncertainty flitting across his features.

"I wouldn't if I were you, Justin. Chaucer hates you even more than I do." It was my turn to smirk. I could read the conflict as clear as day. He was frightened by Chaucer but didn't want to back down, admit defeat. Chaucer leaned forward and Justin stepped back.

I heard the back door open again. "Katie? Can I talk to you, please?" Aiden stepped out from the kitchen and stopped short. "Oh, excuse me." His gaze ran over Justin, assessing the situation. Chaucer was still growling, the fur between his shoulders standing up. Aiden moved forward, towering over Justin's slim athletic five feet nine inches. Aiden's muscles flexed as he crossed his arms. "Kate, will you introduce me to your friend?"

"He's not a friend. This is my ex-husband, Justin Cady."

"So, that's it, is it?" Justin had found his voice. "You've already found another man to take care of you. How long, Katherine? How long before you jumped into some other man's bed?"

"Gee, I don't know. I've kinda been juggling two of 'em. This one and one that's even bigger and better-looking."

Justin spit out, "Whore." Before he could finish his sneer, Aiden had him slammed against the wall. He'd grabbed Justin's perfectly pressed white button-down and was holding him by the fabric he'd fisted at Justin's throat. Justin struggled, turning red.

"Apologize." Aiden looked huge and frightening as hell as he made the demand.

I put my hand on Aiden's arm. He didn't relax his grip, but he let me take over. "I wasn't trolling for dates on our honeymoon. I didn't cheat on you throughout our marriage. That was you. Watch who you're calling a whore."

It was impossible for him to maintain any dignity while Aiden held him. "Yes, fine, I apologize. That was beneath me."

Aiden didn't release him so much as bounce him off the wall.

I straightened my spine. "Why are you here, Justin? You didn't travel three thousand miles to tell me you think I'm pathetic." Aiden's hands fisted. "What do you want?"

Tipping his chin, arrogance returned, he said, "The car, Katherine. I want my car. It's perfection."

I smirked. "Yeah, not so much anymore."

"Side panels and windows can be replaced. The mechanical precision cannot." His eyes shifted to Aiden, quickly assessing. "I saw it parked in back. I have my own keys and it's mine. I'm merely being considerate, telling you I'm taking it."

A bitter laugh rushed out. "Oh, yeah. You're nothing if not considerate. Whatever. Take the car. It's not like I have fond memories of it." My hand fell to Chaucer. "Or that it fits us. Okay, are we done now? Have you said all the hateful things you needed to say?" Not waiting for an answer, I went on, "Yes? Good? See ya, Justin. Our lawyers can hash out the rest. This is my home now, and as you have no business in Bar Harbor, we never have to see each other again."

"Let me walk you out." Aiden held out his hand, leading Justin toward the kitchen. Justin walked quickly through the restaurant and out the back door, with Aiden close on his heels.

I stood, trying to absorb how my day had so suddenly changed. It seemed impossible that I had just been admiring the walls and picking out dishes. Aiden walked in a few moments later. He was shaking out a hand before he noticed me watching him.

Expression tender, concerned, he asked, "Are you okay?"

I was doing fine until he started in with the kindness. My eyes flooded and I turned away. He grabbed my arm and pulled me back to him, crushing me against his chest. But I wasn't having it. I pushed him away.

"Stop. I don't like you any better than him."

His shoulders slumped. "I know. I—" He stuffed his hand in his pockets. "Something you said. I realized I was acting just like—I was being an asshole—"

"Yes. My point exactly. Thank you." I slapped my thigh. "Come on, Chaucer. We're out of here."

"You don't have a car."

"But I have feet." I picked up the catalogs and opened the front door. "Lock the back on your way out." I didn't look at him, couldn't look at him, as I locked the front door. Who the hell did he think he was? Rushing in, looking all hot and fierce, and then giving me his don't-hate-me-because-I-dumped-you sad eyes.

When we started walking up the street, I realized we were missing something. "Your leash was in the car! Damn it. Even when Justin's not here, he sucks." I tapped my leg and said "Heel," bringing in Chaucer close to my side. How many miles away was Gran's house?

A few minutes later, Aiden's truck pulled up next to us, keeping pace. The window rolled down. "Katie, are you really going to walk the two miles home?"

Pfft. Two miles. "That's nothing, right, buddy?" Chaucer watched Aiden, but kept pace by my side.

"Most of it uphill."

Sighing, continuing to stare straight ahead, I stopped. "How steep?"

"Very. You'll probably need climbing ropes, crampons, a harness."

Bland look engaged, I turned to the open window. "Really?" I needed a special bat backpack so I'd have it at all times.

"Yes, *really*. And as I'm headed that direction, anyway…" He leaned over and threw open the passenger door.

Chaucer started for the truck. I hissed, and he sat, looking back and forth between us. I pulled my phone out of my back pocket and tapped the screen. "Hey, you busy?…Awesome…Chaucer and I are walking up Main. Could you give us a lift home?…Great! I'll explain on the ride." I glanced over at an annoyed Aiden. "And could you hurry? I've got a creeper lurking."

"Please, let me drive you home. I need to talk to you." He sounded hurt, the self-centered jerk. I was the injured party, not him.

"I need a lot of things, too, Aiden. First and foremost, people in my life who like me, who make me feel good about myself—like the guy who's racing over here to take me home. What I don't need is a man who makes me feel like crap on a regular basis. One who pulls me close and holds me tight, who waits until I begin to trust and start to feel steady, and then walks away."

I grabbed the open door and looked him in the eye. "I'm not here to fulfill your secret adolescent dreams. And I'm not the proxy for every woman who's ever done you wrong, either. We all get our hearts broken. Grow up!" I slammed the door and continued walking up Main, Chaucer by my side. Bear would find us.

CHAPTER THIRTY-TWO

Aiden

I DROVE AROUND TOWN, down along the water, up through Acadia National Park, my thoughts cycling. She was right. I had the greatest woman in the world, and I'd dumped her. With extreme prejudice.

I parked by a river and pulled out my phone to look at that stupid pity mug shot for the hundredth time. Those big green eyes, so lost, that fiery hair she'd tried to tame, that adorable look of outrage on her face, it killed me. She killed me.

When the sky turned pink in its setting, I was no closer to a way to win her back than I had been when she'd walked away from me on Main. I was a jackass. A doomed, heartsick jackass. There were a few things I could do, though, and it was long past time I manned up and did them.

I pulled up to Katie's house an hour later. I didn't go to her door, instead walking around back to the woodpile. I'd made a promise I'd neglected to keep. That needed to stop. A lot of things needed to stop.

Chaucer's huge head watched from the window, but he had yet to alert Katie to my presence. Interesting. I'd chopped three logs into quarters before I heard the back door open.

"Please, leave me alone. Stop doing this kind of thing." Katie stepped to the edge of the porch, her arms crossed.

"I promised to chop your wood over a month ago. I'm sorry I'm late."

She sighed. "Is this some kind of weird Maine tradition? In California, when we don't like someone, so much so that we feel the need to humiliate them in public, we just stop all contact with that person. We definitely don't trespass on their property to make kindling."

"Can you turn on the light?"

Mumbling something about a bat, she leaned in the back door. The porch light flashed on. She grabbed a coat from just inside the door and put it on.

"You should have those things on motion sensors. It's safer," I said. *Chop, chop, chop.*

She peered into the dark beyond our circle of light, and shivered. "Whatever. Listen, can you just leave?"

She and Chaucer stood side by side and watched me chop four more logs. When I picked up an armload of quartered pieces and carried it to her wood box, her eyes followed me, brows furrowed.

"Can I ask you a question, Katie?" I put another log on the chopping block.

She hugged herself. "Is it why haven't I pulled out my granddaddy's shotgun yet?"

"Can we wipe the slate clean? Pretend we're meeting again right now for the first time? As if Pops asked me to chop the wood and I came back that same day to do it?"

"No."

"Can we call it a wash, then? You broke my heart when I was fourteen. I broke yours at thirty."

"I thought we agreed I was twenty-five. And what the hell are you talking about? I never broke your heart." She tucked her hands in her jacket and stamped her feet, confusion clear.

"That last summer you visited. It took me nine summers to work up my nerve. I finally approached you to ask you to the bonfire beach party. You turned away from me and laughed, said I was a little kid." I leaned on the ax, trying to read her face.

"I did not! I would *never* do that!"

"Except you did."

Spinning, she stomped to the back door, muttering under her breath. She turned back, arms crossed tightly. "I have no memory of this. None. Are you sure it was me?"

I explained the whole encounter, what was said, what she wore. She gazed off into the night, confusion obvious. When her face cleared, she said, "Are you shitting me? I was talking to Daisy about her little brother, her six-year-old little brother who said he wanted to marry me. I never even saw you!"

She moved away again but stopped. "And even if I had done that, what the hell, dude? What is the statute of limitations on hurting your feelings? I was fifteen. Are you such a petty manchild that you'd nurse that hurt for fifteen years? Holy crap! If that's the case, you'll never get over being dumped at the altar."

My chest hurt.

"Leave. Don't make me call another cop to arrest you."

CHAPTER THIRTY-THREE

Kate

I CLOSED AND locked the door, then switched off the lights. When I heard his truck pull away, I walked through the house and stepped out to the front porch. The night was cold and clear, stars blazed in the sky, surf pounded in the distance. It should have been beautiful. I sat down heavily on the top step, the will to move draining out of me.

Chaucer lay down next to me, leaning into my side. I wove my fingers through his fur. "Who does that? Who gets all sweet and romantic, making a person think she's understood and cared for, and then dumps her, citing an imagined slight from childhood? Men suck."

I rested my temple on the top of his head. "I thought I loved him, Chaucer." I remembered Aiden's arms around me, the tenderness in his eyes, the kisses he trailed down my neck. *No.* I clenched my fingers in Chaucer's fur. I wasn't going to think about that Jackhole anymore. He made his choice. He chose his hurt over me. I wanted to sob. Instead, I stood and walked back into the house, locking the door behind me.

I climbed the stairs. "I got rid of two men in one day. At least I'm becoming more efficient." Bear had talked to Connor about the Bronco sitting out in front of his house. Connor doesn't drive anymore. He tried to give it to me, but I said it was only a loan. And then thanked him profusely.

I walked into the bedroom, Chaucer following me. "Our lives are filled with good things." I hugged my baby. "Let's get some shut-eye. Lots to do tomorrow!"

When I turned out the light and climbed into bed, the tears finally came. Hidden in the dark, I allowed myself to mourn for what could have been. I loved him, but I'd get over it. Eventually.

CHAPTER THIRTY-FOUR

Aiden

THE GUILT WAS CRUSHING. I drove along the dark, cliff-side road where I'd found her weeks ago, sitting in her car, unsure of what to do. Pulling over into the exact spot she'd stopped, I followed her lead and reflected on my choices. I'd taken a woman who'd been cheated on, stripped of money and communications, struggling to live in a house I'd let fall to seed, and I'd decided she had it a little too good.

I couldn't remember ever feeling this level of shame. I liked thinking of myself in heroic terms, the way Katie had described me to Pops. She was right, though, what she said today. Being heroic when there was little cost to you isn't heroic. As soon as my heart was on the line, I turned cowardly. My chest constricted. I was a bitter, lonely coward. But I didn't want to be. I wanted to be the hero she deserved.

I drove to Pops's place. He'd been trying to give me relationship advice for years, and I'd been brushing him off. I was an idiot. He and

Grandma had been married for forty years. Happily, lovingly married for forty years. He grieved her passing, his heart broken, but he never wallowed in the pain, didn't blame the world. He eventually fell in love again and had another wonderful relationship. I should have been taking notes.

The lights were on, but Pops may have fallen asleep in front of the TV. I'd raised my hand to knock when he opened the door.

"What's the matter?"

"Why would you think—"

He waved me in. "You wouldn't be showing up unannounced this late for a chat. So, what's the matter?"

He sat in his chair and I took the couch. "I panicked and fucked up."

He nodded slowly, thoughtfully. "And how are you going to fix it?"

Blowing out a breath, I said, "I don't know. That's why I'm here."

"Well, you better tell me the whole story, so we can figure it out." He stood and headed toward the kitchen. "I think we're going to need a couple of beers for this."

After he returned and handed me a bottle, I went over all of it. I skated over the sex, but judging by the way he was glaring at me, he'd put two and two together. The man wasn't stupid. By the time I'd finished, he was up and pacing.

"You're my grandson and I love you, but I can't remember wanting to punch a man this much, not for a long time."

"Feel free to take a shot. If I could, I'd punch myself."

"On one hand, I want to help you get your girl. On the other, I want to protect her from you." He studied me. "I guess it depends on who I'm looking at. Are you the Aiden who took a slap from a mean old woman to protect another kid, or are you the Aiden who led Katie on and then dumped her?"

I sat, elbows on knees, my head in my hands. "I don't know. I want to be the first, but I'm afraid I'm the second."

"It's our choices, Aiden, that show who we truly are. Who are you choosing to be?"

I looked up at him, grinning. "Did you just quote Dumbledore to me?"

His face reddened as he gestured to the TV. "I was just watching—doesn't matter! It's true." He crossed his arms defensively, waiting for an answer.

"I love her, Pops. I want to be someone she can rely on. Someone she could love."

"And how are you going to prove to her that you're worth taking another chance on?"

I dropped back, sprawling on the couch. "Why do you think I'm here, old man? You're the expert. What should I do?"

Smiling, he sat down. "I am, aren't I? It's about time you realized it."

"Well?"

"Well, what? This is your mess. You figure it out." He got back up, went to the door and opened it. "If you love her, then you'll know what she needs. It's not a question of how you can get her to love *you*. You need to decide what you can do to love *her*." He opened the door. "And you need to do that on your own."

I scrubbed my hands over my face. "You're right." I stood. "Thanks for listening. And for the kick in the butt." I walked past him and stopped on the porch. "'What she needs.' I'll work on that. Thanks, Pops."

CHAPTER THIRTY-FIVE

Kate

THE CLOTHES I'D kicked off in the middle of the night lay on the floor. The pillow was still damp with tears, but it was a new day, the beginning of a new life, one I was going to embrace. I had my own house. Thank you, Gran. I was going to open a restaurant. Thank you, Connor. I had access to a handyman with an unlimited supply of kisses and inappropriate butt grabbing. Thank you, Bear. I had a full woodpile. Get bent, Aiden.

When I took Chaucer downstairs for breakfast, I found a letter taped to the pantry door. Points to Aiden for knowing the first place I'd go, but again with the breaking and entering? I was getting his ass arrested. And I wanted my key back, freaking pushy cop!

I fed Chaucer and then let him out, all the while staring at the envelope with my name in Aiden's handwriting as though it were a rabid snake.

After a cup of coffee and a piece of toast that I couldn't choke down, I womaned up and tore the letter off the pantry door. I swore that, if he made me feel like crap again, I was telling his grandpa on him.

Dearest Katie,
I can't begin to apologize for how I've treated you. I was so sure, you see. So sure I was right. I think, looking back, I felt wronged—through no wrongdoing on your part. I've been in love with you since I was five years old. You were the one all girls and then women were compared to and found wanting. You're gorgeous, but that's not it. Well, not all of it. You're funny and kick-ass. You're kind and so smart. Every woman has paled in comparison. As a kid, I waited for summer like it was my birthday, Halloween and Christmas all rolled up together. Summer meant you.

But then you stopped visiting, and all the light and color in my life drained away. I waited for you, assuming you'd be back, that it was just an off year. I spent that first summer planning what I would say or do to get your attention, so sure that the next summer you'd be back. But you weren't. I felt abandoned. I know that's stupid, but it's how I felt.

Alice used to complain that she didn't think I was fully committed to her. After she took off, I assumed that was how she justified leaving me for another man, but maybe she was right. I'd lost my heart to Katie Gallagher a long time ago.

Even now, after I've hurt and betrayed you, I can't stop thinking about you. Working, driving, sleeping, eating, it doesn't matter what I'm doing, thoughts of you bombard me, my hands on your soft, freckled skin, your flame-colored hair fanned across my chest, your kiss-swollen lips, your giggles and moans...

I've been a COMPLETE ass. I'm sorry for every time I mocked and doubted you, every time I left you to fend for yourself with no food or money. Honestly, I know I don't deserve your forgiveness. I'm counting on you being an infinitely better person than me, and hoping you'll take pity on my lovesick ass.

And I do love you, Katie. Make no mistake. You stole my heart early, and it's been yours ever since. If you can give me another chance, I'll spend my life grateful that such a kind, funny, strong and glowing woman allows me to worship at her feet. And cupcakes! I promise a lifetime supply of cupcakes. And dog treats. What I'm saying is, name your price.
Love,
Aiden

A key dropped out of the envelope.

Tears blurred my vision. Chaucer plopped his head in my lap. "He's promising a lifetime supply of dog treats. It's a pretty good deal." He snuggled in. "He says he loves me." I scratched Chaucer's furry, bearlike head. "What do you think? You're an excellent judge of character. Do I risk it? Again?"

A car pulled up in front of the house. I checked the clock. Six ten. Who the heck? I went to the living room and looked out the front window. Aiden's truck. I hadn't decided yet. Chaucer trotted over to the front door. His tail wagging a mile a minute. When I didn't rush to open it, he jumped up on the door, his front paws against it.

"Yes, fine," I said, pulling him down. "You've made your point. And I'm sure it has nothing to do with all those doggy biscuits he gave you. But he will have to wait a little bit longer."

I needed a shower and some think time before I saw him. Thirty minutes later, I walked down the stairs, my hair in wet ringlets, my face clean and freckled, wearing faded jeans, a black thermal tee and Grandpa's fisherman's sweater. I sucked in a deep breath and opened the door.

Aiden was standing on a ladder, installing something.

Heart squeezing at the sight of him, I asked, "What are you doing?"

Aiden startled. He turned to look at me, climbing down the rungs. "Sorry. I know I should have asked first, but I needed to get started, to be doing something other than sitting here, waiting, making myself crazy—er." He motioned to my front yard. "So, Pops gave you his Bronco," he said, nodding his approval.

"Loaned. I'll give it back."

"No. It's a good rig for you two. Pops doesn't drive anymore. I'm sure he told you to keep it."

Yeah, he did. We'll see. I pointed at the eaves over the porch. "Seriously, what are you doing? To my house. Without my permission."

He fumbled with the box, his cheeks coloring slightly. "Motion sensor security lights. I just, uh—" he shrugged "—I wanted to make sure you'd be safe."

I turned away. He looked so contrite, I wanted to hug him, but I wasn't ready. I hadn't decided. His truck was overladen with gardening supplies. I motioned to it. "Did you just rob a garden center?"

He watched me apprehensively, before speaking. "No. You said once that you liked the idea of adding flower boxes along the porch rails—"

"When did I say that?"

"When we were in bed, talking about our homes growing up. I described mine, and you said you'd always wanted a pretty little house with flower boxes, overflowing with blooms."

"I did?"

He grinned. "Well, I might have been running my hands all over you at the time, but you did say it."

"Oh." I felt my cheeks heating.

He stepped closer. "I know the first frost will be hitting us soon but... Well, I didn't know which flowers were your favorite—" he shrugged again "—so I got all of them."

I stared at the truck, willing my brain to make sense of what Aiden was doing. I walked down the steps and leaned over the side of the truck bed. It was a veritable mobile nursery, and that wasn't even all of it. He'd already off-loaded some flowering trees, which were sitting on the ground by the open truck gate. There were even more wedged into the cab. I turned to him, gesturing vaguely at the truck. "You want to make me flower boxes?"

"No. I'm not a carpenter. Bear's doing the actual building." He put his hands in his pockets. "I haven't slept. I was doing some soul-searching, trying to figure out how to get you to care for me again, but I was hitting a wall. I went to see Pops and he helped me shift my thinking. It isn't about me. It's about you. What could I do to show Katie I see her, I know her and I love her?

"I thought about the flower boxes you wanted, so I sketched ideas. I woke Bear up before dawn—he's unhappy with me right now—to show him the sketches. He said my design ideas sucked, but that he knew exactly the type of flower boxes this house needed. I made him get up and start working on them. He'll bring the first set over when he's done, make sure you like them. Although he said he didn't think you knew any better than I did what design would be complementary to the house. Or something like that. He might have used the word *organic*. Honestly, I stopped listening. He can be pretty snotty if you wake him up too early."

That made me smile. "Like a bear."

He chuckled. "Yeah, exactly."

I turned back to him, bracing myself. "Aiden, I get it. You're sorry, but this thing—" I motioned between us "—I don't know if I can do this again." He started to speak, but I cut him off. "To be completely honest, it would make it a lot easier on me if you didn't do stuff like this." I turned back, waved at the truck bed. "The grand romantic gestures are hollow when there's nothing backing them up. You said you love me, but what happens when you get cold feet again? Do I get dumped *again*? I was with a man for ten years who never loved me, who constantly made me nervous and uncomfortable in my own skin. And with you, I feel like I'm always preparing for the rug to get pulled out from underneath me."

"Katie—"

"No, really. You should take all these back."

I reached into the truck and pulled out a pot of sweet peas. "Except this one. I love sweet peas. I'm keeping this one as payment for emotional damages." I turned and walked up the steps, never looking back at Aiden.

"Katie, can I say one more thing?"

I didn't turn around. "I really wish you wouldn't."

"Please."

"Can you wait until I get in the house and close the door? You can talk all you want then." I reached for the front door.

"Will you go out to dinner with me tonight?" His voice was a low rumble.

Instead of opening the door, I leaned in and banged my head against it a few times. I was cut short when a hand appeared, cushioning my head from the hard door.

"Please, don't do that, sweetheart. I love that head and all the hilarious, ridiculous, profound thoughts rolling around in it." He spun me to face him, took the flowerpot from me, setting it on the porch, and then held up a bakery box. "I also brought lots and lots of cupcakes."

"Don't. I'm not strong enough for this." Against my will, tears fell.

He put the box on the porch next to the plant, before his hands dived into my hair as he tipped my head back. "Please, don't cry. It kills me." He leaned forward and kissed away my tears. "I love you, Katie Ann Gallagher. I always have. I can't live without you. I thought I could, but I'm a stupid, stupid man. You are my heart. Please, say you'll give me another chance."

I blinked rapidly, trying to see him better. "But—"

"Forget what I said." He shook his head. "I mean forget what I said before about my not doing love. Remember what I'm saying now about loving you wholeheartedly and not being able to live without you."

"Seriously, Aiden, lithium. I really think you need some kind of prescription mood stabilizer."

He pulled me toward the steps, went down one step and then found my mouth with his. He nibbled and soothed, his lips brushing softly against mine, drawing me back to him, willing me to forget the hurt, to embrace the love. Could I?

I'd spent much of last night trying to talk myself into hating him, but I couldn't. He'd screwed up, but he'd owned it and tried to make up for it. I thought about the security devices and the flowers dripping from his truck. The man knew how to make amends, I'd give him that.

The sound of tires on the drive disturbed the stillness. Aiden held on to me, one hand possessively covering my butt. He shook his head. "Worst timing ever."

Bear climbed out of his truck. "Katie! What the hell? I thought I was the only guy you made out with on a regular basis."

I started to laugh, but Aiden gave me a fierce look. "Not anymore, you don't," he said and kissed me again, and I forgot all about our visitor.

"Ahem. Right in my way, people. Move it indoors."

I broke away from Aiden, laughing and smacking away his searching hands. "Ooh, let me see!"

Bear held up one of the flower boxes. It was perfect, with rounded edges that mirrored the rounded stones of the cottage. "I left it unpainted so you could see the box, but I was thinking either a whitewash to match the rail or a soft, muted blue gray to match the hues of the rocks themselves. Which would you prefer?"

I clapped and grabbed his arm, pulling him down for a kiss on the check. "It's beautiful, Bear! I love, love, love it! And I want the blue gray." I spun back to Aiden and hugged him, resting my chin on his chest and looking up. "Thank you for doing this for me." I stared into his eyes and felt my heart lurch. "I love you, too, you know."

He let out a breath and held me tighter. "Good." He tilted his head toward the house, lifting his eyebrows. "Do you want to take this inside now?"

I laughed and smacked him in the chest. "No way. We're gardening. I need to go get my gloves and a trowel." I turned to Bear. "How long before you have them up, and I can start adding plants?"

Bear paused in his measurements and shrugged. "Maybe a week? Aiden said you wanted them all around the house. I need to build and paint them first, then I'll install them."

"Oh, okay. Thanks, Bear. Well, then, have a good one." I grabbed Aiden by the wrist and dragged him through the front door. "Our plans for the day have changed."

He kicked the door closed. "Thank God." He shoved me in front of him, and we ran up the stairs, desperate to find one another again in the violet room at the top of the steps. "Move faster, woman. I've got plans for you, and they're going to take a while."

I giggled and ran faster.

When we got to the bedroom, he pulled my sweater over my head, throwing it at the door, closing it. He kissed me senseless and then picked me up and tossed me onto the bed. "Welcome home, Katie Gallagher."

EPILOGUE

IT WAS A FRIGID, snowy morning in Bar Harbor but Nellie's Kitchen was warm and crowded. Neighbors ate and chatted, calling out to one another. Katie was cooking in the back, Chaucer lying in the doorway to her office, watching her.

Connor sat in his usual spot, the last table, closest to the open door of the kitchen so he, too, could watch her and talk with her.

Kimberly waited tables four mornings a week before she drove to the university for classes. The arrangement worked out well for all involved, and it meant Jack was often in, eating breakfast with Connor so he could be served by his daughter. He said it never got old for him.

Aiden walked in and headed straight back to Connor's table. He always knew where to find him at this hour. "Hey, Pops. How are the pancakes today?"

Connor looked up from the bundle in his lap. "Hmm? Oh, well, little Miss Helen here is especially partial to her mama's banana mini pancakes, aren't you, Nellie?" Connor kissed the head of his beautiful, redheaded great-grandbaby.

Aiden leaned forward and kissed his daughter, too. She was the spitting image of her mother, all curly red hair and big green eyes, but she had her daddy's chin. No one else seemed to agree with him on that pronouncement, but he was sticking with it.

He left Nellie in the very capable hands of her great-grandfather and went in search of his wife. She was pouring batter onto the griddle while sausages and bacon sizzled to the side. Aiden grabbed a piece of bacon off the strainer, narrowly avoiding the hand smack Katie aimed at him.

"Morning, sweetheart." He leaned in and kissed her. She smiled and went up on her toes to kiss him back.

"Good morning. Are you keeping the town safe from ruffians and ne'er-do-wells?"

He gave her a long, deep kiss. When he pulled back, he said, "Your pancakes are burning."

She jumped, swinging back to the griddle. "Damn it! Stop distracting me. Go sit down with Connor. I'll bring you something to eat in a minute." She pushed him toward the doorway and out of her hair.

"Hey, Chief, leave the cook alone. We're hungry." General chuckling followed the shout.

Aiden flashed a devastating smile. "Sorry,

folks. Pops said he wanted redheaded great-grandbabies. Plural. I was just doing my best to follow orders."

Katie came rushing out of the kitchen to the amusement of all. She placed a plate in front of Aiden. "There. Put that in your mouth instead of talking so much." She leaned over and kissed Nellie's sticky cheek. "How's my sunshine?"

"She's bright as a new penny and sharp as a tack." Connor handed her another pancake to smash and eventually eat. "Now, what is this talk of plural great-grandbabies?"

Katie placed a hand on her still-flat stomach. "Well, that's something we've been meaning to tell you."

* * * * *

If you enjoyed the quirky, feisty heroine in this love story by debut author Seana Kelly, you'll also love these Harlequin Superromance books:

HER SECRET SERVICE AGENT
by Stephanie Doyle,
AIRMAN TO THE RESCUE
by Heatherly Bell,
PICKET FENCE SURPRISE
by Kris Fletcher.

All available at Harlequin.com.

Get 2 Free Books,
Plus 2 Free Gifts—
just for trying the Reader Service!

HRLP17R2

Get 2 Free Books,
Plus 2 Free Gifts—
just for trying the Reader Service!

Get 2 Free Books,
Plus 2 Free Gifts—
just for trying the Reader Service!

HARLEQUIN
HEARTWARMING™

HWI7R